KNIGHT'S LEGION MC

SAVAGE
STORM

NAOMI PORTER

Naomi Porter/Ocean Dreams Publishing

www.naomiporter.com

www.oceandreamspublishing.com

Publisher's Note: This is a work of fiction. Names, characters, places, and incidents are a product of the author's imagination. Locales and public names are sometimes used for atmospheric purposes. Any resemblance to actual people, living or dead, or to businesses, companies, events, institutions, or locales is completely coincidental.

Book Layout and Cover Art ©2021 Cat at TRC Designs

Ordering Information:

Quantity sales. Special discounts are available on quantity purchases by corporations, associations, and others. For details, contact the "Special Sales Department" at the address above.

Savage Storm/ Naomi Porter -- 1st ed.

ISBN: 978-1-952423-28-4

KNIGHT'S LEGION MC

SAVAGE STORM

CHAPTER ONE
STORM

Just kill me now.

The first Friday of the month. Karaoke night. I'd rather be on my bike, heading south to my hideaway and wreaking-havoc on my liver with a bottle of Jack. Battling my demons alone-sounded spectacular compared to the shit bleeding through the speakers in The Bullet.

I sure as fuck didn't want to listen to songs about love and cheating. Country music was depressing shit. Gimme classic rock and guitar solos any day of the week.

Millions of other things were better than watching drunk folks singing and stumbling their way through twangy songs. Most of them were tone-deaf, even more couldn't read the words on the monitor while jacked up, and *all* of them sucked.

Yeah, I was a ray of fuckin' sunshine. Like most days. What else was new?

Tucked away at our corner table, my brothers and I observed the crowd. Naturally, I didn't do menial shit like this. My road captain, Track, convinced me to come out and meet with Lynx. Turning down a request by my treasurer simply wasn't done. Karaoke it was.

The reason for the outing? Money.

As president of Knight's Legion MC, I agreed to come because, well, like I said, money. The Bullet was one of several legitimate businesses the club owned in Bastion Township. We took that shit seriously. Not everything conducted under the club was on the up and up, but most were, like The Bullet.

"Karaoke brings them in masses." Lynx's hazel eyes darted around the room. He didn't see people; he saw dollar signs. All he ever thought about was ways to increase the club's profits, which was why he was my treasure. Lynx was a ruthless and determined, licensed CPA. He made sure KLMC's coffers overflowed with cash and the numbers checked out.

"I hate karaoke," I grunted, tossing back a shot of whiskey and welcoming the smooth burn. Too bad the amber liquid didn't deafen the noise threatening to make my ears bleed.

The locals loved the outdoorsy vibe in the log building. One could say the wooden floors, plank walls and stone hearth made it cozy. It wasn't the sort of place I'd hang out—but whatever, the patrons liked it.

There was a stage where bands played and drunks sang karaoke in front of a small dance floor. The best part? The big ass bar where we made all our money. We loved the Minnesotans' hard-earned cash.

The Bullet kept the Knight's Legion in Bastion Township's good graces. Along with our gun shop, auto body garage, tattoo parlor, and gym. The latter two were squeaky clean, like the bar. I was working on making the rest legit.

"Shit. Admit it. You wanna get your ass up there to belt out 'Crazy Train.'" Track guffawed, banging his chest. "You love Ozzy."

I glared at the fucker. We were friends well before we became prospects and patched in together. The Knight's Legion sealed our bond, making us brothers forever.

"Piss off!" I mouthed, giving Track the bird.

Lynx tapped the table to get our attention. "Like it or not, karaoke brings in three times the green than any other evening. I propose we add another night or two… or three." Lynx held my gaze—Mr. All Business. The Bullet was his baby. He managed the shit out of it with top-of-line bartenders and dependable employees who kept the customers happy.

I reclined in my chair and crossed my arms over my chest, sweeping my gaze over the joint. On the stage, the old man singing was downright awful. The inebriated crowd cheered as he coughed his way through some song about a barbecue stain on a dude's shirt. No fuckin' clue what it was about.

It didn't take long to consider Lynx's proposal. I was confident he wouldn't let me down. "Add another night. We'll see how it goes."

A victorious glint flashed in his eyes.

"Hey, Storm. Can I get you anything?" Nancy asked, her big eyes locked on me, nearly swallowing me whole. Damn, could she be any more obvious about what she wanted? Like my cock between her legs. Nancy wasn't an awful-looking blonde with dark roots. I just wasn't interested.

"Or do anything for you." She licked her bottom lip as if the gesture would tempt me. Yup, just as I thought. Women didn't get it. Some men couldn't be seduced by offers of sex.

Or maybe it was only me.

I took what I wanted when I wanted it, and where I wanted it. Such was the life of a motorcycle club's president. Women were eager to please me, and I usually let them.

But not tonight. "We're good."

She leaned in and whispered, "I'm off at eleven if you change your mind."

"Noted." I had no intention of taking her up on her offer. The pussy around here never did it for me. I had sampled some. But that was years ago. It all had felt the same, right down to the women looking alike. Blondes with dark roots, heavy eyeliner, and very little clothing to hide their assets. A dime a dozen. Okay, for a quick fuck but no substance, no variation.

Substance? Why the fuck did I care about substance? Good, intelligent women didn't stick around. They wanted more than what the club life offered and couldn't handle the danger. Of course, if my dad hadn't screwed every club whore my mom might have stayed.

Lynx clucked his tongue. "If you ain't gonna tap that, I will."

"Have at it. Not interested." I took a long pull of my beer. Should have gotten a second shot of Jack instead.

"Not interested? What's with you lately?" Track eyed me suspiciously. "I haven't seen you with a kitten in weeks."

More like months, but I would never admit my dick spent more time in my hand than in a pussy.

"Got shit on my mind. No time for drama." When I turned thirty last fall, I realized my life was half over. I had been fortunate to escape death a few times. But my days were numbered. The Reaper would eventually catch up to my savage ass.

"Drama? Our girls know better, Prez. And if they don't, I'll give them a refresher," Lynx said on a grunt.

Lynx was full of shit. A softy when it came to women. I flicked my eyes to Track's and we snorted. "Nah. Leave it for now. Anyone else complains, I wanna hear about it."

Lynx nodded, finishing off his beer.

Now leave me the hell alone about women.

The night of my thirtieth birthday, I'd stretched out in bed after getting sucked off by Carla, my go-to club kitten—and stared at the ceiling fan. Even now, I couldn't recall which other kittens I'd been with. Nor did I care. To me, to all my club brothers, pussy was just pussy, a kitten's or otherwise.

Knight's kittens were club whores. Other clubs called them *sweet butts*. Our kittens were carefully selected and vetted before allowed into our clubhouse. I also made sure they were Grade-A, disease-free pussy for my brothers. In return for their services, the club gave them protection and support.

But shit, I just wasn't interested in any of them these days. Not even Carla, my personal pussycat, did it for me. She was off-limits to my brothers. Call me an asshole, but I never liked to share anything. Not even club whores. As president, I didn't have to.

Some kittens dreamed of becoming my old lady, the king's queen, but it'd never happen. They were only there to serve, nothing more, and never in my bed.

On their knees in the bathroom? Sure.

Up against a wall? Absolutely.

Bent over and face down on a table? My favorite position.

In my bed? Fuck no. I wouldn't allow the stench of pussy in my room. It was sacred. Only for me.

Some older members suggested getting an old lady since I didn't like to share. No fuckin' way. I didn't have the patience to deal with a needy woman. The only thing I cared about was my MC. My brothers. The Knight's Legion family. Period. End.

A commotion near the stage grabbed my attention. Clapping, whistling, and shouts of "foxy lady" had me sitting up in my chair. The last thing we needed was for a bar brawl to break out. Shit like that rarely happened, but The Bullet had seen a few over the years.

Lynx was on his feet for a few seconds before getting a thumbs up from Ire, assuring all was well. Ire was a KLMC member and the head bouncer.

I relaxed back into my chair, scoping out the joint. My mind was chaotic, as always this time of year. If I pinned Carla down on a table, it might help relieve the pressure building inside me. I'd fought this feeling of wanting more for over a decade. But when June arrived each year, it reminded me how women didn't stick around. Reminded me of my own past sins. Strangely, it was worse this year and I didn't know why. Maybe a quick hookup was just what I needed. I felt a little backed up, even though I jerked off my morning wood each day. My own hand was no substitute for a warm pussy.

Yeah, I'd do just that before I left town tomorrow. No question, Carla would be thrilled. She was always complaining about how she missed me. It'd been months since I let her blow me. Tonight I needed a release, and Carla would be happy to do the honors.

MADELINE

"Honey, you'll be great." Kim nudged me toward the stage. How in the hell did my friends convince me to sing karaoke?

"Great?" Tara snorted, rolling her eyes, more than a little tipsy. Or maybe not. Out of our teacher group, she was the wildest of the bunch, even before three screwdrivers. I could never tell if it was the drinks or just her personality. "She'll be fan-freaking-tastic! Now get your sweet ass up there and belt it out like I know you can."

Catcalls came left and right. When I heard "foxy lady," my stomach roiled. "No thanks. Everyone here is drunk. It's not like they'd appreciate my singing. Besides, I haven't been on stage for a long time."

"You're not singing for them. You're singing for us." Kim dragged me by the hand the last few steps. "School is out for the summer. Kick it off with a song. Now go shake your pretty little behind and stop being a baby."

I glared at her. "Baby" always struck a nerve. It was my brothers' favorite thing to call me when we were young. I pursed my lips together, mustering all my courage. *No baby here. Not by a long shot.*

"Fine."

Kim and Tara squealed, clapping as I made my way to center stage. Tara had told the DJ I'd be singing "Before He Cheats" by my girl, Carrie Underwood. I could sing her songs all night long, but this one had special meaning. *Never gonna be a fool again...* I glanced over my shoulder, giving the DJ a slight nod. A deep breath held in my lungs. *I can do this.* The music started, men whistled, and the crowd roared—stupid drunks. For all anyone knew, I sucked balls. Luckily for them, I didn't. I was damn good. There weren't many things I was confident about, but my ability to sing was one.

I can do this. Get into the zone and let the people blur into nothingness. I'll be fine.

CHAPTER TWO

STORM

My sights landed on the reason for all the enthusiastic activity. I sucked in a deep breath as my stomach tightened.

Long, dark hair, ivory skin, and an hourglass shape took to the stage in a white sundress. Heat raked over my skin. She must've not known the overhead lighting would illuminate the curves of her inner thighs, leading up to the promised land.

Fuckin' hell, I had an instant boner. The heavens opened, shining a spotlight on her petite, lithe body. I blinked, swearing I saw a halo above her head. She fisted a piece of her skirt and her powerful voice knocked me back to reality. This angel belted out the song like a professional.

Standing like a moth drawn to a flame, I approached the stage where this sultry singer swayed her hips. Her eyes were closed, cheeks rosy, and Christ, she poured everything she had into her performance.

Did she have any idea she was sending off come-fuck-me vibes the way she shimmied her shoulders and puckered her lips?

Mine rang in my head. *M-I-N-E.*

"Hey, Prez, where you goin'?" Lynx hollered. I ignored him, focused on every fucker in front of the stage, throwing out catcalls and propositions.

She was going to be mine—even if only for tonight. Carla became less than a distant memory.

I assessed the drooling assholes, vying for her attention, stalking to the side of the stage where she'd exit.

She tossed her long brown hair off her shoulders, and her eyes flashed open, looking over the tops of the crowd. There was a storm brewing in her sparkling eyes. Goddamn, she was beautiful. My gaze traveled over the thin straps of her sheer white dress to her full bust, then her hips and down to the hem. A little farther were gorgeous knees and brown, well-loved western boots with a cross stitched on the front.

Shit, she *was* a real angel.

My heart thudded against my ribs, rattling me to the core. My cock painfully strained in my jeans. I hadn't felt this alive since…well, maybe ever.

As the song neared the end, two women blocked the exit, dancing and cheering. Friends of hers, I assumed. I hung back against the wall, crossing my arms over my chest and waited.

What did I intend to do?

What did I want to do?

Sink my aching cock into her warm, wet pussy. This beauty looked different from most of the women around—with her dark hair and genuine smile—but I sensed everything about her was different. I couldn't explain this draw I felt toward her. I should've walked away. Erased her from my memory. But I'd do no such thing. For the first time in months, I wanted to be inside a woman's heat, more than in her mouth.

Suddenly the crowd erupted. *Angel* curtsied, holding a piece of her dress out with a radiant smile. She shuffled across the stage, then hopped down the stairs.

This woman shined brighter than the sun. The sheer force of her joy knocked the air out of my lungs.

"Girl, you rocked it." A redhead hugged Angel and bounced on her toes, jostling my little songbird all around.

"She sure showed us," the older woman added.

"Booze helped. Damn, it's exhilarating being up there." Angel fanned her face, and her eyes met mine. They were as blue as the clearest skies. She didn't pull her gaze away.

She stared back.

Fuck, yeah.

I issued her a single nod. In return, I got a full-on million-dollar smile. Complete with straight, white teeth behind her teasing lips. Her friends tugged her away to a table in the back. I followed Angel, ready to pounce on any motherfucker who dared to lay a finger on her.

Some guys stood, giving her a standing ovation. Older guys. Boring as fuck looking guys. She bowed to one, then the other. Grabbing what appeared to be a glass of water, she fanned her face again and talked a mile a minute. I longed to hear what she was saying over the music.

Damn, she was a gorgeous little creature.

I hung back a few yards from her table, unsure of what to do. Usually, I took what I wanted. My club's kittens couldn't refuse. Outside of the clubhouse, I didn't mess with women. Most feared bikers and stayed away because they didn't understand the MC life. Others were curious but never stuck around long term. I'd seen quite a few brothers nurse broken hearts with booze and club pussy when an outsider couldn't hack it.

The only words a coldhearted bastard like me could offer them was, *It's not the end of the world.* I'd send them off with a few kittens and wish them well. Problem solved, right? Guys like my brothers and me didn't do love. The ones who attempted to romance a woman quickly learned our kind wasn't cut out for sweet affections. God knew I didn't have any patience to deal with the inevitable drama that came with women.

Except, this beauty—

"Can I get you anything, Storm?" Nancy appeared in front of me, putting a hand on my chest just as Angel looked my way. "Quickie in the john?"

Shit.

Angel's electric blue eyes dulled as she shrugged a bare shoulder and turned back to her friends. A breeze of indifference blew my way.

Sonofabitch.

"Storm, baby?"

"Get gone, Nancy." As an employee, the same rules applied to her as they did the kittens. Nancy may not have clubhouse privileges, but being pushy or needy wasn't acceptable. We'd never even hooked up, but I knew she'd wanted to for a while now.

"But—"

I growled, jaw ticking. "Did I stutter? Get. Gone."

Nancy's hand fell away. When she left, my woman wasn't at her table. I scanned the room, my heart rate kicking up a notch. What the fuck was that about? My heart racing for a woman was as foreign as a woman refusing me. It never happened. Period.

Where the hell had my songbird run off too?

Track got my attention, pointing to the hallway toward the ladies' room. I could always count on him to have my back.

Wasting no time, I made my way to the bathroom, half tempted to barge in. But I wasn't a total heathen. I sure as hell didn't want to frighten her. So I waited, leaning against the wall.

Several minutes later, the door swung open. As I had planned, her face met my chest. I gripped her trim waist. She felt fantastic. So much my cock twitched with excitement.

Her eyes went wide, her face instantly red. She was a little thing, now that I held her up close. Her head didn't even reach my chin. I could snatch her off the ground and run out the back door before anyone noticed. "Oh, God! I'm sor...sorry—"

"Damn Angel, I sure like hearing you yell." Yelling my name in the throes of passion while I fucked her senseless would be even better.

She attempted to step back, but I didn't release my hold on her. Judging by the rise and fall of her tits, she enjoyed my touch.

"Excuse. Me." Her attitude changed from sweet to don't-fuck-with-me. Her hand went to mine, trying to push it off her waist.

Not happening.

"Buy you a drink?"

Her eyebrows pinched together as her eyes narrowed. "No, thanks. Let me pass."

"I'll let you pass if you have a drink with me."

She rolled her eyes. Fuckin' rolled her eyes. "How charming. Not interested."

"Didn't ask if you were interested. Asked if you'd have a drink with me."

She leaned back, raking her pretty eyes up and down my body. They flitted, over my arms and legs, lingering on the bulge in my pants, for far longer than I expected. Finally, they landed on the patches stitched on my cut.

I smirked at her attempt to act indifferent, unaffected. She didn't fool me; her pink cheeks were a dead giveaway. Angel wanted me as much as I wanted her.

"Knight's Legion Motorcycle Club. *President*, impressive. But a biker? Yeah… Not interested." She shook her head, seemingly forgetting I had a hold of her waist. I imagined the rest of her body felt as spectacular, if not more.

But reject me? Hell no.

"You don't know me," I hissed through clenched teeth. A woman who judged upon first sight? This was why I avoided women outside my MC world.

Except this woman was different. There was an energy about her I'd never felt before. It reached all the way into the marrow of my bones. I hoped she wasn't some kind of witch who'd cast a spell on me just by breathing the same air.

"Exactly the point. I don't plan to know you, Mr. Biker President." She rolled her eyes again. Saucy little shit. "Now, let me pass."

"No." I crossed my arms over my chest, spreading my legs apart to block her way out of the hallway.

What the hell was I doing? I should let her leave. Be done with Miss High and Mighty. But I couldn't. Some voodoo shit had to be the reason for my reaction to her.

"You've got to be kidding me." She snorted, shaking her head. "You don't intimidate me. What're you gonna do? Kidnap me? With all these people around?" She tossed her head back, laughing as if finding me humorous. "Good luck."

Damn, I wanted to kiss her neck. I glanced behind her, dramatically turning my head behind me. "Don't see anyone around."

Her face fell slack, a flicker of fear skirted across her face. Not exactly the reaction I wanted, but she should fear me. Everyone did.

"Madeline? Everything okay?" One of her friends approached, giving me the evil eye. "Come on, honey." She reached her hand out.

Madeline hesitated and cut her baby blues to me as if seeking my approval.

Good girl.

"Go on. I'll catch you later, Angel." I winked, stepping out of her way.

As she took her first step, I couldn't help myself, needing to touch her again.

"Madeline…" I grabbed her hand, reeling her into me. Our bodies molded together perfectly.

Fuck yeah.

The surprise on her face was adorable as I whispered at the shell of her ear, "I can smell you. You're soaking wet for me. Don't leave without giving me your number." I ghosted my lips over her lobe, inhaling the heavenly scent of her hair. "Okay?"

She shuddered on a gasp and didn't say anything. Her body stayed close to mine.

Our heat mingled as she stared into my eyes. The pull to her was intense. Maybe I was playing with fire, but right here, right now, I didn't give a fuck. The sweet scent of her, all of her, drove me forward.

"You hear me?"

She nodded.

"You gonna follow my orders?"

Something flashed in her eyes, and she bit her lip, considering me. I ran my hand over the curve of her hips as I waited for her reply. Finally, she bobbed her head.

"Mhmm."

"Good girl. I'll be waiting in the corner." I let her friend drag her away.

What the hell was I doing? No matter. This woman was fresh pussy. Nothing more. Hell, she could sing while I fucked her eight ways to Sunday, then I could go a few months again, just my hand and me.

Yeah, I only needed a taste of something different.

Scratch an itch, then I'd be golden.

CHAPTER THREE

MADELINE

Biker dude wants my number? Why?

My heart raced as Kim tugged me to our table. I felt his fiery gaze on my back, smelled the smoke as it engulfed my dress—searing my skin. He was nothing short of a raging bonfire like at the parties I used to attend back in high school.

Dangerous. Deadly. But oh, so devilishly handsome.

Ridiculously ornate silver rings adorned his long, thick fingers. There was a skull with ruby eyes on one, a diamond cross on another, and a serpent wrapped around his middle finger. I had to admit, I liked how his fingers dug into my waist. It immediately put my thoughts into the gutter—of him holding me so tightly, fucking me without mercy. I was instantly wet and tingling when the image entered my mind.

When my face smashed into his concrete chest, he smelled of leather and musk, all man with a hint of Downy fabric softener like my mom used. The combination could've been addictive if I had allowed myself to be near him, be *with* him.

I would do no such thing. This man was bad news. Not suitable for me or any woman, really.

My practical side halted when I looked into his dark penetrating eyes. I was in trouble. His gray depths pulled me in, wrapped around my throat, and held me there. The biker dude was hauntingly beautiful with a trimmed black beard and a military-style crew cut, longer on top and short on the sides. I'd like to feel his thick coif between my fingers and his scruffy chin brushing against the sensitive skin of my inner thighs.

Oh man, I was in *big* trouble.

I dropped into my chair and shifted uncomfortably. Biker dude had been right. I was wet—soaking wet. And he smelled me? My arousal? God, please… He was lying, right? If not, I was mortified.

"What was that all about?" Kim asked, eyeballing me. "Because honey, I didn't take dark and dangerous as your type."

Tara set her drink on the table, her eyebrows raised. "Who's dark and dangerous? What'd I miss?"

Kim leaned toward Tara and whispered, "Behind you. At your seven o'clock. But don't look yet. He's watching her. Like. A. Hawk." Kim's gaze flicked to the side, then back to Tara.

He's watching me. A shiver speared down my spine. *Dark and Dangerous* was watching me? I reached for my rum and coke, gulping it all the way down. It did nothing to temper the rich molten lava of desire running through every inch of my body.

"Oh girl, those men are hot." Tara whisper-shouted in my ear. "Which one is he?"

Was this what having an out-of-body experience felt like? Unable to move. Talk. Think. Blink. But my wet satin thong was a clear reminder this weird situation was, in fact, real.

What was happening to me? No man had ever made my mind whirl or my body heat into an inferno of lust. Surely not a biker.

Well, not exactly true. I drooled over Captain America's bare chest and big muscles regularly. I had a thing for clean-shaven men with blue eyes, or rather, I only allowed myself to notice a specific type of man.

Mr. Biker President was not at all what I sought out, yet he had me clenching my thighs after one brief encounter. My nipples were painfully hard. My skin sizzled from his searing gaze. My heart thundered. A man like him was dangerous and controlling. He couldn't be after more than my body and a sleazy night of sex. Heck, I bet he only wanted to get his rocks off, and five minutes later, he'd be gone.

"Drinks on the house," a server announced with a tart expression. "Courtesy of the Knights."

"Who are the Knights?" my friend Ray asked. "I'd like to thank them." He went from slouching in his chair to sitting upright as if intrigued. He adjusted his round metal-framed glasses on his oval-shaped face. His beady eyes scanned the room. Ray didn't fit in with the country folk in the bar. He was more of a grunge rocker sort of fellow.

"No need. They don't like to be bothered."

"Then why the drinks?" Ray tilted his head, hiking a dark brow.

"Ask her." The server pointed her long red talon at me.

I glanced at the scowling bleached blonde, setting the drinks on the table. It was the same woman who'd had her hand on Mr. Biker President's chest. Was she his girl? Or one of many?

"Get you anything else?" Daggers shot my way when she slammed down a pen and napkin in front of me.

What the hell?

"No. Thanks." I looked down at the napkin where it had a message: *Your number here.* An arrow pointed to a blank spot. I slowly looked over my shoulder at Mr. Biker President. His eyes were locked on me. No smile. Just an intense stare. A hungry, intense stare.

Was he for real?

"He bought us drinks and wants your number." Tara grinned like a fool.

"It appears so. Maybe we should leave. This place isn't really our scene." I fidgeted with the hem of my dress, hoping no one else could smell my soaked thong.

The biker dude had to have been screwing with my head, or maybe he was part canine and could sniff out a needy pussy everywhere he went. I wasn't the least bit interested. Nope. Not even slightly. Apparently, my throbbing clit hadn't gotten the memo.

"Elementary school teachers can take a walk on the wild side." Chad lifted his beer bottle and chugged. I watched as his Adam's apple bobbed in his long neck. He let out a satisfied sigh and wiped his mouth with the back of his hand. He was a P.E. teacher at Heritage Elementary School, where the five of us worked. Though he didn't look it with his thick, wiry auburn beard and long hair—resembling John Lennon."It's summer break. Let's live a little."

Ray chuckled. "Maybe we could join their club."

"Oh, mercy. I don't think you two have what it takes." I shook my head. In fact, I was sure they didn't have what it took. The men in the corner weren't giving off friendly vibes as they eyed my friends and me. Or was it just me? Were they trying to intimidate me? I would be lying if I said it wasn't working.

"I work out." Chad flexed his bicep and kissed it. He was a few years older than me, a runner and youth leader at his church. A super nice guy.

"I'm solid as a brick wall." Ray patted his beer belly. "I can drink anyone under the table."

Hmm, holding his liquor might count for something in a biker club. But I doubted it was enough to gain entry into the MC. The fourth-grade teacher also played bass with local guys at the armory and the occasional wedding or event in Winters Township. Maybe his band could play at one of the club's parties.

I stifled a giggle at the thought of Ray and his buddies playing

Top 40 covers for a bunch of outlaws.

"Either of you ever been on a motorcycle? Because I'm pretty sure riding one is required to be in a biker club." Tara hissed with laughter, holding her stomach. She was twenty-three, my same age. We'd gone to college together in the Twin Cities and were still roommates. After graduation, we'd both wanted out of the city and were hired at Heritage. Tara taught second grade and I taught kindergarten in the room three doors down from hers.

Ray tossed a handful of popcorn into his mouth. "No. They're dangerous." He munched away, reaching for another handful.

"That counts you out, friend." Kim patted his squishy bicep. She was the oldest in the group, a seasoned fifth-grade teacher and divorced mom of two college boys. Tara and I had become her pet project when her sons left home last year. She'd said she always wanted a daughter, and now she had two: us. Neither Tara nor I had balked; we loved Kim like a mother.

"I can ride a dirt bike." Chad grinned, stealing the bowl of popcorn away from Ray.

Ray scowled. "Hey!"

Tara snickered. "Well, then. Go right on over and talk to them. Maybe they have an application tucked in one of their vests."

"Cut," I corrected.

"Huh?" Tara turned toward me with a look of confusion on her face.

"What they're wearing. It's called a cut, not a vest."

Chad's eyes bulged in my direction. Not at me, but above my head. A tan arm covered in ink crossed over my shoulder, his hand splayed out on the table.

I gulped as an extended index finger tapped the napkin. "Where's your number, babe?"

The voice was different. Less intimidating. The arm was leaner but still muscular. And the skull ring with the ruby eyes was missing. I craned my neck to see who was behind me. This man had a charming smile, hazel-colored eyes, messy, short blond hair. He appeared friendly. Reasonable. Nice.

"Damn babe, you're hotter up close." He squatted beside me at eye level. "Make the prez happy and scratch your digits here on this napkin. Okay, darlin'?" He appeared to study me, then my friends.

"She's right, by the way. It's a cut." He tugged on his leather collar.

"What are you, his errand boy?" I fluttered my eyelashes, hoping to soften him up so he could get his prez to leave me alone.

Kim and Tara sniggered at my sides while Chad and Ray stared in awe.

"Something like that." His smile faded. "You gonna play hard to get babe? 'Cause I'll warn you, the prez always gets what he wants."

"Really?" I squared my shoulders, feeling a challenge coming on. I was done with men who believed they mattered more than women—misogynistic pigs.

"Yes, ma'am."

"I already told the *prez*," I made air quotes for dramatic effect, "I wasn't interested."

Errand boy's eyebrows shot up. "You what?"

"Did I stutter?"

"Fuck me into next week, darlin'. You got a pair of steel balls for being a hot little number."

"Could you be any more condescending? And rude?"

His eyes glittered with mirth. "Just jot your number here, pretty please." He tapped the napkin again.

"No." I crossed my arms over my chest. Give a stranger my number? Did I look gullible? I practiced what I preached to my kindergarteners—stranger-danger and don't fall for the lost puppy trick.

"Aw, fuck," he muttered.

"Tell your prez to find someone else. I'm sure there are plenty of other *hot little numbers,*" I made air quotes again, "around who'd thank their lucky stars Mr. Biker President wanted their digits."

I picked up the pen, and in capital letters, I wrote: NOT. INTERESTED. Then I waved the white paper in front of the errand boy's face. With a snarl to his lip, he snatched it from my hand and stalked off.

Victory!

I smiled at Tara and Kim. "That's how you do it, girls." They both clapped and bumped shoulders with me. Adrenaline pumped through my veins. It was a phenomenal feeling.

A crash from the back corner made me jump. I turned around as the prez stormed out of the bar, leaving his chair tipped on its side. The two guys with him were smirking at each other. When their gazes landed on me, they each blew me a kiss on their way out the door.

Suddenly, I didn't feel so victorious. I got a weird twinge in my stomach.

"You sure showed them, honey." Kim nudged my elbow. "Proud of you."

"Except she's missing out on a good time with the prez. Don't you think it's time you get back in the saddle and start dating again? Surely you're over that cheating asshole." Tara arched a suspicious brow.

"I'm over Dane. Have been for a long time. I just don't trust men." Especially a man who thinks he can demand my number as if it's owed to him.

The bleach blonde huffed behind me, cleaning up the mess left in the prez's wake. I sort of felt bad for her. She appeared to want him and had probably been with him a time or two... or ten. I found myself sizing her up. She was curvy with a nice pair up top. Too much eye makeup and bright pink lips—but whatever. To each their own.

Tara shrugged. "So? You don't have to trust him to have fun with him."

"Uh-uh. I want more than what he can give me. Guys like them don't have girlfriends, wives, or committed relationships. They have one-night stands and fuck-buddies." I wouldn't be either.

"How do you know so much about bikers? First, the cut and now their relationship preferences." Tara stuck a cocktail straw into her mouth and slurped down her screwdriver.

"I don't really know much. Back home, Toby's best friend's dad was a biker. His wife had left him because he'd cheated on her. I'd overheard my mom and dad talking about it. Dad said outlaw bikers don't practice monogamy. Of course, back then, I was like nine or ten and didn't know anything about anything." But I did now, hence not being interested.

"Well, don't let Dane screw with your head."

Too late. He already did.

"Some of them are monogamous. I think if you're an old lady, it means something special? Kinda like marriage." Kim's lips twisted like she was thinking hard.

"How do you know about old ladies?" I asked.

"*Sons of Anarchy*. But if I remember correctly, the prez on the show cheated on his old lady too. Stay away from bikers, honey. You'll only end up with a broken heart."

Okay then. Never saw the show, but Kim probably knew more than me on the subject, if perchance there was some truth in the TV series. Kim also had first-hand experience with a cheating husband, much like I had with Dane. I had dodged a bullet, unlike sweet Mama Kim.

"I take it we won't be coming back here for karaoke again?" Ray shoveled another handful of popcorn in his mouth.

"Nope. Not me. Once was enough. Bastion might be too rough for us. We should stick to our own township." I glanced around the bar. People seemed to be having a good time laughing and drinking. No other bikers were around. I probably would've come back if it weren't for fear of seeing Mr. Biker President again.

From then on, I'd stay in Winters where bikers didn't regularly roam the streets—and a muscular, hot-tempered, brooding outlaw didn't have his sights on me like I was a piece of meat he wanted to chow down on.

He sure was pretty to look at, though. And my silky thong was totally drenched.

CHAPTER FOUR

STORM

This time of the year hurt like a bitch. Old wounds, that never fully healed, ripped open. The guilt I carried every single day made it difficult to breathe. I hated who I was and what I'd done.

For the next several weeks, I'd live in my own personal hell until I boarded up my shameful past. It always happened when summer arrived and school ended. My demons would rise out of the graveyard deep inside me. Fuck, it hurt something fierce, too.

I rocked in my weathered leather office chair. The muscles in my neck and shoulders were stiff as iron. Alone with my thoughts was a dangerous place.

The walls were closing in, the air growing thicker as shame and regret choked me. I needed to get on my Harley and get lost for a while. A couple of days was all I needed.

But the angel at The Bullet kept me from leaving on my annual retreat. I felt pathetic for letting a woman get to me. What the fuck was happening to me?

"Prez?" AJ appeared in my doorway. He was our newest prospect and had been babysitting our bikes at the bar. When I'd barreled out after getting the first rejection of my life, I'd given AJ orders to follow the girl in a white sundress and brown western boots.

Madeline.

That was three goddamn hours ago. My mind had conjured up different scenarios of her with other men. I imagined her flirting and dancing. Maybe even singing another song, shaking her hips on the stage, and turning all the dicks in the bar hard as stone.

Mostly, I'd spent the last few hours torturing myself over a woman who made it clear she wasn't interested, and it burned me the fuck up.

"What ya got for me?" I rocked my chair.

"She left with her friends half an hour after you."

"Really?" Color me surprised.

"Yeah. Nobody bothered her. I followed them to Casitas Mexican Restaurant. An hour later, she drove the older woman home. She lives in Winters—"

"Winters Township? No wonder I hadn't seen her in Bastion before. What else?"

"I think she lives with the redhead in a single wide in Rosecrest Trailer Park. I sat around until the lights shut off. I assumed they went to bed, so I came back to report to you."

"Does the trailer park look safe?" Why in the hell did I even care?

"Yeah. Well lit. Some yards had kids' playsets. Others had gardens. She's quite the looker." AJ waggled his brows.

My jaw twitched when I felt a weird flicker in my chest. I didn't like it. Was it jealousy? I didn't get jealous over anyone, ever.

I narrowed my gaze. "Don't be eye-fuckin' her. Get me?"

"Yes, Prez."

"Be at her place by six. I want a full report of what she did all day by seven." Once I knew what Madeline had been up to, I could leave for the lake.

"Six in the morning?"

"That a real question, prospect?" I never had the patience to deal with stupid questions on a good day, so right now, I really didn't have any. Madeline snubbed me. Prospect was eye-fuckin' her. Now the question? Not a good combination.

"No."

"Don't let her see you. Don't talk to her. Don't even rake your eyes over her body. If you get a boner for her, I'll know." I leaned forward in my chair and picked up the switchblade I kept on my desk. I snapped it open, studied the sparkling clean blade, and shot AJ a menacing look. "You jack off to her? I'll cut your balls off and feed them to you."

The prospect slowly swallowed, Adam's apple vibrating. "Yes, Prez."

"On your way out, send Track in."

He was gone in two shakes, and Track appeared just as fast.

"Yo. What'd you do to the prospect? Guy looked like he saw the Reaper coming for him." Track dropped into the chair in front of my desk and crossed his arms over his chest. His eyes went wide upon seeing the blade in my hand. "Shiiit. What'd the little fucker do?"

"Nothing. Got him on a task. Made sure he understood my expectations."

Track eyed the switchblade. If anyone could read me, it was him. "The girl." It wasn't a question. "I assume he's found her, so whatcha gonna do about her?"

"Nothing. *Yet.* Tomorrow night, I'm leaving for the lake."

Track knew the drill. "K."

"If you or Raul need anything, Boxer is your man. Shit hits the fan while I'm away—"

"Know it works, Prez." Track reclined in the chair. I could tell he had more to say. Probably about Madeline. "Anything I need to know about her? For when you're gone, I mean."

"Nah. Don't worry about her." All I knew was she lived in a trailer park in Winters, but Track didn't need to know those details. Hell, I didn't even know why I was so curious about her. Probably something to do with my marginally bruised ego or some shit. Subconscious crap quacks babbled about. I doubted I would even make a move on her.

Why open the door to complications?

"What about the Hunters?"

"Just watch them. Boxer will handle it if there's any trouble." My enforcer was indispensable. We'd served in the Marines together and I trusted Boxer with my life. I studied the blade, admiring its sparkle as I twisted it. "Not a word about the woman to anyone." I lifted my gaze to Track's.

"You don't even need to ask."

"Wasn't asking."

"Are you taking a prospect with you?"

"Have I ever?"

"Shit, Storm. Things are different this year."

I slammed the knife onto the desk and growled. "I don't need protection."

Track didn't so much as flinch. He wasn't wrong. We were heading into some shit with a small nomad MC looking to put roots down in the area—*my* area. It was why bringing a woman into my world would be stupid. I couldn't afford to be distracted. It would be too fuckin' dangerous for her and I wouldn't put my brothers or club at risk.

"Don't you, though? This woman has you unhinged." He leaned forward in the chair. "The Hunters are the least of my worries. You're more of a danger to yourself because you want her. You're considering her. Don't."

"Who the fuck do you think you're talking to? I'm your goddamn president!"

"You're my best friend. I've never seen you like this over a woman. We're one-percenters. Outlaws. We said we'd never bring a woman into our world, or fall in love."

"Aw fuck. Nobody is talking about love. You saw her." I rocked in my chair, scratching my beard. "She's exquisite, an angel. I just want a taste of something... different."

"Don't go there, brother. That's all I'm gonna say, don't go there."

We stared at each other for a long second. My guess was this woman—Madeline—lived an untarnished, drama, and risk-free life. *I should leave her alone to find a safe, boring man.*

Wished I was someone who could just walk away.

But I wasn't.

CHAPTER FIVE

STORM

Seven o'clock on the dot, AJ waltzed into the clubhouse bar and locked eyes with me. I waved him over to the council's table, where I sat surrounded by some of my brothers. Raul, my VP, sat on my left. He was Track's father and I liked sitting between them. Boxer was next to Track.

I cut my gaze to the end of the table, where Lynx smirked like a dumbass, trying to get a rise out of me. He couldn't stop talking about Madeline and her pretty, blue eyes and sassy mouth. If he kept it up, I'd be forced to break his straight nose.

Kittens milled about the room in lacy G-strings and bras in a rainbow of colors, offering their services to patched members at the bar or playing pool. They weren't permitted to approach the council's corner table. It was off-limits to women unless invited—and we *never* asked a woman to join us at our table.

"What ya got, prospect?" I turned my attention to AJ. Even though the table was full, I didn't want to put off hearing about

Madeline. I might not have wanted anyone to know about her yesterday, but tonight, I didn't care whether my brothers knew or not.

I hated how I was all over the fuckin' place with this woman.

The table fell silent as my brothers listened with interest.

"She's a busy lady."

I tilted my head to look the boy in the eyes, then smirked. "Looks like she rode your ass all day."

"Since seven in the morning." AJ was a good guy, young, did every shit job given to him without complaint.

"Lemme hear it."

"Okay." He exhaled. "She watered the flowers on her porch, then hopped into her car with her roommate and met the older broad she was with last night. They went to Sugar Bliss."

"Sugar what?" Lynx screwed up his face.

"Bliss. Sugar Bliss is a bakery," AJ explained.

"Oh, yeah, yeah." Lynx raised his glass to his lips, smirking.

"Continue," I snapped. Fuckin' Lynx didn't need to know every damn detail. There was only one bakery in Winters, for fuck's sake. The asshole was really starting to grate on my nerves.

AJ nodded and exhaled another breath. "They sat inside for a while, eating and drinking coffee, then went to Heritage Elementary. When she stayed inside for over an hour, I went to check on her. She was cleaning a classroom. Lots of people were doing the same. Figured she's a teacher there. Kindergarten from the looks of the room. ABCs and numbers on the walls. Her friends are probably teachers too."

"Ain't that sweet, a kindergarten teacher. Must like kids." Track snorted. *Asshole.* He knew my thoughts on kids and white picket fences—they weren't for me.

And yet, I needed to know everything about this woman. I hadn't stopped thinking about her. It was stupid. I could see she didn't fit in with the MC life, but I just couldn't stop myself.

"Continue," I grunted.

"From there, she and the roomie went to the bank, a salon—"

"Salon?" Images flashed behind my eyes of Madeline getting her long, gorgeous hair shaved off. Or what if she dyed it blonde? Shit, it would break my heart. Then I couldn't wrap her magnificent mane around my hand and tug on it while I buried my cock deep inside her.

I shook myself out of the depressing thoughts running rampant in my head. "Is her hair short now or blonde?" My dick was on the verge of shriveling up if the prospect answered yes to either.

"Nah. Just a trim from what I could tell."

Relief washed over me, and it shocked the hell out of every nerve in my body. What was going on?

"What else?"

"They all got pedicures. Afterward, she and the redhead went to the market. She hung out at home for a couple of hours, doing household chores—vacuuming and shit—from what I could tell from the front window. Later in the day, she took a plate of treats to her neighbor."

"Neighbor?"

"Yeah, a little white-haired lady. They chatted for a good long time sitting in lawn chairs in the yard and eating cookies."

"You were watching her?" I hiked a displeased brow.

"N…no. Just occasionally glanced. After visiting with the old woman, she went on a two-mile run," he paused, gulping, "it was kind of hard to stay out of sight following her down a dirt road not far from the trailer park."

"And?" I barked, chest squeezing tight. Running alone on a dirt road was not safe with the Dirty Hunters in the area. Shit! My pulse kicked up a notch.

"She returned home and stayed in until I left."

"All right. Tomorrow I want you to do a few drive-bys and report to Track."

"Going somewhere, Prez?" AJ scratched the back of his head. I glowered at him for asking a question about my personal shit. "Get gone, prospect."

AJ retreated in a flash. I watched him sag atop a stool at the bar and raised his hand for a beer. He needed to spend some time in Boxer's gym. His endurance was lacking, but Boxer could get him into better shape in no time.

"Sounds like the girl is sugary sweet." Lynx chuckled, drumming his fingers on his old-fashioned glass. "A teacher. Kids. Flowers. Cookies."

"Make your fuckin' point," I growled at the motherfucker.

"She's a civilian. An innocent teacher." His steely gaze met mine.

"And?" I gritted out, ready to put my fist through his teeth. As if I didn't know anything about Madeline. She sounded as wholesome as apple pie. I usually viewed a girl like her as off-limits.

"Just sayin' you might want to reconsider pursuing her."

"Enough!" Raul slammed his hand on the table, knocking over empty beer bottles. He pushed out of his chair and stood, eyes blazing with fury as he pointed his finger at Lynx. "Show your president some fucking respect. All you assholes." His finger rounded the table, landing on each man.

All eyes were on Raul. For almost fifty, he was still a scary motherfucker with black hair slicked back and a constant scowl on his mug. He took no shit from anyone and always had my back. Track was a younger version of his father. I was proud to have both of them on my side.

Ever since Uncle Matt lost his battle with colon cancer, Raul had been an angry cuss. Not because he wanted to hold the gavel. No, being president didn't matter to Raul. He just missed his brother, his best friend. They started the Minnesota chapter together twenty years ago when Uncle Matt and my dad fell out. Yeah, Raul missed my uncle about as much as I did.

I lifted my tired ass out of the chair and gripped my VP's bicep, still rock solid. "Thanks, old man. But you know these fuckers don't mean any disrespect." They really didn't. They were looking out for the girl and me.

"Doesn't matter. They flap their jaws too damn much." He was right. They did. Most times, I didn't take them seriously.

"All right, I'm hitting the road. Whip these boys into shape while I'm gone." I tossed my brothers a shit-eating grin. "Ride them hard."

"You bet I will."

"Mind yourselves." I threw up the bird, stalking out of the bar.

I carried myself up a flight of stairs. The loud music faded as I turned toward my room in the council's wing.

When my door came into view, I growled low in my throat.

"Hey, Storm. Been waiting for you." Carla grabbed onto my cut, pushing me against the wall as if the bitch owned me. She rubbed her tits against my chest, cupped my dick, and whimpered. "I've missed you so much, babe." She was wearing a purple bra and matching G-string. I never liked the color purple because it was my mom's favorite.

My massive hand wrapped around her wrist and squeezed until she screwed up her face, eyes bulging in pain.

"You're hurting me," she cried.

"Don't fuckin' touch me again," I hissed, forcing her to back up. The bitch had some nerve laying a finger on my cut. Knew better too.

"W… what's the matter with my man?"

"I'm not your anything." Shit, this woman was getting out of control. "What the fuck you doing up here, Carla?" Everyone knew the council's floor was off-limits unless invited. I had the presidential suite, naturally.

"It's been a while. Thought you might need me—it's June, ya know. I know how you get this time of year." She didn't know anything about me, stupid woman.

"If I ever see you up here again, you're out."

Her lip curled into a snarl. "Fine." She jerked her wrist out of my grasp and rushed down the hallway to the stairs, dramatically swinging her bare ass and arms.

Bitch.

Shaking my head, I unlocked my door and entered my sanctuary. Next to my king-size bed, I went to the window to gaze out at the blue sky. It reminded me of Madeline's blue eyes.

What the fuck are you doing, Storm? Forget her.

Women were nothing but trouble—distractions—high maintenance. I didn't have the time or patience to deal with one. I didn't want that kind of pressure or stress.

What I needed were peace and solitude. Time to serve my atonement. None could be found at the clubhouse or with Madeline in the next town over.

In a couple of days, I'd return from my getaway in a better frame of mind. My demons would be locked away… until next year.

As for Madeline? It was best to just leave her alone. I had no business getting involved with a boot-wearing, cookie-baking kindergarten teacher.

A fucked up man like me had no business with an angel.

CHAPTER SIX

MADELINE

I inhaled a deep breath, welcoming the warm sun on my face. Lake Waleska was just as I remembered it. I had hoped this little weekend getaway would be what I needed. A little peace and solitude to replenish my soul. Just me and my thoughts.

Instead, tears pooled in my eyes. Loneliness engulfed my heart as memories of my family's last time here rolled in like an epic wave.

My brothers were wild and crazy teenagers, along with their friend KC who'd been invited to come with us. I was the little princess back then, a position I relished and abused often. What ten year old wouldn't milk it?

They were the most protective guys to ever walk the planet. All week I'd heard, *Be careful, Maddy. Another can of pop, Maddy girl? Wanna piggyback ride, little Maddy?*

God, those guys had spoiled me rotten. Naturally, I'd eaten up every bit of their attention. They were my heroes.

Except KC wasn't my brother. He was super cute and sharp as

a tack. Funnier than my brothers, and stronger too. He gave the best piggyback rides, bouncing me around and spinning us in a circle. I'd giggled so hard my stomach ached. Unlike my brothers, KC never dropped me. He protected me with his life.

All my friends had crushes on KC, like I did. But he hadn't noticed any of us. Too young to think anything about.

I had loved being at the lake. Dad fished all day while Mom had read by the water. The guys had a blast just goofing off. I had never been happier. That summer was supposed to have been the beginning of a new family tradition.

But tragedy struck my family the following year, changing our lives forever. We never made it back to Lake Waleska.

Days after my brother Tommy's funeral, KC moved away. When I asked my older brother, Toby, if he'd gone to his mom's place (KC's parents were divorced), my brother just shook his head. We never saw KC again. Within ten days, I'd lost two people I loved dearly.

Though I missed my brother terribly, he was gone forever and never coming back. But KC hadn't died, so losing him hurt more. Knowing he was somewhere in the world and I couldn't talk to him had broken something in me. I'd cried for years. Still cried every now and then. His leaving had left a hole in my heart that hadn't found a bit of healing in twelve years. He'd been my first love and always would be. I never got to tell him how I felt.

My chest ached as I carried my beach bag to a spot near the shoreline. The weight of memories threatened to crush me. Images of Tommy filled my mind, like a shot of whiskey burning all the way down my throat. KC's smile made my insides rot. Maybe coming had been a mistake.

Activity abounded around me. Large inflatable rafts were perched on the water and jet skis whizzed by. Chatter and laughter circulated through the pleasantly warm air. It all felt so familiar.

The only thing missing was my family and KC. We'd had so

much fun together. I would do anything to rewind time to have one more day with Tommy and KC.

Blinking back my emotions, I spread my plaid blanket. I dug into my bag, taking out a bottle of water, a bag of loaded oatmeal cookies I'd baked yesterday, sunscreen, and the latest John Grisham novel. No sappy romance books for me. Give me suspense and danger any day of the week. I didn't want to read about love at first sight—insta-love as Tara called it—or happily ever afters.

I wasn't opposed to love. Heck, one day, I hoped to meet my perfect match, fall in love, get married, and have a family. But not now. Not for a while. A long while.

Heavy-hearted, I sighed and sent up a quick prayer for peace— like Mom always advised me when I was anxious. *You can do this.*

I got comfy on my stomach, lost in the sweetest thoughts of my childhood. A laugh broke from me while remembering my brothers and KC's silly antics. I swiped away tears and cherished the joyous time I'd had with those I loved. They'd live on in my heart forever.

Rolling on my back, I ditched my denim shorts and tank top to soak up the sun in my bikini. It was a glorious June day. The school year was over, and I had all the time in the world and no place to go. All I wanted was to relax and remember the past—the good old days.

Sleeping in the sun, a gravelly voice startled me awake.

"Madeline?"

I jerked, eyes popping open. A tall, crazy-muscular man in royal-blue striped boardshorts loomed above me. I couldn't make out his face behind dark sunglasses. Well okay, so I wasn't looking at his face. My eyes were glued to his six-pack abs.

"Sorry?"

"You're Madeline, right?"

Maybe.

"Who's asking?" With a body like his, I might want to be the person he was looking for.

He squatted beside me and removed his shades.

My heart lodged in my throat. I knew that face. "You!"

Mr. Biker Prez was here? At Lake Waleska?

"Happy to see me, are you?" A cocky grin stretched across his handsome face.

"Shocked is more like it. You're not following me, are you?" God, was he stalking me?

"Maybe." His eyes raked over my legs, stomach, and chest. Shit! I'd forgotten I was in a bikini. "Or maybe it's kismet."

"Eyes up here, *Prez*." I snapped my fingers. "Kismet? Yeah, right. When did bikers start using words like kismet?" I lifted up on my elbows, stifling a laugh. *Kismet*. Was he trying to impress me?

"Polka dots look good on you." He sat beside me, on *my* blanket with very little space between us. His long legs stretched out in front of him, and his thick thighs touched mine. I clenched down low and prayed he couldn't smell my instant arousal over the sunscreen I'd put on earlier. "Whatcha doing here?" He ignored my question. Albeit a sarcastic question but still, *rude* to disregard it.

"Sunbathing." How weird was it that we were both wearing blue and white?

"I see that. Been watching you for over an hour. Worried you'd get sunburned when you fell asleep. You here alone?"

Creepy biker stalker for sure. Crap. What was I gonna do?

"What are *you* doing here?" I disregarded his question like he had mine.

"Asked you first."

"Are you here alone?" I was determined to not share anything about myself. My heart rate rose the longer I imagined him watching me for an hour. Was he stalking me? Goose bumps sprouted on my arms at the thought. The crime investigation shows I liked to watch flashed behind my eyes. Would a stupidly sexy biker kill an innocent woman sunbathing on the shoreline of a lake?

Jeez, get a grip. He's not here to kill you. All I knew was that he was a biker—the president of an MC. That only meant one thing, *dangerous.*

"Yes." His dark eyes burned into mine. "Gonna answer my questions now?"

"No."

His eyebrows shot up. "Shit. You're one tough little lady, aren't you?"

I rolled my eyes. "Listen, I'm here to relax and enjoy the sun. I'm not looking for... company."

He smirked. "Me either. No harm in relaxing together, though. How about you don't bother me, and I won't bother you?'

"I haven't bothered you."

"Baby, in that bikini, you're bothering me big time." He stroked his cock with a wry grin.

Oh, my God!

"Now, shh, let's soak up the sun. But first, rub some of that sunscreen you've got there on my chest." He stretched out next to me, crossing his arms behind his head. My eyes zeroed in on his massive biceps.

Mercy, he was a magnificent specimen of strength and sex appeal. But his sexiness didn't matter. He was a biker. This was my damn vacation.

"Um, rub some on yourself, Mr. Prez." I tossed the bottle onto his gut.

He didn't so much as flinch when it landed on his abs.

"Storm."

"What?"

"Call me, Storm."

"What kind of name is Storm?"

"Road name." He took my hand, squirted lotion in my palm and put it flat on his chest. "Don't miss any spots. I want an even tan."

"You arrogant jerk." I tried to pull my hand away, but he wouldn't release it. "Let go of me!"

"Chill, baby. Let's enjoy our second chance." He moved my hand over his pecs. Jesus, they were firm. "See, ain't that nice?"

I gulped. It *was* nice.

The feel of his hot skin against my hand and his warm scent tickling my nose were doing strange things to me. My core fluttered and twisted. Dammit, if I wasn't getting wet for him.

I didn't want to feel this way about Mr. Biker Prez. People like him broke the law. Hell, he'd probably even killed someone or… a lot of someones. And could kill me.

No, he wasn't my type. The furthest thing from it. He needed to leave.

"Storm, I'm not playing hard to get or trying to be difficult. I meant what I said at The Bullet. I'm not interested." *Be firm, resolute. Don't waver, and he'll go away and never look back.*

"Didn't ask if you were interested, Angel. I'm interested."

What. A. Jerk!

The gall of this man. He was just like Dane. I sure as hell didn't want to be with someone who didn't respect me. Or tried to control me.

"That's where you're wrong. I matter," I yelled right in his face, my heartbeat roaring in my ears. Every muscle in my body coiled. No man would tell me I didn't have a say. No man would ever control me again. "What I want is just as important as—"

Storm grabbed the back of my neck and crushed his mouth to mine. I struggled against him, fighting to keep my lips sealed shut. The persistent bastard worked his robust and skilled tongue, breaking through.

I inadvertently moaned as a bolt of lightning shot into my pussy. How could I moan? Moan!

Storm chuckled. "I always win, Angel." His hand cupped my ass cheek, yanking me astride him. He deftly flipped me onto my back, trapping me beneath his substantial, concrete body. Then, well then, he kissed the hell out of me.

Every taut muscle in my body relaxed, turning to liquid. I stopped fighting when I tasted spicy cinnamon on Storm's tongue, burning the taste buds right off mine.

"Fuck, your mouth is heavenly." The thin fabric of his trunks did nothing to hide the hard ridge of his cock digging into my pelvis. His long, thick cock.

My mind whirled. I was on a public beach frantically making out with a biker... a stranger. And I couldn't stop. Hell, I didn't want to stop. Admitting the truth to myself scared the crap out of me.

What was I thinking? I couldn't get involved with this man. I wasn't stupid. Nothing would ever happen between us, other than passionate sex. I would only be another notch on his belt.

The longer he kissed me, the less I could think straight. Maybe for once in my life, I could be a little reckless and take from him like he so obviously wanted to take from me. *One and done*, wasn't that what cocky douchebags called it?

He was rubbing hard between my legs. I enjoyed the friction a little more than I should.

"Storm, there are families around here. Children. They shouldn't see you dry humping me."

He froze, mouth on my neck, dick pressed against my mound. There was nothing left to the imagination regarding its size; I felt it all. No question, I wanted to experience it in its entirety. Lord, help me. My brain had to be short-circuiting.

Storm pulled back, staring into my eyes. "Your hips are moving too. *We* are dry humping each other."

Shit, he wasn't wrong. I was an active participant and hadn't even realized it. *Shit, shit, shit!*

For as hot as my face felt, it had to be fire engine red. "We shouldn't be doing this."

"The fuck we shouldn't." His lips were on mine again, and I whimpered with need. Whimpered!

Who the hell was I?

"Storm. I don't know you. I don't just hook up with a guy I've had a two-minute conversation with. That's not me."

"Shit. You're right."

I'm right?

"What?"

He climbed off me, adjusted his erection, and started shoving my things into my beach bag.

I felt strangely bereft without his body on mine. I missed his lips on my neck, his hands roaming over my thighs and hips.

Seriously, what was happening to me?

"What are you doing?" I asked in a breathy voice as I sat up.

"Cleaning up your shit so we can go." He said it as if it were a no-brainer.

"I can't go anywhere with you."

"Madeline, I'm not going to hurt you darlin'. Let's grab dinner, go back to my room, and get to know each other. After a couple of hours, we'll get to know each other in the nude." He winked with the most adorable boyish grin. It may have seemed impossible for him to look so cute—given his black beard, hulking muscles, ornate rings— but it was there: a boyish smile and sparkling gray eyes.

Melt my freaking heart.

CHAPTER SEVEN

STORM

No woman had ever been on the back of my bike, but I wanted Madeline on it. I must've lost my goddamn mind. There was no other explanation for this insanity.

After one taste of her soft, pliable lips and sweet, eager tongue, I was doomed. Kissing Madeline on the beach with the sounds of laughter and splashing only yards away made me fuckin' happy. And nothing ever made my serious, brooding ass *happy*.

I'd been coming to Lake Waleska for the last eight years to torture myself. To remember all I'd done and lost and those I'd hurt back home.

All year I kept shards of pain and guilt buried deep in my soul. Then the first weekend in June, I let my guard down to thrash and bash myself while away from my brothers and clubhouse. Nobody needed to see that shit.

But now Madeline was here.

Fuck. I shouldn't have approached her.

When she'd strolled by, lost in her thoughts, I hadn't announced my presence. I'd wanted to, but couldn't decide how. For over an hour, I'd watched her set up her spot, entranced as she rubbed sunscreen over her curvy lithe body, nibbled cookies, and wiped away tears. It was like my soul needed to take all her pain away. I already carried my own. What was a little more?

Nobody had joined her. She'd come alone as I had, and I found myself intrigued. Even though I'd decided last night to forget about her, seeing her again changed that. I couldn't take my eyes off her.

She'd nodded off. Dudes passed by her with drool dripping down their chins. It fuckin' did me in. I didn't want anyone gawking at her. Eye fuckin' her while she slept. So, I'd tossed my box of Hot Tamales into the trash, dusted off my swim trunks, and succumbed to the magnetic pull drawing me to her.

It felt like fate had brought us to the lake, away from my clubhouse, so we could… Hell, I didn't have a clue why two completely different people would be brought together. But here we were, and I wasn't about to argue with fate.

Turned out, Madeline had a room in the same lodge as me, four units down from mine. We parted ways to clean up. I had every intention of not spending any more time apart from her for the rest of the trip.

One last check in the mirror and I was ready. I felt naked without my cut, but I'd decided to leave it behind this evening. Maybe for the whole time I was with her. I wanted Madeline to see *me*, something I never wanted anyone to see.

She was different. I couldn't put my finger on it, but oddly, it was like I'd known her in another life. There was a familiarity about her. It comforted me. Some crazy shit right there.

Dressed in my favorite faded jeans, a black tee, and biker boots, I was about to head to her room when my phone chimed with a text.

Track: Little lady's been MIA since this morning. AJ is freaking out.

Shit, I'd forgotten I had the prospect watching her. He probably feared not getting patched. The problem was I didn't want anyone to know I was with Madeline. Not yet, anyway. I just wanted this to be about us. Not the club. Not my brothers. Hell, not even my past was invited on this little getaway.

Storm: Leave her be until I get home.

Track: You okay?

Storm: Yes

Track: K

With that interruption dealt with, I continued down the hallway and tapped on her door with my knuckles.

"Coming!" She called out. No shit, I sucked in a breath. I wanted nothing more than her *coming* all over my dick.

The door opened. Madeline blindsided me in a floral printed sundress and her hair up in a messy bun. Her tan skin shimmered. I'd never seen anyone more devastatingly beautiful.

"Hi there," she greeted with a dazzling smile. "I just—"

I cut her off with my mouth on hers, pushing her against the wall. Soft whimpers encouraged me. Her hand gripped my neck, and I went for it, lifting her up for a passionate kiss to steal our breath away.

And I didn't do, *passionate.*

I did fast and furious fuckin'.

Kissing was too intimate. I never did it. Well, except one time I angry kissed Carla when she'd pushed hard for it on my thirtieth birthday. I called it quits with her afterward. If my brothers didn't enjoy her oral talents, she'd been gone a long time ago.

"Storm…" Madeline moaned my name, fingernails lightly scratching the base of my neck. She stroked up and down softly, making my spine tingle. What the fuck was I doing with her? "I'm not this person… I've never done anything like this before. But you make me want to."

Fuuuck. This woman had the power to destroy me with her honesty and tenderness.

I kissed the tip of her pink nose as I set her on her feet. She'd gotten a little too much sun and looked adorable. Christ, *adorable*, hadn't been in my vocabulary before now. "Let's go eat, dance, and get to know each other."

The surprise on her face warmed my insides. She brushed her hands down the sides of my head, over my cheeks, to my neck as she considered me. *Sonofabitch.* Goose flesh appeared on my arms for the first time in my life.

God help me. I was putty in her hands.

"Dancing?" A soft smile appeared. At this moment, I'd do anything to keep it on her gorgeous face.

"Yeah, baby. Dancing."

"Where's your cut?"

"You get just me at the lake."

She popped up on her tiptoes and cradled my face in her small hands, an earnest element in her baby blues. I gripped her hips and pulled her body flush with mine. "But I want to know all of you, Storm."

"You will, Angel. Let's go."

What did I just agree to? Somebody lock my ass up in the psych ward.

Madeline didn't push or balk. Damn, everything about this woman was *refreshing.*

In the resort's parking lot, she fidgeted with the hem of her dress, staring at my bike. "I'm wearing a dress, though."

The last thing I wanted during the snow-free months was to be in a cage. Minnesota winters were long and brutal. So being in my truck when I could ride my Harley was the last thing I wanted to do. But for her…

"And you look pretty in it too. Do you want to take your car?"

She chewed on her lower lip, eyeing the bike. She peered down at her dress and sandals. "No. Gimme a sec." She pranced toward her car, popped the trunk, and dug around. The next thing she did was slip on a pair of black western boots and a flannel shirt.

Damn, this woman didn't let anything hold her back. She trotted back, grinning and looking sexier than before.

"Ready!"

"Angel, you're too much." I reeled her in for another kiss. I couldn't seem to keep my hands or lips off her. Everything about Madeline was spectacular. Her plump, soft lips caressed mine like a sensual dance. Her silky skin made me ache to feel every inch of it. Her intoxicating scent was burned into my senses. Soft and airy, yet seductive and sexy rolled into one addictive package. I was royally fucked.

After getting a taste, I secured my helmet on her and helped her onto the bike. She inched closer behind me, thighs pressing against mine, wrapping her arms around my waist. A weird pang hit me dead center in the chest. I ignored it. I did everything I could to not acknowledge the unfamiliar feelings sprouting inside me.

Of course, I didn't run in the opposite direction, either. I fuckin' knew I should be running for my life as if the Reaper were after me.

"Let's hit it. I'm starving," she shouted before I gave way entirely to my inner thoughts.

My bike roared to life, and we were off, heading south to Mason City.

Today was making its way up the charts as the best of my life.

CHAPTER EIGHT
MADELINE

"I've never had so much power between my thighs before." I blanched as Storm's gray eyes turned feral. Slipping my flannel shirt off, I internally scolded myself. *Stupid girl, you don't say something so provocative to a man like him.*

It was the truth, though. Flying down the highway on the back of Storm's bike was electrifying. It was exactly how I remembered it. Only once, when I was a little girl, had I ridden on the back of a motorcycle. I'd loved the freedom back then.

I loved it this time, too.

My thoughts had run wild, reliving our kiss on the beach. I still tasted cinnamon on my tongue. Mercy, I wanted more of his taste. While the warm air tickled my skin, I'd imagined Storm's hands on me. Lifting the skirt of my dress up. His slick tongue skimming up, up, up... It was safe to say I was thoroughly aroused by the time we arrived at the restaurant.

Storm appeared to be in a trance. I tossed my shirt at his face playfully, to pull him out of wherever he'd gone. He caught it before it touched him. A hungry glint sparked in his severe gray eyes. I clenched down low as he held it to his nose, smelling it. Smelling *me*.

I shivered from my toes to my ears, facing burning red hot as lust seeped into my veins.

"Can't be saying shit like that Angel, unless you want me to tear your clothes off and fuck you on the spot." He smirked, tucking my shirt into his saddlebag.

Mercy.

My panties weren't just damp anymore. They were soaked. "What do you mean?"

"You know damn well what I mean." His hand cradled the side of my face, lips a breath away from mine. He hovered above me, stroking my cheek with the pad of his thumb. "Let's eat." His hand fell away, and he took mine, entwining our fingers together.

Shit. No kiss.

I fought a pout as he led me inside the saloon. I shouldn't be bummed. Storm arrived at the perfect time back at the lake, chasing away the sadness building in me. He'd diverted my attention from the pity party I was sure to sink into while missing KC and my family. I owed him big for that. I wondered how he'd like his payment.

Country music played in the background. The delicious scent of charbroiled meats made my stomach rumble.

The sight of Storm had me drooling, along with every other woman in the building. Without his leather cut, he didn't look as dangerous or menacing. Even if he was dressed in black from head to toe. His faded jeans and T-shirt fit like a glove. Storm was sexy as sin.

Double shit. I suddenly felt insecure. What if Storm decided to ditch me for someone better?

Triple shit. An Uber ride back to the lake would blow my vacation budget, seeing it was forty miles away.

"Welcome to Granny's Saloon. How many?" The perky blonde's

breasts peeked out of a blue and white checkered shirt. It was tied in a knot above her belly button, paired with white Daisy Dukes and red western boots. Her hair was in pigtails. She was cute *and* sexy, in a wholesome-meets-porn-star sort of way.

Jesus, she couldn't have been more than eighteen. She was totally fangirling over Storm, too. Anxiety settled in my belly. I had half a mind to disappear into the bathroom and call an Uber that instant. Why delay the inevitable?

"Two," Storm replied in a curt tone. He squeezed my hand, jerking my attention back to him. My gaze flashed up to his stormy eyes.

I turned away, unable to endure his scrutiny as doubt replaced the lust in my veins.

"Right this way," Blondie said.

We followed her, which was a bummer. Her pert ass swayed from side to side like a brass pendulum. No way would I risk stealing a glance at Storm. His eyes were probably locked on her squeezable bottom. Dane's would have been, so I assumed Storm's was too.

It'd taken six months of being blind and stupid before I learned Dane had been cheating on me. A couple of months later, I'd figured out how he picked up women while we were out. Dane had been getting phone numbers while I went to the bathroom or when he'd refill his popcorn in the theater.

He'd always been a little too happy to swing by the market on his way home. The nights Dane had "worked late," he wasn't at the office. The mornings he'd been up before the sun for "a five-mile run," he wasn't running. I'd fallen for all his lies.

All this now hit a little too close to home.

I faced forward as Storm commanded attention throughout the saloon. Men and women equally noticed him. I wasn't surprised in the least. He was seemed slightly taller than my brother's six foot frame. A lot broader and muscular too. His surly expression could stop traffic.

He had this aura about him that said *Fuck with me and you'll be sorry.* Why was I here with him?

His mood had noticeably changed. Just before we'd entered the restaurant, he'd been playful. I distinctly felt the shift, putting me more on edge. I should've never agreed to dinner.

"Here we are. Trina will be your server." Blondie deposited menus on the table. "Can I get you anything else?" she sidled up next to Storm as I dropped into one side of the booth.

I sighed, rolling my eyes. The fun evening I'd hoped for took a swift nosedive.

"Nothing for me. What about you, baby?" Storm slid in next to me.

"What're you doing?" I glanced from him to the spot across from me where his menu was placed.

"Think I'd let you sit alone? Don't want dudes thinking you're available." His hand cupped my neck, and his perfect lips smashed mine.

"Okay then…" Blondie huffed, stomping away. *Good.*

"These lips are the best appetizer I've ever had." Storm nibbled and licked. "What happened to you? I felt you tense and shut down."

"I don't know what you're talking about." *Liar.*

"Right. I won't push." He took my hand and kissed the top, then the palm. I couldn't help but squirm as his beard tickled my skin.

"Storm… People are watching."

"I don't give a fuck, Angel. Let them be jealous."

"Jealous? Jesus, you are a cocky S.O.B., aren't you?"

"I'm here with you, Madeline. Men and women alike will be jealous of *me.*"

"Oh, jeez." I shook my head. Yeah, men and women would be jealous of *me* because they'd wish they were in my boots.

"Hi! I'm Trina," *another* perky blonde said with a high-pitched chipper voice. "What can I get you to drink?"

Storm didn't turn away from me. He simply twirled a loose lock of my hair around his index finger.

"Heineken draft." Storm's gaze dropped to my lips. "What about you, beautiful?"

"Rum and coke, please." I smiled at our server, gawking at Storm. My body trembled under his intense stare and I squeezed my thighs together.

"Be right back with those."

"You're making me nervous and being rude to the server."

"I like making you shiver and clench." He pecked my lips. "Don't care about no one else." He brushed his lips across mine. "Do you believe me?"

"Sure, I believe you." A little, *maybe*.

"Don't lie to me, Angel. I don't take well to it. In fact, I don't take to it at all. Be straight with me. Always."

The earnestness in his eyes speared into my core. I felt like I could be honest with him, but I didn't want to come across as insecure or weak. A man like him should be with a confident woman. But why should I care one way or the other if this was only a fling?

"What are we doing here? I mean, you with me. Look at us. We're about as different as the Easter Bunny and the Big Bad Wolf."

He smirked. "Getting to know each other better. Thought that's what you wanted."

"I didn't think this was the sort of thing a biker did. Date. Much less an MC's president."

"Here we are," Trina chimed, placing our drinks in front of us. "Ready to order?"

I glanced at the menu I hadn't even opened.

"We need a few more minutes," Storm replied, annoyance in his voice, eyes locked on me.

"Sure thing!"

"You're right. We don't date. We pillage and plunder and fuck.

We fuck a lot. Whenever and whoever we want." His voice had an unapologetic edge. "I don't know why the fuck I'm here with you, other than I want to be. I want to know you. You okay with that?"

I gaped, my heart pounding against my ribs. For as close as Storm was to me, he had to have heard its rapid thumping. Shoot, he probably could smell my damp panties again.

"I'm… I'm okay with getting to know you while we're at the lake. No expectations."

"Christ, Angel." He hissed as if trying to remain calm. "I have all kinds of expectations." He claimed my mouth again, hand gripping the back of my neck, the other brushing over my stomach to my hip, tugging me to him.

I moaned against his mouth, hooking my arms around his neck. This man played me like a fiddle with his dirty talk, controlling nature, and sizzling kisses.

I was doomed if I continued anything more beyond our time at the lake. But I wanted to give myself two days of living in the moment with Storm.

Come Tuesday, I'd get back to my normal, everyday life.

CHAPTER NINE

STORM

Madeline was shutting me out. Didn't she feel how fuckin' fantastic the chemistry was between us? Was it the club or me being a biker, pulling her away? I couldn't blame her if she didn't want to be part of the MC life.

The thought of letting her go gutted me. Some crazy shit there. How the fuck could a woman I'd only spent a few hours with affect me so much?

After I'd kissed her senseless and her second rum and coke, Madeline loosened up. We ate and talked about nothing too personal, just music, movies, and other shit while chowing down on some of the best steaks I'd had in a long time. It was nice. She was easy to talk to and a beauty to look at.

But having her in my arms now, swaying to a country song I didn't know, was *spectacular*.

I got the feeling she expected me to flirt with the women working here. *Not fuckin' happening.* I only had eyes for Madeline. If I wanted to, I could have lined up a few warm bodies for my pleasure. Probably would've done just that a year ago.

Jesus, I hated her thinking I'd want another woman. Didn't she know she was gorgeous? And freaking irresistible?

Men continually checked her out. Several times I wanted to knock some teeth across the dance floor laden in sawdust. I would've if Madeline had noticed them, but she was oblivious. It made me want her even more.

This woman didn't play games. She wasn't batting her eyelashes or puckering her lips for attention or to make me jealous. I'd never met a sweeter, more authentic woman.

"This is nice," she said softly. If my cheek wasn't pressed against her forehead, I wouldn't have heard her.

"It is." I kissed her temple. "I want to get you alone, Angel. I'm tired of men drooling over you."

She giggled, tossing her head back. "Stop it. You're crazy."

She honestly didn't believe every fellow in the building was sporting wood for her.

"Not joking, baby. What do you say we head back to the resort? Put on a movie, kiss throughout it, and…" I growled low, thinking of all the things I wanted to do to her. Shit, I was so fuckin' hard for this woman. My balls ached like never before. I had to have her—tonight.

She lifted her head off my chest and stared into my eyes. "And what?"

"And whatever else we want to do."

She blushed the prettiest shade of pink. "Okay. Let's go."

Fuck yeah.

The ride back to Lake Waleska was a blur. I was happy as a clam, just me, my bike, and Madeline. It didn't get better than that.

She held me tighter this time, breasts pressed firmly to my back, fingers playing with my shirt and abs. A couple of minutes after we'd left the saloon, I was as hard as granite. A dozen times, maybe more,

I'd considered taking her hand and putting it on my cock. Just the idea of her stroking me while we rode down the highway nearly made me come.

I refrained and it about killed me.

At the resort, I pulled into the spot next to Madeline's silver Honda CR-V. I pushed my kickstand out. Like a pro, Madeline hopped off and removed her helmet. To my surprise and delight, she leaned into me and planted her luscious lips on mine. It was the first time she'd initiated any physical contact. Goddamn, her lips caressed mine in a sensual, hypnotic way. I couldn't help but melt into her and groan.

"Thank you for dinner." She lightly kissed the corner of my mouth. "And for dancing with me." She kissed the other corner. "I had a great time." Her fingers brushed up and down the back of my head as she deepened the kiss.

Fuuuck.

My head buzzed erratically like a neon sign on the fritz. One second my brain worked, then it didn't. All conscious thoughts flickered wildly. Madeline's lips were electrifying, so potent they turned a stubborn motherfucker like me into a glob of goo.

"My pleasure, beautiful." I gave her a stupid lopsided grin as I cupped her ass cheek and squeezed it a few times. She gasped as I tucked my knee between her thighs. "You hot for me, baby? Been smelling you all evening."

She sighed, looking away. "Jesus, Storm."

"Uh-uh. Don't shy away from me, darlin'. I like knowing you want me." I pinched her chin lightly between my thumb and finger and forced her to face me. "Tell me I'm wrong."

"Are you always this cocky and confident? You could be nice and not embarrass me, you know."

"Embarrass you?" Fuck, I was taken aback by her honesty. I respected the fuck out of it. "You should never feel embarrassed with me. And yes, what you see is what you get." I winked, running my tongue slowly along her lower lip. "I want you too, Angel. You feel it?"

She rubbed her pussy against the top of my thigh like it was the most natural thing to do. I fuckin' loved it.

"Why do you call me Angel?" She slowly humped my leg while playing with my hair. Her eyes were hooded and filled with lust, her tongue darting out teasingly. I could come right this second. I held back with all my power. When I finally blew my load, it would be inside her, not in my jeans.

"When I saw you on stage singing, you looked like an angel with the lights shining down on you. You stole my breath away."

"Wow…" She exhaled and blushed.

"Wow's right. Your room or mine?"

"Huh?"

"Your room or mine? We're having a slumber party."

"What do you mean, a slumber party? I never agreed to a sleepover." Her eyes twinkled with amusement.

"The heat in your baby blues says otherwise." I cupped her mound. She jumped and squeaked.

"There's heat down here, too." I stroked her lightly.

"My room, so you'll have to leave instead of me."

I shook my head. "Won't be leaving you for a second. Not until we both leave the resort at the same time. Even then, you'll follow me home."

"Follow you home?" She hiked her perfect eyebrow, giving me a little attitude.

"Well, I'll lead you to Winters to make sure you get there safely. Then I'll kiss you long and hard until I'm ready to return to my place in Bastion."

She frowned in the cutest way. "How do you know I live in Winters?"

I chuckled, getting off my bike. "Let's get to your room. We'll talk all about it there."

"But—"

I tugged on her hand to get her moving. She watched me with a suspicious eye. I'd have to come clean about AJ tailing her. *Fuck.* I'd spoken without thinking, not something I usually did. Further proof Madeline screwed with my head.

We quietly passed through the rustic lobby, several pairs of eyes turned our way. *The Easter Bunny and the Big Bad Wolf* popped into my head. We did kinda look like that. Madeline and I clashed big time, but I didn't care. The way this woman made me feel—light and complete—mattered more.

Nothing and no one had ever filled the crater-sized hole inside my heart. I'd been hollow there since my mother took off when I was nine. Well, there had been a time in my life when I had sort of felt whole— with the Hamilton family. It had ended when part of me sank to the bottom of Lake Garrison twelve years ago.

Lake Garrison...

In the elevator, my mind started down the painful, lonely road. It led me back to my hometown of Garrison, South Dakota. The mother chapter's home, the original Knight's Legion MC, started by my granddad Frank and his brother Charlie fifty years ago. A couple of months after my birth, my dad moved up the ranks to vice president, then eventually president.

I'd only gone back home once—eight years ago—after my enlistment in the Marines ended. Foolishly I'd thought I could handle being back. But no. It had been too fuckin' painful cruising by my old stomping grounds. And the lake. All the memories, both good and bad, had pelted me in the face like a violent hailstorm.

Nothing compared to having my innards ripped out when I had seen the Hamiltons from afar one afternoon. I'd caused an unbearable amount of pain to the most caring and loving people I'd ever known. They'd made me a part of their close-knit family when I hadn't really had one of my own. They trusted me, loved me, and I'd destroyed every one of them. I would never forget the sound of Mrs. Hamilton sobbing or the sight of Mr. Hamilton's stone-cold face at the burial of their youngest son.

What had haunted me all these years later, even more, was the little girl with two missing front teeth—my sidekick. A sassy firecracker I had protected from her rough and tumble older brothers.

On the day of the funeral, she'd clung to my side and soaked my shirt with her tears. The only words she'd spoken, dozens of times throughout the day, still tortured me. *Why did he have to die? Why? I want him to come back.*

I still hated myself for shattering her world and severing off a limb of a kind, loving family who'd welcomed me into their hearts and home.

I hate myself...

Delicate fingers skimmed over my cheek. Her soft touch and concerned gaze pulled me out of my thoughts. So sweet. So goddamn kind. So wrong for someone like me.

I was all wrong for someone like her. Madeline deserved better than anything I could ever offer. I wouldn't destroy another innocent's life.

"Hey, you okay?" she asked in the melodious voice I'd come to love in only one fuckin' day.

"Yeah. Got stuff on my mind." The elevator door opened. I took her hand and led the way to her room.

"You don't look fine." She wrapped her free hand around my forearm. I couldn't let her touch soothe me. I needed to resist her magic, the spell she'd cast on me.

"I'm fine."

"I'm a good listener." She stroked her thumb over the top of my hand. Dammit, I wished I could confess my sins to this angel, but I didn't want her to know a savage monster lived inside me.

"I'm fine, Madeline," I snapped, louder and harsher than I'd meant to. "Unlock your door."

"O-kay." She dug out her keycard from her small bag, inserted it in the slot, and when the green light flashed, I shoved the door open. She entered, and when I didn't follow, she turned around, her baby blues filled with confusion. "Come in."

"Listen, I have some things to do. Today was great."

She was in front of me in a flash, a hand pressing on my chest. "What's going on? Did I do something wrong? Offend you?"

Jesus Christ, she thinks she's the problem.

"Nah, you were perfect, Angel. But honestly, Easter Bunny, meet Big Bad Wolf." I tapped my chest above her hand.

"Oh, come on. Don't turn my words on me. Not after spending the day together."

"Madeline—"

"No! You feel the connection between us, like I do. I know you do. You want me. I've heard it in your voice and seen it in your eyes. I know we come from two different worlds, and yes, your MC scares me a little, but I'm willing to give it a go if you are."

"That's just it. We're *too* different. And 'giving it a go' isn't enough. You need to be sure of what you want, and you're not."

"You haven't even given me a chance. We've only had one *amazing* day together."

"Doesn't matter. I should've left you alone."

"No—"

"Don't you get it? I'm not good for you!"

"Storm, don't do this. Whatever happened in the elevator, let's talk about it. Something changed in you, but I'm here. I want to help you."

"You can't." I removed her hand and stepped out of her doorway. "Bolt the door."

"Stop! You can't go!"

"Fuck, Madeline. It was just one goddamn day," I scoffed like the bastard I was. Making light of the phenomenal day we had. We had a connection. I felt it deep in my heart. Some crazy ass shit after only one day. One day of being in heaven… with my angel.

"You're absolutely right." She squared her shoulders and lifted her chin. "Have a nice life, Storm." She closed the door and bolted it. For a few seconds, I got a glimpse of a strong, determined woman, but the soft whimpers on the other side of the door showed her tender, vulnerable side.

I hurt her.

"Fuck," I hissed, stalking to my room. I blew through the door and went to the brown paper bag on the nightstand. The Jack Daniels I'd yet to open. I hadn't needed it, because I had Madeline. It seemed she chased away the demons lurking in my mind before they fed on my soul.

Tonight wouldn't be about drinking myself stupid because of the sins of my past. Somehow those mattered less to me now than they had in a long time. Tonight they could sleep in the graveyard of my agony. Getting plastered was about Madeline. Numbing every piece of me that wanted her. I needed to get her out of my head and move on.

Who was I kidding? I was a fuckin' idiot if I believed that was possible.

All it had taken was one song, one touch and one kiss, for her to imprint on my goddamned heart.

CHAPTER TEN

STORM

"The Dirty Hunters are dead! I'm about ready to string the little maggots up by their ears and use them as a punching bag!" Boxer paced in my office, hands in tight fists with a sizable bulging vein in his neck. "Jill is freaking the fuck out. Wolf, oh, he wants blood."

"Where's he at? I don't want him to go off half-cocked." I cut my eyes to Raul and Track, leaning against the wall next to my desk. It was safer to stay out of Boxer's path. My enforcer rarely lost his shit, but when he did, it was best to keep the fuck out of his way.

"I told him to stay with her and to wait for your orders."

"Good."

"Shit, Storm! You know how hard Jill has worked to build her boutique. And now it's gone! Up in fucking flames! I know it was those motherfuckers!" Boxer seethed with his fingers entwined behind his head, biceps flexed. When we were in the Marines together, no one had ever messed with him.

"We need proof." Although I had no doubt, the Hunters had torched Jill's clothing boutique. All kinds of shit had been popping up ever since I'd returned a week ago from the lake. A patched member's old lady's car had been vandalized—tires slashed, windows shattered.

But none of us had overreacted. It could've been a bunch of high school punks, for all we knew.

Then, when Hero had gone to work at the club's gun shop, the front of the building was covered in graffiti. Upon investigating it, *DH* was found in small lettering. No question DH stood for Dirty Hunters. Fuck, it had made my blood boil.

So when the call came in from Wolf in the middle of the night, it had nearly sent me over the edge. Jill was Boxer's sister; he was a council member. The Dirty Fuckers were striking the leadership.

The last week had been a shitstorm. AJ reported several Hunters roaming the streets in Winters when he'd gone into town to drive by Madeline's place.

Yes, I still had AJ keeping an eye on Angel. With all the shit going on, I needed to make sure she was okay, even if I had no intention of seeing her again.

The Hunters hadn't shown their faces in Bastion, though. Coward, little cunts. But in Winters, they'd been out and about as if it were their hometown, their territory.

Boxer dropped into the chair in front of my desk, breathing hard. "I convinced Jill to go visit her friend for a few weeks."

"Her *best* friend?" Track had a taunting glint in his eye.

Boxer glared. "You got something to say, brother?" The two stared each other down.

As president, I knew all my men's backstories. Including the women they loved, if there were any. Boxer had a woman he'd pined over since he was eighteen. I'd heard all about the girl he called Snow, when we'd met in the Marines. Snow was Jill's best friend. She lived in Seattle with her "douchey boyfriend." Those were Boxer's words, not mine.

"Just wasn't sure if you meant Snow."

"Fuck off! You damn well know I meant Snow, you motherfucker!"

"Calm your ass, Boxer," I barked. After nine years, you'd think Boxer would be over her, but I understood not getting over a girl after meeting Madeline. I was sure I'd never get over my Angel.

"I told Jill the club would get the mess cleaned up. Her apartment was upstairs, you know. I want to give her and Wolf my room when she gets back. I'll take a room downstairs until they find a new place."

"That's fine." I stroked my hand over my beard, thinking. "The club will cover whatever her insurance doesn't. Grizz is checking the surveillance cameras for the boutique and gun shop. We need to amp up security all around."

Raul stepped forward. "What do you want us to do?"

I looked between him and Track. "This shit smells of war. They're hitting us softly, trying to annoy us, get us to react emotionally." I cut my gaze to Boxer. "We will *not* give them what they want."

"So, they're just fucking with us for what?" Track stepped beside his dad.

"Sounds like they want Winters. I fuckin' won't let them get it." Madeline's pretty face flashed behind my eyes. "There are more of us than them. If we screw up, we could get thrown in jail. Then the Hunters would overrun us."

"Shit…" Boxer gripped the back of his neck.

"I want to know what the fuck they're planning!" I slammed my hand down on the desk. "We need to find out where they're hiding, where they've set up their makeshift camp. I want all men involved!"

"I'm on it," Raul left my office.

"I need to check on the gym and see Jill before she leaves. I'll be back in a couple of hours," Boxer grunted on his way out.

"Damn…" Track plopped into Boxer's forsaken chair. "Word on

the street is, Hunters are soliciting women in Winters to work for them. Five-hundred a day…"

"Fuck!" I didn't like hearing this shit was going on in Madeline's town.

Track leaned forward, elbows on his knees. "You know it's only a matter of time before they notice her. She's too beautiful to miss."

My eye twitched, leveling my gaze on his. "AJ is still watching her."

"I know. I pay attention around here. Don't think it'll be enough to protect her, though." He squeezed the bridge of his nose, blowing out a long breath. "We also gotta think about Justin's daughter, Emilee. She's in and out of the clubhouse all damn day. Same with Tina. Good thing Sugar and the boys are gone."

"Yeah, they won't be back for a couple more weeks." Sugar had taken the twins on a road trip back east to visit National Monuments and go to DC. "I'll talk to Justin about his daughter. Raul will handle Tina."

Track nodded, but I could tell he had something else to say.

"What is it?" I rasped.

"Do you want to talk about what happened at the lake?"

"If I wanted to talk about it, I would've fuckin' talked about it."

"And Madeline?"

I never lied to Track. I hated any form of lying with a burning passion. When asked a direct question, I answered it truthfully—just as I expected my men to do.

"She was at the lake." I paused, reeling in my emotions. "I couldn't believe it. We spent the day together on Sunday. As we were going back to her room, I started thinking about how bad I was for her and how she deserved better."

"Aw shit, Storm."

"I took her to the room and left her. Walking away is for the best."

"Not if it's making you an angry cuss."

"I was angry before Madeline."

"You spent the day with her? The whole day?" His lip curled. *Asshole.*

"Most of the day. Took her out to Mason City for a steak dinner, a little dancing, and a whole lotta kissing. It ranked up there as one of the best days of my life. But like she said, we're different. The Easter Bunny and the Big Bad Wolf."

He screwed up his face. "Yeah, no idea what you mean, but I'm sorry, man." He shook his head, sighing. "Wait... You took her out on your bike?"

Should've known he'd key into that minor detail. It wasn't so small, but more like a fuckin' significant deal for me.

"Yes."

"Christ, man. No woman's ever been on the back of your bike."

"I know. Enough. Let's go to Jill's boutique. I want to see the damage in person." I rose from my chair and cracked my neck. Talking about Madeline wasn't easy to do.

Damn, I miss the hell out of her.

Track and I rolled to a stop in front of Sister Chic Boutique. I squeezed the shit out of my handlebars as we sat on our bikes, staring at the broken glass. The front windows were gone, only gaping holes left. Black soot surrounded the windows in Jill's second-floor apartment. My gut twisted into knots. If she and Wolf hadn't gotten out... I didn't want to imagine what might've happened.

"Incoming..." Track jerked his chin as Sheriff Jim Hendricks parked his car next to us.

The sheriff wasn't a friend or foe to the club. He was Sugar's father, so family. He didn't bother us if we didn't deal in drugs, prostitution, or sex trafficking. But we had him on our payroll, of course, and he turned a blind eye to our weapon runs. Transporting

guns was the only dirty part of our club. I was working on getting us
out, but we weren't quite there yet.

I needed to fulfill the promise I'd made to my uncle before he
died, getting Tina's daughter home safely. But it required a lot of
money. Weapons were where the big bucks were at.

Hendricks strolled my way. "Storm, this doesn't look pretty." He
studied the building.

"Nope, not at all." I followed his gaze to the shattered glass.

"Accident?" He peered through the destroyed windows.

"Isn't it always?" As if I'd call it anything else. The club didn't
need the authorities up our asses, sniffing around. We dealt with our
own problems.

"Any casualties?" He gritted his teeth.

"Not to my knowledge." I hated this song and dance. I should be
grateful to have the Sheriff on my side, but we had to keep up public
appearances. Locals strolled by, eyeing us. They knew Jim's daughter
was an "outlaw's woman" and connected to the club. To Sugar's face,
they were nice, but they talked behind her back. People sucked. Sugar
was the sweetest woman and made sure the club donated to schools
and homeless shelters.

Madeline came to mind. If anyone was mean to her, I would tear
them to shreds. It was why I needed to leave her alone. If she was with
me, it would destroy her reputation. She was a sweet, cookie-baking
teacher, for Christ's sake. Too, too good for me.

Hendricks chuckled, gripping his belt. "I hear there are some
Hunters in Winters."

I hiked a curious brow. "Oh yeah? What else you hear?"

"Sheriff Bush isn't happy. He worries about the safety of his
town, but that weasel Miller assures him they're just passing through."
Hendricks shook his head. He didn't like any of the deputies in
Winters.

"How the fuck would Miller know anything about them?" I fisted my hands.

Deputy fuckin' Miller had been a thorn in my side for far too long. He was a scrawny, dimwitted prick.

Track growled low. "Winters is Knight's territory. Another MC coming in should make him nervous."

"One would think." Hendricks rocked on his heels, thumbs hooked into his belt. "The Knights have been in this area for over twenty years. Not sure what Miller is thinking. He's an asshole. Never takes anything seriously."

"I agree with you there." I looked sidelong at Track. His jaw twitched as he glared at Hendricks.

"So, what are you going to do about this?" Hendricks looked at the brick building, turning to me for an answer.

I shrugged my shoulders. "Rebuild."

"I meant—"

"Know what you meant, Sheriff…" I sighed. "Let's go." I nodded to Track.

Hendricks stepped back. "I spoke to Eve this morning."

"Oh yeah? You tell her about this?" I jerked my chin toward the boutique. She'd sent me a text this morning like I'd asked her to do every day. I knew she and the boys were okay, but I wasn't sure if Hendricks would tell her about the fire.

He shook his head. "Nah. You don't need to worry. I knew you'd want to tell her."

My Uncle Matt trusted the Sheriff. I wished I could too, but I only trusted my club brothers. "I'll tell her when she gets back. Don't want to ruin her trip."

"I figured as much. Let me know if you need anything." Hendricks nodded, strolling to his vehicle.

The only thing I'd ever need from Hendricks was to turn a blind eye. Everything else, I'd handle.

Time to pay Sheriff Bush a little visit. Make sure we're all on the

same page regarding the Hunters in Winters Township.
Maybe I'd catch a glimpse of Madeline while I was there.

CHAPTER ELEVEN

MADELINE

Why did I let Tara and Steph talk me into line dancing? All I wanted to do was binge-watch *Sons of Anarchy*. Clearly, I was an idiot obsessing over all things MC.

That past week, I'd read two MC romance series. Holy crap, they were violent. I chalked it up to being fiction. But then, a lot of extreme shit happened on the *SOA* show. Again, fiction.

I couldn't get enough of it either.

The character Jax Teller reminded me of Storm in some ways. He was definitely some nice eye-candy. Seeing his backside was a bonus.

I'd found myself trying to find similarities because I was so damn furious at Storm. How could the jerk get me so into him and then leave me in my hotel room all hot and bothered? It was a beyond shitty thing to do.

Since I hadn't fessed up about Storm being at Lake Waleska, I had no choice but to go to The Wild Hog with my girlfriends.

I so didn't want to be here.

Loud country music drowned out my thoughts regarding Storm. People danced and drank, having a grand time. The booze tickled my fancy, but then I'd just received my third rum and coke, so I was nearing my limit before being drunk off my ass.

What could I do? Only suck it up… and drink until I didn't give a crap anymore.

Tara and Steph kicked it up on the dance floor. The brats ditched me for the first guy who asked them to dance. Traitors.

"Would you like to dance?"

I tipped my head up, straw in my mouth, to a tall, handsome man smiling at me. Blond hair combed to the side, sky-blue eyes, clean-shaven. He had on tight-fitting jeans and a pair of western boots.

I raked my eyes up and down the length of his body several times. My mother would approve. She would've hated Storm, but his guy? He would get Sara's seal of approval. To receive my mom's blessing was the pinnacle achievement. Storm would've never gotten it.

His smile grew wider. "Do you like what you see?"

"Maybe. You a farmer?" Farmers were hardworking, stable, family-oriented men. They fell in love and had a boatload of kids. This man was the kind I once looked for when I went out.

Until *Storm*. The man who may have been hardworking but stable and family-oriented? No way. Storm didn't seem like the kind of man to fall in love, get married, and have even one kid.

Why was I still thinking about him? He needed to get out of my head, so I could move on. Maybe I could move on with Mr. Farmer.

"Yes, ma'am. Am I scoring points?" He reached his hand out. "Dance with me, beautiful."

Weirdly, my body heated, even though I wasn't all that attracted to Mr. Farmer. A strange feeling came over me. Like I was being watched. I swooped my eyes to the left but didn't see anything unusual.

Mr. Farmer cleared his throat as he waited for my reply.

"Oh, um…" I set my glass down and turned my head slightly to the right.

Stormy, narrowed gray eyes were on me. Not at all who I expected to be at the bar. What was up with the murderous look on his face? I held his gaze for a long second, swallowing down the lump of emotion choking me. Were my eyes playing tricks on me? No. The man haunting my thoughts and dreams was breathing the same air as me. Desire bloomed in my core. I glanced away quickly and smiled at Mr. Farmer.

"I'd love to dance." A slow song started. What luck. Let Storm see what he'd thrown away.

Tara and Steph waved. They were dancing close with their guys—a pair of twins, kind of creepy. The men even looked identical. The alcohol must've been getting to me. An image of the four of them screwing flashed behind my eyes. Really creepy and sickening, but whatever. At this point in the evening, anything went.

"I'm Josh, by the way." His hand splayed out across my lower back. For a split second, I thought he'd said Jax–like Jax Teller from *SOA*, but then realized I'd heard him wrong.

"Hi Josh, I'm Madeline." I rested my hand on his shoulder as we swayed old-fashioned style, with my hand in his and a foot of space between us.

Josh was tall but not taller than Storm, or as hulking. He was lean and fit. I suspected he didn't have any tattoos, unlike the one I'd seen on Storm's back and bicep at the lake.

Stop thinking about Storm. Stop comparing Josh to him.

"Madeline… A beautiful name for a beautiful woman." Okay, was he trying to be corny? Cliché?

Even so, I blushed, totally turning beet red. I dropped my chin to my chest and smiled. Josh was sweet and adorable, but he didn't set me on fire or turn my panties sopping wet the way Storm had.

Speaking of… Storm was still at the bar with… Sheriff Bush?

Strange. I'd met the Sheriff at Heritage. He ran the D.A.R.E program at school. Storm's eyes were on me, I think. It was hard to tell from this distance. One of his MC brothers was with him. I recalled seeing him at The Bullet the night I'd met Storm.

"Do you live in Winters?" Josh asked, turning us.

I couldn't see Storm anymore and it made me want to pout. "I do. And you?"

"Just outside of town. Do you come here often?"

I shook my head. "No. Not really. You?"

"First time. A buddy of mine talked me into it."

I laughed. "My girlfriends talked me into it too." But it wasn't my first time here. I wasn't so sure I believed it was his first time at The Wild Hog. Whatever.

A deep belly laugh rumbled out of him. I didn't care for it much. "I'm glad our friends talked us both into coming out tonight."

Before I could respond with a lame reply—like *Those, swell friends*—or something equally stupid, he turned us again.

Storm was directly in front of me, standing to the side of the dance floor. The Sheriff was gone.

When our gazes met, he gestured with his finger to come here. I rolled my eyes and ever so slightly shook my head. His brow furrowed, lips pressed thin. The guy with him said something, but Storm didn't take his eyes off me. He mouthed, *Come here*, and a thunderous fury blew my way.

Despite my innards twisting into a knot, I slid my hand up the back of Josh's neck, hoping to make Storm jealous. My little move caused Josh to reel me in closer, and he put his head next to mine.

Storm's lips said *Fuck*. Then he mouthed, *Come. Here.*

Eyes locked on his, I played with Josh's hair. I didn't enjoy it half as much as running my nails over the base of Storm's neck. Nor did I like the way Josh smelled. I thought I caught a whiff of Irish Spring soap. My dad's favorite. The opposite of sexy to me.

Josh turned us again, the song finishing soon after. He kissed the top of my hand. "Can I buy you a drink?"

I looked to where Storm had been. He was gone. I scanned the bar but didn't see him anywhere. Guess he didn't want to talk to me after all.

I was disappointed. Maybe I only needed to see Storm again to help get over him. To stop thinking about him. Except, seeing him increased my frustration.

"How about that drink?" Josh asked with a charming grin.

"Sure, why not..."

CHAPTER TWELVE

STORM

"**G**imme another," I barked at Copper. When Track and I returned to the clubhouse, I went straight for the bar and my favorite stool. I'd been in the same spot the last two fuckin' hours.

I felt like I might go insane as images of Madeline dancing with *Cowboy Dick* pummeled me.

"You could've dragged her off the dance floor, y'know."

I glared at Track. "Like a fuckin' caveman? Think that would've made her happy?"

"Since when do you care about making a woman happy?" He eyed me, taking a pull of his beer.

"Fuck off." I gritted my teeth. Fuckin' Track.

A hand brushed over my thigh. "Hiya Storm. Looking a little stressed tonight. Something I can help you with?" Carla purred, rubbing her body against my shoulder like a cat.

Dammit. I didn't need her shit tonight, but maybe… Maybe she was just the thing I needed to get Madeline off my mind. Nah, I hadn't lost all sense.

"Not in the mood for you."

Her hand stroked my crotch just like I knew she would—nothing. I felt nothing. Not a twinge, zing, or jerk of my cock. Carla kept stroking. I didn't object since I needed to test out my dick.

Track grumbled, but I couldn't understand what he said.

I tilted my head toward him. "What?"

Track lifted his bottle to his lips. "You keep that shit up, and you'll be guilt-ridden in the morning."

"You okay, Storm?" Carla had a perplexed expression on her face. No doubt because I wasn't getting hard for her.

"Get gone, Carla." I brushed her hand away.

She pouted, slithering away.

"I don't need you babysitting me, man."

"Appears you do if you're letting Carla get you off." Track made a gagging face. He never liked Carla. Fake tits never did it for him.

They didn't do it for me either, but I never messed with Carla's. Didn't need to when on her knees with my dick in her mouth or bent over a table. Why she kept coming back for more was a mystery.

Why I kept fuckin' her showed just how fucked up in the head I was with women.

Well, before Madeline.

Until Madeline, I didn't talk to women, romance, flirt, or dance with them. I sure as hell didn't kiss them as if my life depended on it. And not one woman before Madeline made me as rock hard as she did.

"Shit, Carla did nothing for me. My dick is dead, and my balls are hiding." I drained my glass. "I don't know what to do about her."

Track looked sidelong at me. "Who, Madeline?"

"Yeah."

"Well, what do you want?" Track watched me with a curious glint in his black eyes.

"Brother, I think you know what I want. Don't make me say it."

The bastard always tried to get me to talk about my feelings. No dice. Feelings were for pussies.

"Then go after her."

I shook my head. "I'm no good for her."

"She's a grown woman. Let her decide for herself."

I slid my empty glass away from me. "I'm going up to bed."

Track huffed in frustration. "Okay. If you wait too long, you just might lose her to another man."

I grunted, stalking away. *As if I don't know what I stand to lose.*

I had been waiting for over an hour for Madeline to run by this spot. Last week AJ reported her running through the park every morning. I hoped she hadn't changed her route.

I needed to talk to her. To… Hell, I didn't fuckin' know what I would say or what I expected.

After seeing her at The Wild Hog Saturday night, I'd felt like I couldn't breathe. Like she was getting farther and farther out of my reach. I didn't know what the fuck was happening to me. I couldn't even call her, because we'd never exchanged phone numbers. And I didn't know her last name so I couldn't hunt her down beyond AJ's tips.

Sure, I could have gone to her house, but with the Dirty Hunters roaming around, I didn't want them seeing the president of Knight's Legion at her place.

My stomach tightened as a blur of yellow was heading my way. A jogger.

Holy. Hell.

Was it Madeline?

I squinted. The closer she got, the faster my heart hammered.

It was my Angel.

I perked up on my bike, debating whether to get off or stay put. Either way, she couldn't miss me. As her pace slowed, I knew she'd spotted me. I'd been eyeing a bench near a tree and planned to ask her to sit with me. Damn, I hoped she'd say yes.

She pressed her fingers to the pulse point on her neck, her free hand on her hip. As she approached, I couldn't see her gorgeous baby blues behind her dark sunglasses. I sensed she was annoyed by the way her lush lips were in a thin line.

"Morning, Angel."

"Hey… What're you doing here?" She stayed several feet back.

"Wanted to talk to you."

"We have nothing to talk about." She crossed her arms over her chest, looking tasty in spandex. Yellow sports bra trimmed in black and matching leggings with a black stripe down the side.

But the beads of sweat in her hairline and across her chest? Fuck, I was rock hard in less than sixty seconds. My cock wasn't dead. It lived only for her.

"Sit with me." I jerked my chin over to the bench.

"Don't think so. If this is about the other night, get over it. I do as I damn well please."

I swung my leg back, getting off my bike, and went to her. "Sit with me." I took her hand. She jolted but didn't pull away. Her heated body and the scent of her hair tortured my senses. My stomach tightened. I wanted her so damn much. The way her chest rose and fell, I ventured she wanted me too. We sat on the bench, but she kept a foot of space between us like I had the fuckin' clap. Sassy little shit.

"I don't see the point in talking. You were loud and clear at the lake."

"I wasn't in a good place. I've got shit in my past, Angel, that haunts me. You deserve to be with someone better than me. Someone who isn't the president of an MC."

"I suppose you're right. Lord knows I have a horrible track record with men. I guess I should thank you for saving me from myself." She faced forward but I saw her rolling her eyes behind her sunglasses. "Why are you really here?"

Miss Attitude. Damn. She was not making this easy for me. "Because I can't stop thinking about you. I should've let you decide for yourself instead of making the decision for you."

"Yeah, you should've. I'm a grown-ass woman, y'know."

I couldn't help but laugh. Madeline didn't think it was so funny, though, and pursed her tempting lips together.

"Go to hell, Storm." She was on her feet. I grabbed her just as fast, pulling her back. She landed right next to me, and I tucked her into my side. "I don't want to do this with you." I filled my hand with her thigh, holding her to me. Touching her screwed with my head. Made me weak.

"I'm sorry, Angel. I'm sorry for everything." Just like that, I turned into a walking pussy. I never apologized for shit. If my brothers found out, they wouldn't let me live it down.

"Fine. You're sorry. Apology accepted. Now let me go." She tried to move my hand. Not happening. "Let. Go."

"No." I kissed the side of her head. "Don't want to."

"Look." She stopped struggling and faced me. So damn beautiful. "I've had a lot of time to think about… stuff. Let's face the truth, Storm. You can't give me what I want. So if you're looking to just get between my legs, as tempting as it sounds, I'm not interested."

Fuckin' hell, her words slayed me.

"How do you know I can't give you what you want?" I bit back, furious she was again rejecting me. For being the asshole who had walked away from her, I deserved it.

"Okay. You're right. I don't know." She turned toward me, exhaling an exasperated breath. "So tell me, Storm, Mr. Biker President. Do you see marriage and children in your future? You up for cheering in the stands at your kid's hockey games or playing tea party with your little girl? What about stringing up Christmas lights on the house?"

"Angel, I—"

She raised her hand. "Do you see yourself snuggling on the sofa with your wife? Or watching a chick-flick and holding her when she cries during the happy, sappy parts? Honestly, Storm, you don't come across as the kind of guy who fits that mold."

If her words didn't slay me before, they just shredded me now. I scratched the back of my head, jaw tight. Nausea settled in my gut as I imagined her doing all those things with someone other than me.

"Madeline?"

We both turned toward a male voice. Fuck, it was the dude from the other night. The muscles in my neck coiled as he gazed at her fondly.

"Hi, Josh." She stood.

"Where are you going?" I grabbed her hand.

"Seriously? Let go." She jerked her hand out of mine.

I sat there like a dumb fuck as she chatted with Josh. They smiled and laughed. Madeline's squeezable ass taunted me, along with her long braid. I wanted to wrap it around my hand, tugging it hard as I drove my cock into her warm pussy.

I fuckin' needed to possess Madeline in every way possible and make her mine. Mine.

"Good seeing you, Josh." She smiled and waved, and I wanted to throw up.

"Yeah, you too." Josh nodded, eyes raking over her body as she waltzed back to me. The fucker. I should poke him in the goddamn eyes.

Madeline stepped between my legs, bent so she was eye level, and cupped my face. "Is he still watching me?"

I glanced at the prick and grunted, skimming my hands up the sides of her thighs. If she was going to be this close to me, I was going to touch her. The silkiness of the fabric allowed my hands to feel every curve. My mouth watered, desperate to have her, taste her… fuck her. She sighed. "I'm not into him. So just go with this, so he'll get the hint."

"Go with what?"

"This…" Her lips were on mine, kissing me softly. Jesus, my head whirled in delight.

I pulled her onto my lap and took control, plunging my tongue into her sweet mouth. We groaned as our tongues warred for dominance. This was what I'd been missing, what I needed. She was who I wanted. Angel was my heaven on earth.

Abruptly, Madeline pulled away and looked back to where Josh had been.

"He's gone. Thanks." She was off my lap faster than I could stop her. "I need to go. I'm meeting friends for breakfast."

"What the hell, Angel? You can't kiss me like that and then leave." I was fuckin' hard as steel, dick aching, and she was leaving me?

"It wasn't a real kiss. It was acting, so Josh would see I wasn't available. He wants to take me to dinner."

"The fuck it wasn't real. We weren't acting, and you know it as well as I do."

She shook her head and removed her sunglasses. "Just stop. I know what I want, and you're not the man to give it to me."

"Fuck," I hissed low as a woman passed us pushing a baby in a stroller. Worst timing ever, considering what we were talking about. "How can you be thinking long term when we barely know each other?"

"Because I want to fall in love, get married, and have babies." Her eyes teared up as she revealed a part of herself.

Dammit, I blanched at her wants and felt deep in my bones how much they meant to her. None of it was anything I ever wanted before, but I'd be a liar if I didn't admit I'd thought about the very same things as of late.

"Jesus, Angel," I muttered on a sigh.

"It's what I've always wanted, Storm." She looked away. "I need to go."

"Not like this. Give me your phone number. Let's have dinner. Shit…" I rubbed my hand over my beard. Why the fuck was I pushing this with her? "We'll figure it out, Angel."

"No, we can't. Big Bad Wolf, meet Easter Bunny." She patted her chest, tossing my words back at me. I could see her fighting to stay in control of her emotions, to not let any tears fall.

It gutted me to see her this way. "Angel…"

"No." She took off running, and I let her go.

CHAPTER THIRTEEN

MADELINE

I bit my lip before licking it. It had been four days since I saw Storm in the park. Four days of remembering the kiss I gave him. How could I be so stupid and kiss him?

"Sunbathing in the front yard sucks. We should be on a beach in Mexico or Fiji," Tara complained.

I didn't bother lifting my head to see her pouty lips. I was confident they were jutted out, as always. "Agreed." I'd do just about anything to be anywhere else.

"Maybe we should take a little vacay. We have all summer free to do whatever we want."

"Maybe."

"Where do you want to go?"

I shrugged my shoulder closest to her. Anywhere. I would go anywhere so long as Storm wasn't there.

"A cruise could be fun too."

I sighed with longing for the vast open sea. "Yeah."

"Will you talk to me? One-word responses aren't doing it for me. I'm tired of trying to figure out what flew up your ass since you returned from the lake. What happened with the nice guy you met at The Wild Hog? Josh, right? Has he called you? Texted you. Talk to me, Mads. What's going on with you?"

The roar of a motorcycle made me still before I could reply. I listened, waiting for it to fade away, but it didn't. In fact, I was willing to bet it stopped in front of our place.

Did Storm find me? Wishful thinking. I hadn't heard a peep from him since the park. Not like he had my number to call. But he could've been more persistent. He could've interrupted my morning runs. I didn't change my route, hoping he might be on the same bench waiting for me. But he never was.

I was lying on my stomach with my bathing suit top undone to avoid tan lines, facing the front porch. All I could do was look over my shoulder and see if it was him.

Not happening. I wouldn't put in any effort for Storm. If he wanted to talk, it was going to be all on him. He had messed with my head and heart. No chance in hell I'd make this easy for him.

"Afternoon, lovelies," a raspy voice called.

Lovelies? That didn't sound like Storm. The hairs on my arms prickled, uneasiness clogged my throat.

"Hi," Tara chirped, flipping over and sitting upright. She had on a bandeau top and didn't care about tan lines. "Are you lost?"

"Ah, yeah. Think you'd like to show me around?"

"Tara," I whispered through gritted teeth. "Don't." I still hadn't turned around to see the face of the man who made my skin crawl.

"Sorry, but I'm hanging with my friend." Tara paused as if considering him. "You one of the Knights? I'd think you'd know your way around these parts."

Jesus, this guy was a biker? Had Storm sent him to check on me? Nah. Why would he be lost if he was a Knight?

"The Knights are a bunch of pussies. I'm a Dirty Hunter." He clicked his tongue.

Bile rose into my throat. My pulse whooshed in my ears, feeling exposed and vulnerable. If a biker stopped at our place, it meant he wanted something. Shit, this was bad. I was too afraid to turn around, not wanting him to see my face. Were there more coming? The hairs on the back of my neck prickled like a porcupine at the thought.

"Whatcha doin' in Winters then?" Tara poked around. I wanted to know what they were doing here too. This was Knight's Legion territory. Everyone knew it. From what I knew about MCs, which wasn't much, they didn't like other clubs on their turf.

He cleared his throat. "Just checking it out."

"Then what?" Tara grabbed her Diet Coke off the small plastic table between us.

Okay, Tara. Let it die so he'll leave.

"Not sure. Maybe I'll see you around." The sound of his bike roaring to life sent a wave of relief over me.

"Bye." Tara waved all smiley and shit. She took Minnesota nice to a whole new, dangerous level. Not me, though. I wasn't from Minnesota. I was born and raised in South Dakota, where an outlaw MC ruled the area. Hell, there were a lot of MCs. Sturgis was several hours west of my town and hosted the largest motorcycle rally in the world. From an early age, I'd learned to keep my mouth shut and my eyes down.

I slowly peered over my shoulder. The dude was ginormous. Like the Jolly Green Giant statue in Blue Earth. Except this guy didn't look so jolly with his bald head, pitted face, and leathery skin. The man must've had a severe case of acne back in the day. He was covered in ink from his neck down to his hands. From what I could see, even the sides of his head had tats.

Yeah, he looked nothing like Storm and his brothers. They were drop-dead gorgeous biker gods.

I wanted to see the emblem on the back of his cut, but he went too fast as he rode off. The Dirty Hunters didn't sound nice. I also didn't appreciate him calling the Knights a bunch of pussies.

"Damn, I hope those guys are just passing through town." I flipped onto my back, holding my top to my chest.

"Why? He's just another biker. What's the harm?" Tara guzzled her pop.

"Not all bikers are created equal. There are some horrible clubs out there." I'd seen a couple growing up. People went missing or wound up dead in a creek. I remembered a time when tensions were thick in my small town. Silence had befallen our mostly joyful community when a menacing group of bikers wreaked havoc for months on end. The local MC, which I couldn't recall their name for the life of me, had their hands full. They had lost a few members too.

I wished I'd known about the Knight's Legion running Bastion and Winters before I'd signed my teaching contract. I wouldn't have met Storm, for starters. I wouldn't be, once again, stuck in the middle of a potential club war in my own backyard.

"You sure talk like you know a thing or two about them."

I stood from my chaise, cupping my breasts to hold my top in place. "A little, I guess. I'm going inside to shower before I get sunburned." I bit my bottom lip. "Just stay away from the Dirty Hunters. I have a bad feeling about them."

"But, the Knights are okay?" She narrowed her eyes as if trying to draw a connection.

"Didn't say that either." I retreated inside to wash off the grime of sunscreen baked onto my skin. Washing thoughts of Storm down the drain sounded good too.

Later that evening at the armory, I was on my second rum and coke. The stupid shower had done nothing to strip Storm from my mind. I shouldn't have been surprised. The jerk monopolized my dreams at night and controlled my daydreams. It pissed me off that I couldn't get him out of my head.

It'd been a few weeks since the day we spent together at Lake Waleska. I still tasted him on my tongue and felt his large hands flush on my back when we slow danced. No other man had ever made my panties soaking wet.

The kiss I'd planted on him in the park only made me remember what I was missing. Kissing Storm made my body buzz with need. When his hand brushed along the sides of my hips and gripped my ass, I'd almost orgasmed. Pathetic, right?

Running away from him hadn't been easy, and I'd regretted it immediately. What would be the point in trying to figure us out? He'd said love, marriage, and children weren't something he wanted. I wouldn't be an easy lay for him. Even though I wanted more than anything for him to screw my brains out, just once.

Yeah, I knew better. Once would never be enough. I could tell by the off-the-charts chemistry we had. I'd never get enough of Storm. Never.

I growled low in my throat, gulping the remaining liquid in my glass. I just wanted to forget about Mr. Biker Prez. Listening to Ray's band wasn't helping either.

"Girl, what gives? You look about as happy as a flaming hot, puss-filled pimple." Steph snorted, nudging my elbow. "It's summer vacation. Us teachers should be happy."

I bobbed my head in agreement. All my teacher friends were thrilled to be on summer vacation. Usually, I'd have been happy with them... If it weren't for a particular biker, who'd invaded my every thought and made me feel things I'd never felt before.

"I'm convinced something happened while she was at the lake, but she's not talking. She hasn't even accepted Josh's dinner invitations. She's ignoring him." Tara studied me as she enlightened

Steph. This girl believed she was the authority on all-things-Madeline.

"What happened, honey?" Steph cooed as if talking to one of her kindergarteners.

"Just... You know... Tommy." My chest squeezed as the partial lie left my lips, but they'd both accept it without question. I was a horrible sister. My little getaway was supposed to be about my brother. I didn't want to go home to visit his grave. I'd thought the lake was a perfect alternative. Then Storm appeared unexpectedly. Thoughts of my brother drifted away in the breeze.

"Gosh darn it, Mads." Tara's arms flew around my neck. "I'm so sorry I forgot the anniversary of his death. Worst friend ever."

"It's okay." I patted her arm. It really was. From the moment Storm blew into my life, like an F5 tornado, I'd been utterly consumed by that devastatingly handsome biker. Worst sister ever.

"No wonder you've been down lately." Steph made a pouty face. "Get you another drink, honey?"

"Sure." Why not get drunk? Anything to forget about him.

Just as Steph hopped out of the chair next to me, a quartet of bikers entered the armory. They strutted in as if they owned the joint.

On a panicked gasp, I gripped Steph's hand to stop her. "Wait."

My first inclination was the Knights had come to cart me away. Then I rolled my eyes at the ridiculous image my mind conjured. Storm didn't really give a shit about me. He'd probably already found a better, more accepting woman who fit into his MC life. A siren in a leather mini skirt barely covering her ass, sans panties, of course. Horny-ass bikers probably demanded easy, fast as lightning access to pussy.

My stomach churned at the thought of Storm with another woman. Kissing her, touching her, smelling her juices like he'd smelled mine.

Bile shot into my throat. I rushed to the bathroom, covering my mouth with my hand, clinging to the nearest toilet and emptied my stomach. Gawd. I never should've eaten those nachos. The rum and cokes didn't help either.

Tara and Steph entered as I gagged and heaved.

"You okay, Mads?" Tara collected my long hair in her hand. "Steph, hair tie."

"Got one right here." Steph regularly wore at least three hair ties on her wrist.

I wiped my mouth with toilet paper and stood after Tara secured my hair. "Thanks. I probably drank too much." Lie. My vomiting incident had Storm's name written all over it. "I think I'll cut out early tonight." Then I could wallow over my pathetic life and not be a party pooper.

"Yes. Good idea. Rest up. Don't want you missing the Fourth of July barbecue out at the lake. I can give Tara a ride if she wants to stay," Steph offered, knowing I'd brought Tara in my car.

"Dang, I'd forgotten about the barbecue." Just further proof of how much Storm had infiltrated my mind.

"Seriously? You are off your game." Steph chuckled. "What do you say, Tara?"

She had no idea how messed up I was. I exited the stall, rinsed my mouth, and washed my hands.

"Sounds good to me, unless Mads wants me to go home with her." Tara's sable-colored orbs focused on me.

I preferred Tara left with me. The bikers who'd entered weren't Knights, they were Hunters, and pitted-leather-face was with them. They freaked me out. I hated the idea of my friends being around them.

Could I have been making a big deal out of nothing? Judging these bikers before I even knew their names? Most looked scary, but they also had a soul. Right? Even the scariest.

"I'll be fine." I smiled, drying my mouth with a paper towel.

"Cool! We'll escort you to your car," Tara said in a perky voice.

The second we left the bathroom, the awkward, tense vibe in the armory reminded me of home—during the MC war which had claimed the lives of several innocent locals.

Eyes darted around the room and seemed to avoid the bikers. Ray's band sounded less vibrant than ten minutes ago.

Goose bumps spread across my body. I didn't want to be here, but I also didn't want to freak out. My spine jerked upright. *Fake it till you make it* flashed in my head. I could appear strong and confident as I left the building, instead of panicked and terrified.

The warm evening air wrapped around me like a cozy blanket. Just as fast, it choked me. A row of motorcycles greeted us. They were guarded by what I remembered were called prospects. One stood at each end.

"Jesus, what is going on here?" Steph whispered as we made our way to the parking lot.

I didn't reply, keeping my eyes locked on my car, key fob in hand, thumb on the alarm button.

"Dirty Hunters, I think," Tara said in a quiet voice.

"Are they a gang?"

My heart raced, feeling eyes on the back of my neck. My bare arms were cold and clammy. I'd never been afraid for my well-being like this before. Could it be the alcohol making me hyper-paranoid?

"Biker club," Tara replied. "I guess it's different."

I swallowed thickly—just a little bit farther.

"They look intense," Steph said just above a whisper.

"And scary," Tara added.

Made it! I unlocked my door and jumped into the driver's seat.

"Sure, you want to stay?" I glanced back at the two guards. I'd been right; they were watching us.

"We'll be okay. These guys are probably just looking for some fun." Steph snorted. "Little do they know, this is Winters Township, ain't nothin' fun to do here on a Friday night."

Tara laughed. "So true. Get some rest, Mads. Emotional stuff is exhausting."

She nailed it. Emotional stuff was crushing me. Just not about who Tara thought. Who fell hard for a guy, a biker no less, so quickly? I felt ridiculous. Had I been drawn in by his sexy bad boy looks? Because he was a biker? I should make an appointment with a therapist.

"Okay. Call if you need a safe ride home."

"Will do." Tara shut my door. I locked it, waiting until they were safely inside before I left the parking lot.

On my way home, I was extra vigilant. In Winters, after six in the evening, it looked like a ghost town. Stoplights blinked yellow for drivers to yield down the main road. Local merchants were home with their families.

But after nine o'clock during the summer, when the sun finally faded into twilight, it was easy to spot the single headlight a half a block behind me. I bit the corner of my lip as I white-knuckled the steering wheel.

Was one of the Hunters following me? Maybe it was only a random guy on a bike. I'd seen a few in town. I wasn't usually a paranoid person, but it felt like times were changing in Winters.

To test my gut instinct, I pulled into the drive-thru at Arby's. No cars were in line, so I rolled my window down and ordered a four-piece mozzarella stick and a small chocolate shake. They would both go into the trash, but I wanted to appear like I was out getting a late-night snack.

Once I collected my purchase, relief washed over me as I continued toward my home. But then the single headlight returned.

"Shit, shit, shit," I yelled, palms sweating as I squeezed the steering wheel. I inhaled and exhaled, trying to slow my racing heart.

Some biker creep was for sure following me. I couldn't go home alone, but I also couldn't drive around town all night either.

Downtown Winters was small and quaint. Aside from Arby's and Taco Bell, nothing else was open. I didn't want to go back to the armory.

Then I remembered Walmart was open until midnight.

But what would I do? Hang out in the store until it closed? Then what? Hope for the best? Pray the Hunter got tired of waiting for me?

What other choice did I have?

The Walmart parking lot was mostly empty, affording me a parking spot right in the front. I grabbed my purse, the shake, and mozzie sticks and hightailed it into the store. Tossing the food into the trash, I breathed a sigh of relief.

I'm safe.

CHAPTER FOURTEEN
STORM

"**W**hat the fuck you mean she's been in Walmart wandering around for an hour?" I roared into the phone. The prospect had one job. One fuckin' job: stay out of sight while tailing Madeline.

What does little shit do? Allow himself to be seen—stupid fuck. Madeline was probably shaking in her boots, scared shitless in the damn produce department.

Sonofabitch.

"Sorry, Prez. At this time of night, the town is empty. No cars to hide behind." His voice shook, exhaling a nervous breath.

"Don't gimme your fuckin' excuses, boy." My nostrils flared as I huffed like a bull seeing red.

"What's going on?"

I lifted my gaze to Track, standing in the doorway of my office. He must have heard me yelling over the music in the bar. I waved him off, but the asshole entered anyway and dropped into the chair.

"She buyin' anything?" I turned my attention back to AJ on the phone.

"No. Just looking around with her arms wrapped tightly around her chest."

"Chest? You looked at her chest?" I stood from my chair, rolling my hand into a fist.

"N... no Prez." AJ stuttered. The little shit, he better be afraid. Although only twenty-one, he'd proven himself thus far to be dependable in completing every shit job given to him.

"Prospect, if you don't improve your fuckin' tailing skills you won't get patched next year," I yelled into the phone. Madeline was more important than washing the councils' bikes or cleaning urinals.

I stalked out of my office to the clubhouse entrance. I couldn't have Madeline scared out of her mind. I needed to make sure she was okay after the fuckin' Hunters showed up at the armory. I'd had AJ staking out the place when Madeline and her friend went inside. My gut told me to keep the prospect there, and I was glad I had. AJ had texted the second the Hunters arrived. Then another text came, informing me of prospects drooling over Madeline and her friends in the parking lot. I lost my shit.

Those dirty sons of bitches were not only in Knight's territory, but a source of Boxer's had heard one of the Hunters talking about profiling. Those fuckers were scoping out women in Winters, and Madeline was one of them.

At this point, I was going to protect her with my life. Even if from a distance, I cared too damn much to let anything happen to her.

"Keep watch. I'm on my way." I ended the call and cut my eyes to Track.

"What's up with your woman?" He climbed on his bike.

"She's not my woman." I tugged my keys out of my pocket.

Fuckin' Track just had to be a shit, calling Madeline my woman. So what if I had a prospect watching her every day. I was only concerned about her safety. Nothing more.

"Bullshit, Prez. She means something to you. What's the latest?"

"Earlier today, AJ spied a Dirty Hunter at her house." My heart raced, jaw tight. The parking lot here at the compound was packed for the usual Friday night club party. I'd avoid it. My Angel was all I could think of.

"Fucking hell. That's why your office was a mess of wood and glass." Track started his bike.

I grunted, throwing my leg over the seat. I'd trashed my office in a fit of rage. But it wasn't all about the fuckin' Hunters being at her house. I was still pissed about her dancing with another man and running away from me at the park. I shouldn't be wound so tightly, but I fuckin' missed her.

In the last couple of weeks, I'd been stressed to the max while dealing with the Hunters. I knew Madeline could calm me down with her tender touch and kisses, but she wasn't mine. Fuck, I hated it too.

The Hunters were getting bolder and out of control talking to women in Madeline's town. We hadn't been able to shut them down. I wanted to avoid a full-blown war if I could, so I needed to stay level-headed. But I was going out of mind with worry for the community. More so for her.

"Where we headed, Prez?"

We?

I could've ordered Track to stay put, and he would've obeyed. I didn't need help handling Madeline, but there were four Hunters at the armory. Who knew how many more lurking about. It'd be reckless to go into Winters alone. I might have a short fuse and an erratic personality—up one minute, down the next—but I sure as fuck wasn't reckless.

"Walmart." I pulled out of the gated parking lot.

The roads were clear. Track and I flew down the back roads going 70 MPH. Deer were grazing in the fields. One could've darted out in front of us, but I wouldn't go any slower. The thought of Madeline being afraid compelled me to haul ass.

It was twenty to eleven when we met up with AJ on the side of the building. The boy looked nervous.

"Gimme an update," I shouted, without preamble.

"She's peeked out the double doors twice. Parked on the wrong side. Must've forgotten the doors on the right are locked after ten. She'd have to cross the parking lot to get to her car from the left side."

"Shit," I muttered. "Seen any Hunters?"

"No. You want me to go in and escort her out?"

"Fuck no. She doesn't know you." I inhaled a deep breath. Just the idea of seeing Madeline again had my stomach in knots. "I'll be back."

The store was mostly empty. Employees stocked the shelves, working in the freezer section. I casually strutted through the main walkway, dialing into the sounds around me.

My heart practically jumped into my throat when I heard her laugh. I slowed my steps and followed her melodic giggles to the card aisle. A smile stretched across my face.

She had on a sundress and western boots—white ones this time. The girl sure loved her boots. She rocked them too. Her skin looked tanner, no doubt the result of her laying out in the sun earlier today, in a goddamn bikini. I was furious about it too, but I couldn't deal with that. Not right then. I had other pressing matters.

Her back was to me as I approached. I wanted to wrap my arms around her. My hands ached to touch her, and my lips tingled with need.

"How's it going?" I stuck my thumbs in my pockets to keep from touching her. I needed to play it cool.

She spun around, bug-eyed, and dropped the card she'd been reading. "Storm!" She stepped back, bumping into the card display.

"Hey, you okay?" I capped her shoulder to steady her.

She cleared her throat, pulling out of my grasp. "Yeah, fine. You just startled me. You shouldn't sneak up on people. It's creepy." She picked up the card she dropped and returned it to its spot.

"You seem jittery." My eyes roamed over her beautiful face, down her tempting, lithe body. Fuck. I desperately wanted to touch her.

"Your assessment is wrong." She pressed her lips thin. I couldn't help but smirk. She was putting on a good show, acting tough and in control. I knew better, but wouldn't steal her thunder.

"Okay. Well... Good to see you." I turned around and took a step, faking indifference.

"Storm, wait." Her voice rose an octave higher than usual, sounding frantic.

"Yeah?" I peered over my shoulder.

"Are you... Um... leaving right now?"

I nodded.

"Can you maybe, walk me out?"

I turned around to face her. "Everything okay, Angel?" I furrowed my brow, hating how her hands trembled at her sides.

She sighed, like she was lowering her guard. "No. I think someone's following me." Her eyes teared up.

I freaking lost it, tugging her into my arms. She let me hold her, and damn she felt amazing in my arms. Smelled good too. Fresh and soft. There was no other way to describe it. She wasn't drenched in perfume like some women. It was all Madeline, just as I remembered.

This was where I should confess the dude following her was one of my guys. But I didn't. "Let's go check it out."

Madeline nodded, staying tucked into my side.

"Anything else going on?" I was curious if she'd admit to a Hunter being at her house. Madeline seemed to be an honest person, but had a hard time trusting people.

"Dirty Hunters have been in town a lot this last week. One of them stopped at my place today. Said he was checking out the town.

Asked if we'd show him around."

I fisted my left hand and bit down on my back molars. Fucking Hunters were praying on unsuspecting women—on my woman.

Their game was prostitution. Knights didn't allow that shit in our territory. If people wanted to pay for sex, they'd have to go elsewhere for it. Goddammit, this pissed me off.

"Did you give him your number?"

Her baby blues flashed as we exited the store. Oh, she looked pissed.

"What do you take me for, a stupid woman? Hell no, I didn't give him my number or name. I have a brain, biker jerk." She pushed out of my arms and hot-footed it toward her car.

God, this woman turned me on. I loved her fire.

"I know you're not stupid, Angel." I trotted after her.

"Don't call me that."

"Will you slow your ass down." I reached out and took her hand, spinning her around.

"No! Just stay there and make sure I get into my car safely. I don't need anything else from you."

"I beg to differ, darlin'." I reached my hand up to her face.

She swatted it away. "Screw you, Storm." She took off running, and what did I do? I ran after her. This woman had me by the balls and didn't even know it. She would never know it.

"Why the hell are you running from me?" I caught up to her, grabbed her by the arms, and pushed her against the side of her car. "Fuckin' stop already."

She gasped, mouth popping open. "Let go of me." Her eyes were wild with fury as she struggled to break free from my hands.

Not happening.

"I need to talk to you," I told her as calmly as possible. Damn woman made my heart race. My alpha side screamed to be set free. To unleash holy hell on her pert ass. I fuckin' needed to hold it together.

Forcing Madeline to do anything wouldn't end well.

"No."

"Goddammit, woman. If you don't settle the fuck down, I'm gonna tan your hide so red, you won't be able to sit for a month!"

She froze, her baby blues assessing me. "You wouldn't." Her voice dripped with disdain.

"The fuck I wouldn't. Sometimes a good spanking is needed to tame a wild woman such as yourself."

She pushed out her chin defiantly. "I'd press charges. Assault. Then I'd get a restraining order."

I growled like the savage animal I was, narrowing the gap between us. "Nothing could keep me away if I wanted you."

"Well then, I have nothing to worry about because you don't want me."

"The fuck I don't." I crushed my mouth to hers. Warmth spread across my chest. There was nothing better than having Madeline in my arms, kissing me back through her soft moans. Every hair on my scalp stood at attention, every skin cell tingled, every neuron fired.

I needed this woman in my life. Despite my fear of not being good enough, the shame I carried from my past, or the danger being with me could bring her, I needed her.

"Storm…" she said in a come-hither voice against my lips, "I've missed you."

"Fuck, Angel. I've missed you, too." I softly kneaded her wet, luscious lips with mine.

"Then take me home." She exhaled a lusty breath, fingers playing with the back of my neck.

I pulled back. A ravishing shade of desire veiled over her face. Fuck yeah.

"I'll take you to the clubhouse."

"No. I'm not ready to go there. Let's go to my place." She bit my bottom lip, sucking it into her mouth. I nearly messed my jeans on the spot.

"You sure?"

"Positive."

I hesitated for a second, heart thrumming wildly against my ribs. If I went home with her, if we had sex, I'd never let her go.

Fuck it.

"Okay, baby. Drive me over to the side of the building where my bike is parked, and I'll follow you home."

Her eyes smiled as she lifted on her tiptoes and kissed me softly. It was just a quick kiss, but it held so much promise for what our night would bring.

We got into Madeline's car, and she pulled it alongside the building. The fuckin' smirk on Track's face immediately set me off.

"Are they your friends? I mean, brothers." Madeline peered around me.

"Eyes over here, baby." I kissed her, unable to get enough of her but reluctantly broke away. "Yeah, my brothers. Gimme a minute to talk to them. Then I'll follow you home."

She smiled, a slight blush on her cheeks. "Okay."

I pecked her lips then unfolded my large frame out of her little car. After shutting the door, I tapped the window. "Lock it."

I winked when I heard the click.

"Hey lover boy," Track razzed, not two seconds later. "That was some hot as fuck lovers quarrel. A real spitfire you got there, dontcha?"

"Fuck off." I got on my bike. "I'm following her home. You two can head back to Bastion."

Track's smirky grin fell away. "Think that's a good idea after a Hunter's been seen on her street?"

"It's not really a street. More like a single paved road flanked by two rows of mobile homes," AJ said like he knew his shit. Good, it showed he'd paid attention. "But yeah, Prez. I agree with Track. It's not safe if a Hunter shows up and sees your bike."

I scratched my beard. I couldn't have AJ hanging out all night after watching Madeline all day or have my road captain doing menial shit, either.

I cut my eyes to Track. "Call Copper. He can take the night shift." Copper was two years older than AJ and about thirty pounds heavier, all muscle. He'd also been a prospect for more than a year. Moved up to bartending. He'd get patched, if the table voted him in, in a few months. I looked over at AJ. "Follow me and stay until your replacement arrives. Then I want you back by seven."

"Okay, Prez."

I gave Track a short nod and did the same to Madeline, letting her know I was ready. She bobbed her head and drove off.

Shit, what was I doing? One little heated argument, and I was on my knees, kissing her white western boots.

I was in deep shit.

But deep shit wasn't enough to stop me from following her home. It would take a lot more to keep me away after she'd invited me back to her place.

No chance in hell would I pass up this opportunity.

CHAPTER FIFTEEN
MADELINE

I was thrilled Tara wasn't home when I parked my car in our little driveway. Our single wide looked dark. Stupidly, I'd forgotten to leave a light on in the living room.

When I was with Dane, we always stayed at his place before I moved in with him. He didn't care for my home because I lived in a trailer park and not in a real house—snobby jerk.

Honestly, I'd pushed for Storm to come home with me as a test. It was wrong, I shouldn't have tested him, but Dane had made me skeptical of all men. The last thing I wanted was to have a repeat of the destructive-Dane-years.

I hadn't been totally lying. Going to Storm's clubhouse was intimidating. I needed to know more about his club and what they were about, first. If he hadn't left me crying and cursing him in my hotel room, I would've asked him then.

Which brought me to tonight. What the hell just happened in the Walmart parking lot? I'd been prepared to leave the store with a big scary biker and drive away. Yes, I wasn't looking forward to coming home to an empty, dark house. But I would've managed. Maybe.

That kiss, though. It was all on Storm. He initiated it. I was more than a little happy about it, too.

I wasn't lying when I told him I missed him. It scared the crap out of me—having such strong feelings for a man I hardly knew. But there I was, inviting him home to have sex.

I'd truly lost my mind.

Storm parked his bike beside my car. My stomach fluttered and pussy tingled with excitement.

He opened my door, reaching in and tugging me out of the car. Storm stood so close my face smashed into his chest.

"Angel, it's adorable how you adhere to the speed limit."

"I break the rules sometimes." I walked my fingers up his chest teasingly, burying them in his beard.

"Yeah? I'd like to hear about the rules you've broken." He filled each of his hands with my ass cheeks, lifting me off the ground as if I weighed nothing more than a weightless piece of silk.

I laughed, hooking my legs around his waist and my arms around his neck. God, he was pretty to look at. Probably not what he'd like to be called, but he was pretty, and I could stare at him indefinitely.

Storm carried me to the front door. I unlocked it, opened and closed it, all perched from his muscly arms.

He paused at the door, as if listening for something. It took me only a second to realize he was making sure no one was in here.

"Down the hall, second door on the left." I nipped at his neck, inhaling the scent of leather mixed with his natural musk. Intoxicating. "Do you want anything to drink?"

"Just want you, Angel." He dropped me on the edge of my bed.

"Well, I'm a little thirsty. I'll just grab a bottle of water from the fridge." I stood and was pushed onto the mattress.

"I'll get it."

Okay then, Bossy Biker Prez.

Not sixty seconds later, Storm appeared with the water and a bottle of beer, setting them on the nightstand.

"Why don't you shut the door, Prez?" I kicked off my boots, tossing them into the open, messy closet. I might've been embarrassed if the rest of my room wasn't tidy. Mostly. Every drawer from the dresser to the nightstand was disheveled. I was more of an on-the-surface clean kind of girl.

"Don't want your roomie to see us naked." A devilish smirk appeared on his lips.

I waved him off. "She's seen me naked plenty. I don't want her to see you in your birthday suit. How'd you know I have a roommate?"

"I just know." He winked, removing his cut and draping it carefully over the chair near the window. "She's seen you naked plenty of times, aye? Does that mean you swing both ways?"

"If I did, would you have a problem with it?" I teased, watching for his reaction.

His dark eyebrows raised, and he smiled. "No problem at all. But if you're with me, you're only with me." His black T-shirt came off next. I almost launched off the bed to lick every curve and dip of his rippled abs. The man was a sculpted masterpiece.

"Same goes for you, whether a man or a woman."

"Not into dudes, baby."

"No other women either... if you're with me." My body tensed, sensing he was trying to avoid answering me. I wasn't totally oblivious. A sexy, single, outlaw biker was probably a manwhore.

I was only a conquest.

On *Sons of Anarchy* and in the MC romance books I read, bikers fucked many different women... club whores. It was just what they did. I couldn't be with him if he were with other women while with me.

"I heard you." He removed his belt and unzipped his pants.

"And?"

"And what?"

I was off the bed, unsure if I wanted to go through with this after all. "If this is just a one-night fuckfest, then tell me now. I can handle it—more than handle it. But after tonight, I don't want to see you again. Not in Walmart, or at my front door or the park. Understand?"

Storm jerked me into his arms and held the side of my face against his firm chest. He stroked my back, but he still hadn't said a word.

It was fine. I could have a one-night stand. A night where I forgot about the outside world and his MC. No problem.

Liar.

What I couldn't do was be with Storm knowing he was with other women. Even without a formal declaration, more than one night with him would feel like... well, *more*. For me, it would feel like a relationship. And relationships, even on the most casual level, meant something to me.

"Please answer me," I whispered, pulling out of his arms. "I don't do casual hookups. Not ever. You can screw me tonight if that's all you're looking for, but then I never want to see you again."

"Fuck baby. What the hell happened to you?"

"I was cheated on." The words flew out of my mouth before I could bottle them up. "Betrayed by an unfaithful douchebag who messed with my head. I won't go there again, not with you or any other man. So answer my damn question." I only cared about the cheating part. Storm didn't appear to be the kind of guy who hit women, but then, what did I really know?

Storm was avoiding my simple question, and I felt on the brink of unraveling. He probably had dozens of women at his beck and call. God, who was I kidding? A biker president with one woman? Never gonna happen.

He just stared at me like I'd lost my mind. Maybe I had.

"You know what, don't answer." I ripped my body away from his.

"I want you to leave." And I'd officially lost it.

Whatever.

My house. My pussy. My choice.

I ran out of the room, heart pounding erratically as I swung open the front door. Well, at least this could all end now that Storm saw what a whack job I was, thanks to Dane.

Something flickered outside. I made out the shape of a biker at the end of the street.

Who was he? A Hunter or a Knight? It was too dark to tell which club was watching my house. If I had to guess, I'd say it was a Knight solely because the prez was in my bedroom. Speaking of...

What the hell was taking Storm so long?

"Let's move it along, Prez! I think one of your brothers is lurking around my neighborhood." I shook my head, peeking out the front door.

Suddenly I was swept off my feet, and the door slammed shut.

I gasped. "What're you doing?"

"Lock the door."

I stared into his eyes, defiantly. "No. We aren't doing this."

"The fuck we aren't. Now lock the goddamn door," he roared like some badass king of the jungle. "Fuck it. I'll do it myself." He threw me over his shoulder, slapped my ass hard, and I yelped.

"Jesus Christ woman, you are always trying my patience." He locked the deadbolt and barreled down the hallway to my room.

"Yeah, well, back at you, you, big ass brute!"

Storm tossed me onto the bed like a sack of potatoes. My back hit the mattress, and he was on me before I could react to the sudden impact. He was completely naked.

How did I not notice his lack of clothing after he flung me around like a Raggedy Ann doll?

Not only was he buck naked, but he was sporting the most enormous erection I'd ever felt against my pelvis. I didn't need to see it. I felt his thick, hard-as-stone length.

My mouth watered, clit throbbing as Storm sucked on my neck and pawed at my body.

"Storm..." I breathed out his name. "I... What... Jesus..." I clenched my pussy as his hand brushed along my inner thigh, unbelievably lightly up, up, up until it slipped under my dress.

"Dammit, Madeline," he growled, biting the tender skin below my ear. "From the moment I saw you singing to this moment, you have riled up my emotions, driving me crazy and fuckin' turning me on. No other woman has ever done anything like it before. I won't fuckin' cheat on you." He lifted his head and stared straight into my eyes. "Do you hear me, woman? I would never cheat on you."

"I..." Did he mean it? Or was he paying me lip service? Telling me what I wanted to hear so he could get into my pants?

"Don't overthink, baby."

"But I—"

"I'll protect your heart, mind, body, and soul. I promise. I won't hurt you." His lips covered mine in a heated kiss.

Every cell in my body wanted to believe him. I desperately wanted to believe him. Either I trusted Storm for tonight and fully let myself go, or I protected my heart for the inevitable heartbreak to come. Still, I'd have this night with him, but he wouldn't get all of me. The latter I could compartmentalize. The former could destroy me.

"I want you," I whispered against his mouth, running the tips of my fingers over his broad, sculpted shoulders, down the ridges in his back, and over his taut, muscular ass.

Storm was off me and had me on my feet faster than my brain could keep up with his rapid movements.

"Strip," he demanded in a calm voice. He climbed onto my bed and positioned himself in the middle of half a dozen white pillows I had perfectly placed against my headboard. He looked like an overgrown tattooed cherub floating on fluffy clouds.

I rolled my lower lip into my mouth to stifle a laugh. Did he know how sexy and adorable he was, all at once?

"Hurry Angel, I'm ready to explode here." He stroked his cock from the base up to the tip in a hypnotic motion. Down, up, down, up. Precum beaded at his slit. He left it alone, glistening like morning dew on the petals of my potted petunias.

I licked my lips, parched and desperate for Storm to quench my thirst.

Unexpectedly his hand stopped moving, waking me from the trance I'd been in. My eyes flitted up to his smoldering, predatory gaze.

A satisfied smirk danced across his full lips. "You okay there, Ma-de-line?" He drew out my name like a sensual caress between my thighs.

My hands flew up to my feverish cheeks. Unadulterated arousal traveled through my veins at the mere sight of perfection on my bed. Storm was the sexiest man I had ever laid eyes on. Muscles were everywhere. A groomed beard defining his handsome face in a sophisticated and devilish way. Platinum eyes I could stare into forever. This man had cast a spell on me.

Panties drenched? Absolutely.

Nipples puckered and peaked? Painfully so.

Clit throbbing with urgent need? Fuck yes.

"Earth to Angel... Earth to Angel..." Storm snapped his fingers. "Why look baby, when you can touch?" His deep belly laugh filled the room. Seductive, yet infuriating. Rough yet soulful. "You're killing me, Angel. Get those fuckin' clothes off your luscious body. Pronto!"

I connected the dots to this simplistic puzzle. Him. Me. Sex.

In quick succession, my dress, bra, and panties were removed and tossed aside.

"Now that's more like it. Would've preferred a little teasing as you undressed, maybe a song to go with some gyrating hip action.

Next time…" Storm winked.

"Will there be a next time?" I stupidly asked, being a total buzzkill.

Anger sparked in his eyes. "The fuck you say?"

"Storm… I… Sorry…" I stuttered like one of my kindergarteners caught eating a crayon.

This mighty and fierce man had me bent over his lap in two seconds flat. The sting of a slap on my ass came one second later.

"Storm!" I wiggled to get off him.

Slap.

"What're—"

Slap.

Slap.

"Stop…" The word weakly spilled from my lips. Tears pooled in my eyes at the same time my pussy pulsed, and wetness painted my thighs.

"You sure you want me to stop?"

"I dunno," I whimpered, brain frazzled as I labored to breathe. A mix of pleasure and pain warred within me. What did it mean? I'd been on the receiving end of a man slapping me before but not like this, and I sure as hell never enjoyed it.

Storm lifted my hips and licked the flaming hot spot on my ass cheek. I imagined it bore the mark of his handprint. It would eventually fade…

"You've never been spanked before, gorgeous?" He dotted kisses on my red skin. "Hard to believe a sassy, impossibly defiant woman such as yourself hasn't been punished."

"Storm?" I moaned his name.

"Yeah, Angel?" His fingers dipped between my thighs, discovering how wet he'd made me. He groaned and kissed my ass again.

"Please, I need you."

"That right? You gonna stop saying stupid shit? Stop doubting my words. 'Cause I'll tell you, Angel, I say what I mean and mean what I say."

I attempted to turn toward him, so I could see his handsome face. When he didn't stop me, I straddled his lap and cradled his face in my hands. We gazed into each other's eyes while I stroked his cheeks, his bristly beard tickling the pads of my thumbs.

Something in me shifted. I couldn't put a name to it or a feeling. All I knew was Storm claimed a piece of my heart when I wasn't looking. Each time we were together, every kiss, every touch, the spot grew deeper and more profound. It terrified me too.

Storm could shatter every piece of me.

We hadn't even connected intimately, but I knew once we did, I wouldn't be able to walk away. The attraction I felt, this feeling of familiarity, was intense. It was like I'd known him my whole life.

Scared as I was of Storm's absolute power, I wanted him. It might be a fatal mistake, given he was the president of a motorcycle club. But at this moment, I didn't care.

Rubbing my pussy on his stomach, I peppered kisses over the apples of his cheeks and down his nose. With each kiss, I ground harder, coating him with my arousal.

"Fuck, Angel," he groaned, cupping my breasts and rolling the tight peaks between his thumbs and index fingers.

I threw my head back, picking up speed as I bucked and moaned louder than I ever realized I was capable of. My body was on fire. My pussy swelled and pulsed. The need to come was like nothing I'd ever experienced before.

Storm wrapped a hand around the back of my neck and touched his lips lightly to mine. He took his time discovering my mouth with sensual, languid strokes of his tongue. His appearance didn't scream sensual or gentle. Fierce with a touch of wicked prowess? Absolutely. Yet here he was with his decadent kisses, lulling me into a dream-like state.

"I need a taste, baby." He gently laid me on my back, my head nearly hanging off the edge at the foot of the bed. "Smooth as silk…" His finger skated over my pussy. I was glad he liked my Brazilian wax.

A low, carnal growl sent a shiver up my spine as the mattress dipped at my feet. I was so blissed-out, there was nothing he could do I'd object to.

"Help yourself…" The breathy words eddied from my lips like a sultry plume of smoke. My eyes closed in anticipation of the first oral sex I'd had in a long time.

I had an inkling Storm did nothing half-assed in the bedroom or otherwise. Before I wondered how many women had been in my position, I shut those thoughts down.

I wanted to relish in this man's tongue.

My legs were raised over his shoulders, opening the gateway as he lifted me to his face. With one brush of his tongue and a delightful hum, I was writhing on the bed.

Another broad, slow swipe had me squeezing my head between my hands and gasping for air. My core pulsed and clenched, aching to feel him inside me.

"So fuckin' heavenly, Angel. I can die a happy man after eating the sweetest pussy I've ever tasted."

More pulsing, clenching, writhing. His dirty talk drove me crazy with need.

Storm unfolded me, one agonizingly slow lick after another. The tip of his tongue swirled around my clit, rubbing and flicking. He dipped between my folds, moving through them like a lazy stroll in the park. Like he had all the time in the world.

It was too much. Too intense. Too sensual. Not at all feral and rough like I'd imagined it would be.

One. Two. Three swipes. My thighs shook.

Four. Five. Six. My core tightened.

Seven. Eight. He dove into my sex at the same time he pinched my clit between his fingers.

"Yes, Storm! Yes," I screamed, bucking my hips wildly.

I was close, so close to a monster orgasm. No electronic toys could match what Storm did with precision and ease.

Mercy, the earth shifted in a mammoth explosion. Storm turned feral. Ravenously eating me out with the ferocity of a starved wolf. He bit my clit and sucked on it. I nearly lost my mind. He released it, inserting one finger, then another, and secured my ball of nerves between his thumb and finger.

I moaned and mewed.

Pulling at my hair, wincing from the wicked cocktail of pleasure-pain, pleasure-pain. I never knew how spectacular the mix could be in tandem.

As I reached the crest of my orgasm, Storm launched me into oblivion with an all-consuming, unbelievably slow swipe of his tongue, beginning at the tight rosette between my ass cheeks up to my clit. The sensations pushed me over the edge of ecstasy.

I screamed his name, ripping my orgasm from my core and shattered, digging my nails into his scalp and pushing my pussy into his face.

Storm growled. "Fuck baby. Take it. Take it all."

Expletives poured from my mouth at rapid-fire. Every variation imaginable of fuck, shit, and Christ littered the ozone while I scratched Storm's scalp. I held him in place, riding the wave of ultimate pleasure without any regard for him, without any thought of what tomorrow might bring. I was too far gone. Too overwhelmed by his salacious assault.

Storm's tongue was a weapon, used for the sweetest torture.

And fuck, I was doomed.

Can I keep him? was the last thought to flit through my mind before my eyes rolled back into my head.

CHAPTER SIXTEEN

STORM

I might've killed her. Not long after Madeline's spectacular climax, she'd drifted off into dreamland. My tongue had taken on a life of its own and dominated her. Owned her. I'd fuckin' lost my mind with this woman. She tasted so damn delicious. Sweet, just as I'd imagined hundreds of times since I'd first smelled her cream at The Bullet.

Fuck, I was proud of myself. That "O" was a horrendous son of a bitch, too.

Only a few women had ever gotten my cock *and* tongue between their thighs. But if the lady was lucky enough, she only received what I called a five-second sampling.

I couldn't wrap up my tongue to protect it like I could my dick. Shamefully, not all of the snatch I'd had was the cleanest. What could I say? I only had one-night stands and club whores.

Madeline was unique in every way. She received the epic experience, with no time limit. Her pussy was so addictive, I could've feasted on her all night. It was safe to say she was my drug of choice.

Never in my life had I devoured a pussy that way.

She'd shattered like thin ice, crackling and breaking into tiny pieces, screaming out my name like a prayer. The sight of her was more enthralling than watching her sing on stage.

The woman had held my face to her pussy and jackhammered her hips, taking what she wanted. My sweet Angel wasn't afraid to control me while I loved the shit out of her clit.

And her moans? They were like an erotic song. They almost had me coming right along with her. Almost.

I should've known I'd pushed her too far when she gasped and panted for what felt like days on end, crying out, oh Storm, God, oh fuck, Storm, oh mercy, Storm…

Fuck, her nails were sharp, too. Digging into my scalp as she held me in place. I'd almost pulled my face away, worried I'd die of asphyxiation.

But what a spectacular way to meet my maker. Buried in her sweet as honey pussy. Yeah, I would've died a happy man.

I hadn't even had my cock buried inside her yet, but I already knew I was claiming her. Madeline was mine.

Mine.

I carefully climbed off the bed and pulled the covers back. I'd let Madeline sleep a bit before round two. And there would be a second go at it. I needed inside her and planned to knock her out again with a couple epic orgasms.

I chuckled to myself. *I'm such a bastard.*

Madeline's limp body sagged in my arms. She didn't stir as I tucked the blanket around her. Christ, she was so beautiful with her dark hair fanned out on the white pillow—a true angel. I ran my thumb along her jaw, memorizing the gentle slope of her nose and her perfect lips with a cupid's bow.

This ache in my chest was new to me. I was sure it had everything to do with what tonight meant; what tomorrow would bring.

Being with me just might destroy Madeline's innocence. But I couldn't think about it now.

A noise came from the living room. I instantly tensed without boxers to pull on. I was a commando kind of guy, so I slipped on my jeans, zipped them but didn't fasten the button. I crept out of the bedroom with my switchblade in hand. I was kicking myself for not bringing my 45 Auto. I'd given it to Track to take back to the clubhouse so Madeline wouldn't freak out.

"Ahhhhh," a woman screamed.

I put my hands up in the air. "Shh. You'll wake Madeline."

"Holy balls. You're... you're that... that... biker." She stuttered, letting her purse drop on the floor like it weighed a ton of bricks.

I smirked. "Yeah, and you're the... the... roommate." I mocked her. Couldn't help it. This gal was a riot, standing at the door, gawking like I was a celebrity in her house. I should've been honored, making her dreams come true, and probably her panties wet. I smirked again at the thought.

"Right. I'm Tara. Good to meet you."

"Storm." I shoved my hands in my jean pockets, hoping she didn't see my blade. "I heard a noise, came to check it out. If we're all good here, I'm going back to bed."

"Wore her out, did you?"

I cocked my head, eyeing her and her cheesy grin. I suspected Tara was drunk. "I don't kiss and tell."

"Uh-huh, so you fucked her brains out." Tara giggled, fanning herself. Yup, panties wet. Likely dripping wet by the way her cheeks flushed nearly the same color as her hair. No question, she was drunk as a skunk.

"Since you have all the answers, I'm going back to bed." I turned on my heel.

"Hey, wait."

I stopped and glanced over my shoulder.

"Don't you dare hurt her. She's a good woman. The best woman."

"Noted."

"I mean it. I might look innocent, but you don't want to mess with a redhead. We have evil pulsing through our veins. Don't test me."

I chuckled as she swayed on her feet. I doubted she would remember this conversation in the morning. "You have my word." And with that, I returned to Madeline's room.

After I removed my jeans, I slipped under the covers and spooned Angel. She felt amazing in my arms, warm and docile. Her body molded to mine like she was an extension of me.

How this saucy, adorable, gorgeous fuckin' woman had gotten under my skin, I may never know. But I was damn happy about it. She made me feel shit. Shit I never felt before and never wanted to feel... until her.

I breathed Madeline in and let my eyes drift close.

Strong suction took my cock. My eyes flashed open. Was I dreaming? Only a second passed before a groan escaped my lips. I didn't have a white popcorn ceiling in my room, but I didn't care about no damn ceiling if this was a dream. Not while getting my cock sucked quite vigorously. The broad doing the honors had a suction stronger than a Hoover.

I hissed as my balls drew up, and my spin tingled. I couldn't help groaning again. Fuck, this woman was sucking the life out of me. It wouldn't be long before I painted her throat with my cum.

I lifted my head and was greeted by a full moon inches from my lips. Shit was it a fine ass too. Creamy-ivory with a tan line outlining where her bikini bottom had been. I'd seen this ass before—last night when I'd spanked Madeline.

My Angel. God almighty, she was giving me head first thing in the morning.

I smirked, glancing around her room. The walls were painted the same shade of blue as her eyes. It all became crystal clear. This wasn't a dream. My girl was worshiping my dick.

The best damn way to start the day was with a sixty-nine. How did she know I'd want this?

"Morning Angel," I rasped. "Breakfast is the most important meal of the day." I gripped her hips and pulled her onto my face. "Nom, nom, nom." I swiped my tongue across her delicious cunt, lapping up her arousal.

Madeline stilled and released my dick with a pop. "Storm, stop!"

"Nuh-uh." I licked up her sweet cream and flicked her clit with my middle finger.

She moaned and rocked her hips a little. "But... But I'm sucking you off," she whined so damn cute I smiled.

"And doing an excellent job. Don't stop, baby." I lifted my pelvis so my cock was at her lips, encouraging her to take it back into her warm mouth.

She sighed, shoulders sagging. "I flaked out last night and wanted to make it up to you." The regret in her voice stopped me mid-swipe. "Just let me do this for you. Please."

How could I argue with her desire to please me? My chest tightened as an intense emotion swept through me. Something I only ever felt with her. I set her ass back on my chest and rubbed my calloused hands over her silky thighs. I wanted to soothe her, let her know it was okay.

Giving up control wasn't something I did. Ever. I took what I wanted, controlled everything and everyone in my life. But at this moment, for Madeline, it was easy to give her what she wanted. Too easy. Still, I'd give in this one time. One. Time.

What guy wouldn't want to be on the receiving end of a blow job with no expectation of reciprocation?

Me with Madeline.

"All right, Angel. You win. Have your way with me." I relented, letting her take the reins. None of my brothers better hear about this. The prez didn't give in to no one.

"Thank you, Storm," she said in a soft, musical voice, then took me back into her warm mouth. The angels sang as she blew me into oblivion.

Jesus, now she was killing me.

Her tongue molded to my pulsing cock. My eyes rolled back into my head as she pressed it to the roof of her mouth, stroking the underside in time as she sucked. It wasn't fast like some women did, rushing for the finish line. Oh, hell, no. Madeline caressed my dick thoroughly.

My balls drew up again, spine tingling, thighs quaking. I couldn't inhale a deep breath, only shallow gasps of air as the pressure built, lifting me higher and higher. Fuck, this felt phenomenal.

Madeline hummed when the tip hit the back of her throat. A zing shot straight up to my brain.

"Fuck, Angel. Fuck, fuck, fuck," I grounded out, not knowing what to do with myself. My hands needed to hold onto something, and her pert bottom would do just fine. I filled my hands with her ivory flesh, bringing it to my mouth and sunk my teeth into it.

Madeline mewed, arching her back. Her delicious ass lifted to my face, begging for more. I licked the spot with my teeth marks and made a matching imprint on her other cheek.

"Storm…" she cried out but didn't move away from my face.

Chuckling, I ran my scruffy beard over her sensitive skin just to make her crazy. Selfishly I wanted to flip her onto her back and drive my cock home into her pussy. I wanted to fuck her so hard she wouldn't be able to leave the bed.

I needed inside her. Smelling her arousal was torture. I didn't think I could wait much longer.

Was she dripping even more for me? Turned on? Pulsing with

need?

There was only one way to find out.

I ran two fingers across her entrance. Fuckin' hell, I was right. I collected some of her wetness, rocked my hips toward her face, and sucked off the dew in time with her rhythm.

So damn sweet. Having Madeline's cream on my tongue sent me over the edge.

"I'm close," I grunted. "Fuck baby. You're not so innocent. Your mouth is wicked."

My words seemed to spur her on. She showed me no mercy and I blew, squirting into the back of her throat. It kept coming and coming as if it would never end.

I yelled and cursed, squeezing her hips. There'd be bruises, but I didn't care. I was damn sure she wouldn't either.

Madeline didn't release me until my dick went limp. I expected her to climb off, flash me a victorious smile, but it was like she was frozen in place.

"Was it… okay for you?" Her timid voice sounded nothing like the fierce, take-no-shit woman I was crazy about.

Okay, for me? Was she joking?

"Seriously, Angel?"

"You can tell me. I know I'm not very good at this, but I want you to know I'll learn. I want to learn. Just tell me how you like it."

Where was all this coming from?

"Baby c'mere." I reached for her, but she jerked, shooing my hand away.

"No. Just tell me the truth. I can take it."

Fuck this shit.

I had her off my stomach and flat on her back, pinned to the bed with my body. The air left my lungs at the sight of her.

Madeline's pretty, blue eyes were glossy and brighter against the redness surrounding them. The worry or pain in them caused my heart to slam into my chest, knocking the wind right out of me.

"Don't look at me." She covered her face with her hands. "Please..." Her voice broke.

"Jesus, Angel. What happened?"

She shook her head, not answering.

"I don't know what's happening. Why are you crying?"

"I like you... I want to be with you. But I don't have a lot of experience with sex. I promise I'll learn, though..."

"Are you out of your mind? That was the best blow job I've ever had."

"You don't have to lie. I can take the truth." She shoved my chest.

I didn't budge. Nope. She didn't get to push me away. I wrapped my hands around her tiny wrists and lifted them above her head. My massive frame swallowed Madeline up as I hovered above her. God, she was a little thing—fierce and vulnerable.

"Not lying. Your mouth is heavenly. You can give me head anytime you want." I dropped a kiss on her lips.

She sniffled, blinking back the tears she wouldn't let fall. "Really?"

"Fuck yeah. Why would you think you weren't any good?"

She turned her head to the side as if ashamed. That wasn't okay with me.

"Eyes over here, beautiful."

Reluctantly, she swooped them up to mine. She swallowed, clearly struggling to answer my question.

I asked again. "Why do you think you weren't any good?"

"My ex." I barely heard her quiet reply.

My jaw tensed at the thought of some other guy's dick in her mouth. Goddamn, I really hated the idea of another dude's cock anywhere near her. I recalled her saying she'd been cheated on. Was it by the same guy who told her she wasn't any good at giving a blow job?

"When was this, baby?" I felt a violent storm brewing inside me.

She sighed. "Come on, let's not do this."

"I'm just curious. This guy sounds like an asshole." *And I want to kill him.*

"He was. We were together for almost two years. Broke up six months ago. You're the first guy I've been with since him. Didn't really want to be with anyone after Dane."

Dane. What a pansy name.

I kissed the tip of her nose, then pressed my forehead to hers. "What did he tell you, baby?" Why the fuck I needed to know about this guy was beyond me. I just did. Aside from being curious, who the fuck was I? I never talked this much with chicks. I never cared to know anything about them.

But Madeline was different, and I wanted to know everything about her.

"He said I was subpar in bed, and it was a good thing I had a winning personality, or he'd dump my ass." She closed her eyes tight. Embarrassment radiated off her, skin turning red on her cheeks and down to her chest.

"Fucker," I hissed, wishing I could beat the shit out of him. "What else?"

"Seriously? I don't want to do this." She wiggled her hands, so I'd let her go, but I wasn't ready to set her free.

"I need to know why you're so upset. We're doing this."

"Look, I could never please Dane, okay? Whether it was cooking, cleaning, or how I looked. Nothing I did was good enough. I wasn't good enough. I tried so damn hard to make him happy. To be everything he wanted and needed. Even when he cheated on me, I tried." She worried her bottom lip between her teeth. "He blamed me for him cheating because I was horrible in bed."

"I'll kill him! No. I'll castrate him, then kill him."

"No, it's over. I got out."

"Still, that prick mistreated you."

She leveled her gaze, eyes hard and pissed. "Yes, he did. Are you happy now?"

I rubbed my forehead against hers. "Angel, he lied to you. You're the best I've ever had in bed. And that's saying something…" Shit. Not the road I wanted to go down now or ever. Dumbass.

"Yeah, and how many have you had in bed?"

Knew that question was coming. "A lot. I'm thirty, never had an old lady."

"So, a lot to compare me to. Probably dozens…"

I felt like an asshole. She already believed she was inadequate and subpar, and I just made her afraid I'd compare her to other women—biggest asshole on the planet.

"No. You're the only woman I've wanted more than once."

"Oh, jeez." She rolled her eyes. I didn't like it when she did that. "Somehow, I don't believe you. There's got to be someone you've been with more than once."

"There's a kitten who I preferred over the others." I hated admitting there had been one woman. I didn't want to lie to Madeline. But Carla had been my go-to since the day I let her into the clubhouse two years ago. Not sure why, either. I never liked blondes or fake tits. Carla had both. She was like a favorite, broken-in pair of shoes. Comfortable and familiar. I could take her without any talking or kissing. Minutes later, I'd send her on her way. There wasn't anything more to it.

"Preferred a kitten?" She narrowed her eyes and pursed her lips together.

"Club whore." Alarms went off inside me. I was heading in the worst fuckin' direction with this conversation.

"Oh. Right." She squirmed beneath me as if wanting to get away from me. Not happening. "Like your favorite. The one you chose over and over. Why not just make her your girlfriend or old lady?" She squirmed some more—this time with more force.

Goddammit, I hated this conversation.

"Wasn't like that with her. She's not old lady material. None of them are. They're just there for our sexual needs." Why couldn't I keep my stupid mouth shut with her? I spoke the truth. Even if I preferred Carla, I never wanted more than a quick fuck or head from her. Of course she'd wanted more, but it'd never happen.

"Wow, you use women only to satisfy your carnal desires. How charming." Madeline rolled her eyes again. It was apparent she was disgusted with me. "Just get off me."

What the actual fuck? Get off her?

"No." I gyrated my hips into hers, tempting her with my hard cock. "We aren't finished here."

"Oh, but we are, Prince Charming. You and me, what happened last night, it was only a one-time deal." She thrashed below me, trying to break free. I held her wrists tighter.

"That's where you're wrong, baby. I'm not giving you up." I crushed my lips to hers, stirring her up with my tongue. Let her go? She was crazy. I determined when and if I'd let her go.

"Get. Off. Me."

I ignored her—a big, fuckin' mistake.

She bit my lip so hard I tasted blood. "The fuck, Madeline?"

"We aren't a good match."

"No, shit." I licked my lip. "You didn't have to bite me so fuckin' hard."

"Aw, poor baby. Does the tough biker have an owie? Well, you wouldn't if you'd get the hell off me."

"Stop acting like this. I know you want me as much as I want you." I pressed my forehead to hers. She was huffing and puffing, chest rising and falling. The sight of fury in her eyes only amped up my desire for her.

"You're so full of shit. I'm not a whore, Storm! You can't have me, then pass me along to one of your buddies. I have standards. I believe in monogamy."

I lurched my head back as if punched in the gut. "What did you say?"

CHAPTER SEVENTEEN
STORM

Bewilderment blanketed Madeline's face. Her mouth opened, then snapped shut.

I repeated my question in a fractured voice. "What did you say?" I felt like I was drowning, choking on my own saliva.

"Storm, I'm not the kind of woman you like. The kind you're usually with, a kitten. Please leave."

I clenched my jaw, counting to five before I rained down holy hell on her. "You think I don't know the kind of woman you are? That I'd pass you off to one of my brothers? You fuckin' believe I think of you like a whore?" My voice boomed.

The shock, or maybe it was fear in her eyes, undid me.

I let go of her wrists. Before I could lift off her, she clasped her hand behind my neck, stopping me.

"I… I was just going by what you were saying when you were talking about your kitten."

"Fuck, Madeline. She isn't my kitten. She belongs to the club."

Technically speaking, Carla did belong to the club. I just didn't let my brothers touch her while I was with her. But six months ago that all changed when I released her to them. I leveled my eyes on Madeline's. "Have I made you feel like a whore?" My stomach churned. I'd hate myself if I made her feel like one.

"No, but you said—"

"I don't care what I said. How do I make you feel?" I'd poured myself into her last night, and she didn't feel it?

"You make me feel... wanted. But any woman would feel the same way with you. I mean, have you seen yourself in a mirror lately? You'd give Chris Hemsworth a run for his money in the Sexiest Man Alive contest." Her voice was lighter, but I wasn't having any of it.

"I'll go." I tried to pull up, but she wouldn't let me.

"Please, wait. You're confusing me."

"How?"

"The night we met at The Bullet, you were Mr. Caveman. Cocky and demanding. Like you were looking for a hookup. I mean, I saw the way the waitress was with her hands on you."

"I've never been with her."

"Okay, I believe you. Then we saw each other at the lake, again you were cocky and so confident. You were kissing me within minutes of seeing each other. You swept me off my feet in less than sixty seconds. The day was wonderful, then you left."

I exhaled, looking away. "I had a lot of shit on my mind. I didn't think you should get involved with me because of it. I knew what kind of woman you were. You deserve better."

"Last night... We're kind of volatile, dontcha think?"

"Maybe. But it's not so bad. It's pretty fuckin' fantastic, actually."

"I've been fucked with before. Dane did a number on me. I hate how I didn't see what was right in front of me sooner. I was a blind idiot."

"What do you see in front of you right now, Angel?"

"A strong, devilishly handsome man I want to trust. A man who lights a fire in me, I never want to burn out. A man who calls me Angel. Every time I hear it, he breaks down a little more of my walls." She took my face in her soft hands, stroking my cheeks with her thumbs.

"I've never once thought of you as a whore. I swear. I will kill any man who puts his hands on you or hurts you. And I'm not joking. From the moment I saw you singing, I knew you were special. You were a beacon of light. I need some light in my dark world, Angel." I dropped a kiss on the tip of her nose.

"Then stay, and let's give this another shot." She didn't have to ask me twice. I lowered my mouth to hers. The moment our lips connected, fireworks lit up the darkness inside me.

I kissed her slowly, deeply, sensually. I nibbled on her bottom lip, and she moaned into my mouth. I could listen to her crying out my name for the rest of my life, never tiring of it.

Our tongues lashed together, fighting for dominance as passion ignited between us. Neither of us won the battle. We were equals. Madeline kissed me back, just as desperately. Revving me up for more.

I wanted more. So much more.

Her hands glided over my biceps, taking their time feeling my muscles, squeezing and stroking. It fuckin' turned me on even more. I swear she was memorizing every inch of me. Suddenly she firmly gripped my ass, and my cock jumped.

I broke the kiss, panting. "Shit, Angel. You're driving me wild with your hands."

She smiled, lightly trailing the tips of her fingers all over me. Every spot she touched singed my skin. I hated and loved it all at once.

This woman was claiming me. Owning me. And I fuckin' let her. I didn't take control or stop her.

What was happening to me?

No other woman had been with me longer than a quick fuck or

blow job. Only fifteen minutes tops. Even that long was rare.

I didn't do sensual. Or tender. I sure as hell didn't do romance.

I didn't spend the night with a woman.

I didn't allow myself to feel. Feelings were for pussies. They made you weak. Vulnerable.

But I was doing it all with Madeline. One thing freaked the fuck out of me. It was the way our hearts seemed to beat in time together... as one.

"Condom?" She peppered kisses across my chest.

"I want you bare. I'm clean. You?"

Trepidation appeared in her eyes. "I'm clean and on the pill, but... All those women..." She shook her head. "Storm—"

"I'm clean, I promise, baby. Been tested. Plus, I've always wrapped up my dick."

"Then, why not now?" She hiked a brow as if analyzing me. "We hardly know each other."

I smiled and rolled with Madeline putting her on top of me. "Because I told you, you're special. I haven't been with anyone in months. Now ride me."

"Months, huh? And I'm supposed to believe you, Mr. Biker Prez?"

Her fuckin' sarcastic mouth set me afire. A spark flashed in her baby blues. Little shit knew she turned me on with her sass.

"You don't trust or believe me, then grab my jeans. I'll suit up." I wasn't playing. I'd do this any way she wanted, condom or no condom. "And baby, whether you want to believe it or not, you are special." I slapped my hand on her ass, and she yipped.

"Hey!"

"Don't doubt me again, Angel. Or I'll be forced to punish you."

"Yeah? Well, when do I get to punish you?"

"Another time." I smirked. "You trust me?"

"Fine, fine, fine. I trust you." She took my hard dick in one hand, braced the other on my chest. She lifted and guided in my cock, inch by delicious inch. Shit, she was tight. If I didn't know any better, I'd think she was a virgin. It had been over a decade since I had virgin pussy, but I'd swear Madeline's was the tightest I'd ever experienced.

She inhaled as she worked herself onto me. "You're huge, Storm." Her eyes rolled back into her head, her mouth forming a perfect O as I stretched and filled her completely.

"Your little pussy will shape to me, baby. It'll be all mine. Made just for me. Your ex must've had a pencil dick." For as tight as she was, the dude probably had a micropenis. Served the son of a bitch right.

"Oh, you have no idea." She leaned forward and licked my bottom lip. "Where have you been all my life, Storm?"

"Just been waiting for you, Angel. Waiting for you to get here."

"Now that I'm here"—she swirled her hips, lifted and dropped— "I'm not going anywhere." She raised up and slammed down. "You okay with that?"

"Fuck yeah, I'm okay with it. More than okay."

"Good. Now hold on to me so this ride can start."

"Shit yeah." I gripped her hips, raising her up and pushing her down on my hard as iron cock.

Up and down.

Up and down.

She tossed her back, panting hard and squeezing the fuck out of my dick.

Up and down.

Up and down.

"Play with your titties, baby. Pinch those pink nipples. Gimme a show."

She did as told, tugging and rolling her little buds between her fingers. The stimulation caused her to clench around me like a vice. I nearly blew my load.

Up and down, again and again.

"I'm close, Storm. I'm close," she cried, eyes wild and dilated.

The faster she rode me, the harder I held back. I wanted her to come on my dick before I came inside her.

She bounced, screaming out my name. I didn't think I'd make it, then she seized astride me. The very sight of her shattering caused me to erupt. I drove my hips up, slamming to the hilt, and saturated her insides with my cum.

I saw fuckin' stars. Stars. I came so hard the sensation of it left me breathless—a first for me.

"Oh. My. God." She collapsed forward onto my chest, panting and heaving. We were still connected, and I didn't want to separate from her, ever. After feeling her bare, I never wanted to wrap my dick up again.

I softly brushed my hand over her back as I basked in this euphoric moment. Never had I ever experienced anything like that. I felt like I was soaring through outer space like a shooting star.

Madeline purred. "Mmm, I'm so aroused right now." She wiggled on me. "You're not soft."

"Miracle of all miracles. You do miraculous things to me, Angel."

She laughed. "You're bullshitting me right now, aren't you?"

"Never." I flipped her onto her back. "Let's go again." My mouth was on her neck, devouring her.

Madeline giggled. It was the best sound ever.

This woman made me feel alive. None of the pain usually haunting me reared its ugly face when she was around. My Angel was a beacon of light in my dark world. I was fuckin' keeping her forever.

Madeline was mine. Nothing and no one would ever take her away from me.

CHAPTER EIGHTEEN

MADELINE

I never spent a whole day in bed before. Well, I had when sick with the flu or depressed over douchebag Dane. But never for crazy amounts of sex with a beyond irresistible biker. Tara had banged on my door sometime after ten this morning and hollered, "Going to Steph's. You two are fucking loud!"

Storm and I had laughed our heads off.

Now I was sprawled out on my stomach in bed, blissfully sated while Storm kissed every inch of my body.

The man was on a mission, and who was I to stop him? I wasn't a fool, after all. His mouth on any part of me was out of this world. I tingled all over. Every spot he touched electrocuted me in the best possible way. I was so aroused, wet, and deliriously happy.

"Hey… Why don't you have tan lines on your back from your bikini top like the ones on your ass?"

I hummed as his hands skated up my sides while he licked down my spine. Straddling my upper thighs, I felt him hard again, poking the crack between my ass cheeks. This would be the fifth time today he'd had an erection. I was counting.

Dane and I never spent a lazy day in bed. He never worshiped my body the way Storm was doing. Worshiped. Maybe not the word he'd use, but it sure felt like it by the gentle touch of his hands and soft kisses he dotted on my skin. I felt something more. Maybe *valued*, which I never felt with Dane. Or even *cherished*.

"I had my top unhooked," I answered plainly. It wasn't rocket science. How did he think I didn't have tan lines?

His hands and mouth left me, and I felt the loss acutely. I pouted into my pillow, catching myself before I begged him to continue. I hated asking for anything. Dane had made me beg for everything. I wouldn't do it with Storm or any other man, again.

"You were tanning on your front lawn, right? For the whole neighborhood to see, right? And a Hunter came around, right?"

Oh shit. I thought I knew where he was going.

"Yes."

"What the fuck, Madeline? You don't do that." His voice took on a deadly edge.

"Why're you getting so worked up? It's not like I flipped onto my back. I mean, the thought had entered my mind, but I quickly dashed it away."

"The thought had entered your mind, huh? Are you fuckin' kidding me right now? You better be, Angel, or I will tan your hide!"

I stifled a giggle, trying to not rile him up more. But honestly, it wasn't like we were together yesterday—or any other day before. Even now, he had no claim on me.

"Jeez, Storm. Loosen up. Don't you want me to be evenly tanned? The lines on my chest are so unsightly." I gasped in surprise when he flipped me onto my back.

How did he do that so fast every dang time?

"These lines are unsightly?" He licked above my breasts. "And these?" The tip of his tongue traced the line between them. "Answer me, dammit!"

I would if he wasn't turning me on again. Instead, my back bowed, and I moaned.

"Fuck, you drive me crazy." His mouth covered my nipple, and he suckled vigorously. The intensity of it was like lightning shooting straight into my pussy. I whimpered, burying my fingers into my thick tendrils on the top of my head.

He released me with a pop.

"No. Don't stop," I all but whined, grabbing the sides of his face to see his intense eyes. They were dark and stormy, staring back at me. "Fuck. Me."

"You gonna do that shit again? Suntan without your top on properly?" His jaw twitched like at any moment he would explode. I wasn't sure why he was getting so worked up about this.

Weirdly, I liked his possessiveness. It made me feel protected, cared about. But I knew whatever we were doing today wasn't going to last. He said it himself earlier, he didn't do relationships. So Storm didn't have any right to tell me what to do.

"Newsflash, you don't own me."

He growled, nostrils flaring. "That fucker could've raped you on the spot. Hunters have no respect for women. No moral compass." His voice lowered, his eyes softening. "Do you understand what I'm saying? You could've been raped."

I swallowed a lump of emotion lodged in my throat as my eyes teared up. He clearly cared about me and my safety. "I understand what you're saying, and I'll be careful from now on."

He lowered his head, shaking it, but I lifted it back up, forcing him to look at me.

"I don't tan all the time. I could probably count on one hand the number of times I've done it. Tara and I were bored yesterday. It was a sunny day…" I shrugged a shoulder while stroking the pads of my thumbs across the apples of his cheeks. God, he was the sexiest, most beautiful man I'd ever seen, despite the thunder flickering in his gray depths. I was sure most people feared him, but I didn't.

He relaxed against me, eyes calming and focused on mine. "Don't do it again."

Shit. That sounded more like a command than a request.

"Storm… I—"

"I just need an answer, Angel, before I fuck you." He got between my legs, the head of his thick cock at my entrance. I wanted him more than anything. But it felt like he was controlling me with his dick because he knew I wanted it.

"You can't tell me what to do. I'm not trying to be difficult. I'll be careful from now on. I probably won't be tanning again, anyway. I hadn't done it in years before yesterday."

"Madeline, don't do it again without me."

"What?"

"If you want to tan with your top off, I'll let you, but I need to be with you."

"You'll let me?" Now he sounded like my father.

"Don't get riled up or read into my words. I just want to protect you. Okay?"

Well shit. How could I argue with him for wanting to keep me safe?

"Fine. We'll do it your way. Now fuck me already."

His lip curled as he slid right in. I inhaled suddenly, my mouth popping into an O like I always did when he first entered me. He didn't move as I adjusted to him, then he started even, deep thrusts.

Storm was different this time. His eyes were locked on mine with one of his hands holding my thigh up so he could penetrate me deeper. His other arm was bent next to my face, thumb rubbing my temple.

"You're so beautiful." He kissed me slowly as he pumped in and out, taking his time, in no rush to take me over the edge.

What was he doing?

This didn't feel like fucking. It felt like more. Like he was making… No, I wouldn't allow myself to go there. Storm and I, *this*, it was just sex. Fantastic sex. But there was no way it was more than two people having a little fun.

Okay, maybe it was more for me, something on a deep emotional level.

I felt like I knew Storm. His eyes seemed so familiar when he gazed into mine. The worried tone in his voice when he'd said, "I just want to protect you. Okay?" was like déjà vu. I'd heard those exact words before, and they gave me the same fluttery feelings I'd only ever had with one other person. It was crazy.

I ran my hands over the corded muscles of his broad back down to his ass, trying to spur him on—to get to fucking, but it didn't seem to work. This man was confusing the hell out of me.

A sudden heaviness crushed my chest. I couldn't breathe. Guilt crashed down on me as if I was betraying my childhood crush, Kaleb, when there was never anything between him and me. Nothing other than friendship. How could there be? Kaleb, or KC as we all called him, was my brother's best friend and seven years older than me. But I hadn't cared. I loved him with all my heart.

All these years later, I had never loved any other guy or felt an ounce of guilt when I was with someone else—like Dane—because they never scratched the surface of my heart, which had always belonged to Kaleb.

As Storm rocked into me, kissing me with so much passion, my heart sang for the first time in twelve years. What was worse? I welcomed the feelings blooming inside me when I shouldn't. I shouldn't feel any of this for a man who would never give me what I truly wanted.

The president of an MC wasn't who I ever saw myself settling down with. What the hell was I doing with Storm? How could I let him slip past my walls?

What was I thinking?

I wanted love, marriage, and children. Those were things Storm would never give me.

But right now, with our bodies connected, his lips devouring mine, I shook the past out of my head. I didn't care about any of it. I didn't care about my dreams of a husband and babies.

I only wanted Storm and would take whatever he gave me, today.

Tomorrow I would deal with the realities of our situation. Storm would never be mine the way I wanted him to be. Inevitably, I would end up with a broken heart.

CHAPTER NINETEEN
STORM

Monday morning, we were in *church*. Not a physical one. It was what we called meetings in a large room inside the clubhouse. *Church* had been held thousands of times since KLMC began. Just as many bottles of whiskey had been enjoyed during those meetings. Not much had changed since I arrived here as a pissed-off, guilt-ridden, newly graduated eighteen year old a dozen years ago.

This room reminded me of my time in the Marines. Bland walls, godawful buzzing fluorescent lights on the ceiling, industrial floor tiles. Cold and sterile. Functional. Pictures lined one wall illustrating the club's evolution dating back to when Uncle Matt started the chapter with Raul and Justin. Across from me, a massive flat-screen television hung. Grizzly's desk was off to the side of it. I had some deep conversations with Uncle Matt in here before he died. My brothers and I had had a lot of good times in church. Now wasn't one of them.

"You're putting her life in danger." Track exhaled in frustration.

I cut my eyes to Raul and Boxer. I'd only been back at the club a couple of hours. After being with Madeline, I felt on top of the world, then this motherfucker opened his big mouth. Fortunately, Boxer stayed silent, sitting beside Track.

I stared Track down. I couldn't think of a single thing to say to counter his statement. I *was* putting Madeline in danger. My bike had been parked in her driveway for two days. I'd fuckin' put a giant target on her.

Fuck. What was I thinking?

Boxer cleared his throat. "Copper and AJ reported a few Hunters passing by her place and slowing down in front of it." My enforcer's jaw clenched as if trying to not unload on me.

"Didn't you hear their engines? Didn't you think to check it out?" Track sat forward, bracing his elbows on the table, a concerned expression on his face. I felt like I was getting the third degree. "She's special. You care about her. I get it. I see it. Bring her to the clubhouse where she can be protected."

I shook my head. Bring her to the clubhouse? Let her stay with me in my bedroom? Doing that would be monumental—a statement. The club would see her as my old lady, and I wasn't ready to claim her. I mean, I had. She knew it, I knew it. But I wasn't prepared to publicly announce it.

"You're right. I should've been more careful." What else was there to say?

"What are you going to do about it? The Hunters are getting bolder every goddamn day in Winters. Some of the locals are nervous." Track cracked his neck.

"Look Prez. We need to have eyes there twenty-four seven. On the streets, at some businesses on First Street so we can see what those fuckers are up to." Boxer's voice was even, likely trying to keep me from getting defensive. I appreciated his levelheadedness. I didn't need him giving me shit like Track.

"Grizz has been trying to hack into the town's security cameras. They're the toughest he's seen. You know security isn't his thing. He's doing his best." I rocked my chair, frustrated with myself for being careless with Madeline's safety.

"Well, brother, it ain't good enough." Track paused for a moment. I braced myself, sensing I wasn't going to like what he said next. "Call your old man, have him send his guy to help Grizz."

I cut my eyes to Track and slowly shook my head. "I don't need his help."

Track let out a long sigh. "You're not going to Garrison. He'd come here. We need help."

I scratched my beard. There was one guy I could call who was a genius with security systems. He flew all over the world, setting up systems for major corporations. I hadn't spoken to him in over a decade, since the day before my dad sent me here to live with Uncle Matt and Aunt Eve. But I knew if I called him for help, he'd come.

Then I could avoid contacting my old man.

My chest tightened as it often did when I thought about the past. Did I want to open the vault from my former life? Did I even have a choice? I needed to protect my territory, amp up the security at the clubhouse and the club's businesses. I also needed to keep Madeline safe.

A shitstorm was coming...

I leveled my eyes on Track's. "I'll make a call. Not sure how soon he can be here, but I'll call him." I glanced at Boxer. "In the meantime, I want boots on the ground in Winters. Eyes on Madeline at all times. Make your rounds to the local businesses under the club's protection."

"Got it, Prez."

"You're not bringing her here?" Apparently, Track had a death wish.

Raul and Hero, my Sergeant at Arms, sat stoically as usual. Hearing Track's question made Raul's eye twitch. I knew they weren't happy with me being gone all weekend. But they'd never call me out on it in front of anyone else. Raul was the best VP. Knew when to keep his mouth shut and when to speak. Unlike his son, Track.

Hero was the strong silent type. His job was to protect me when needed. When he wasn't running the gunshop, he also managed the club's small armory of weapons and our runs along with Track.

"No. Not even sure if I'll continue seeing her. If the Hunters think she's important to me, they'll use her to get to me. Can't risk it."

"You're wrong, brother. You're fucking wrong this time." Track dragged his hand across his cheek. Clearly he was exasperated with me. "By not claiming her, you've left her exposed and vulnerable. What are you afraid of? This can't be because of the boy. The second I saw you this morning, you looked happy as fuck. It's because of her. She makes you happy."

"Enough." I slammed my hand on my table, leaning forward, huffing like a bull ready to charge. I wanted to knock his goddamn teeth clear across the room for mentioning the boy. "We're through here. Call church."

"Stubborn son of a bitch," Track muttered, getting to his feet and exiting the room.

Track couldn't tell me he'd willingly bring a woman into this mess. My road captain's heart was just as stone-cold as mine. Or, more like how mine used to be before Madeline melted it.

Angel sure made me feel good inside and kept my demons away. When I held her in my arms throughout the night, I slept. I didn't have a single nightmare. When my cock was buried deep inside her, our eyes connected, I couldn't imagine life without her.

But at what cost?

The club was on the brink of war with the Dirty Hunters. If my gut was right, it was going to be a bloody war. Madeline was safer without me.

Before Raul or Boxer could say anything, my phone rang and I answered.

"Sugar, everything okay?"

My aunt laughed. "Honey, we're just fine. How's my prez doing?"

I flicked my eyes to Raul and Boxer. "I'm good. Where are you?"

"Niagra Springs. It's amazing. This whole road trip has been fantastic. I wish you could've come with us." Aunt Eve was such a sweetheart. Had I gone with her, I would've never met Madeline.

"Sounds great. So when do you think you'll be back?"

"Not sure yet. Maddox and Markey are having the time of their life. They're not ready to return." Sugar sounded relaxed and happy.

"Stay gone as long as you like."

"Why? Is something going on you're not telling me about?" Shit, she was sharp as a tack, just like Uncle Matt.

"The twins will be seniors this year. Once they graduate, you may not be able to get them to leave the club again. Uncle Matt would want you to enjoy yourselves."

She was silent for a long second. "He would want us to have fun. But I have a bad feeling, Storm. Are you hiding something from me? You sound different."

"Just have stuff on my mind. Nothing you need to worry about on your road trip."

"Hmm…"

I needed to give her something or she'd call every day. "It's a woman."

Boxer and Raul's eyebrows shot up. Yeah, talking about a woman was just as weird for me too.

"A woman? Is Carla causing trouble with the other kittens again? I swear to God, Storm, I'm going to pull out her hair!"

Some members entered, putting their cell phones in a basket to be placed outside the room. Only I was allowed to have my cell in here during church, unless I said otherwise.

"No, Sugar. Not her. I met someone."

I listened to my aunt gasp, then murmur, *he met someone*. My brothers took their seats, and Raul put the basket on the table in the hallway and shut the door.

"You met someone? Who is she?" The shock in her voice was palpable. I still couldn't believe how much my life had changed in the last few weeks.

"No time to talk. We're about to have church."

"Are you lying to me so you can get off the phone? What's her name? How long has this been going on? Gimme something, Storm." She was relentless.

"Madeline. That's all you're getting until you get back." I held the phone out. "Tell Sugar, hi," I told my brothers. They mostly grunted but she'd know church was about to begin. I put the phone back to my ear. "See?"

"I guess you weren't lying. Madeline is a pretty name. Can't wait to meet her. I'll let you go now."

My stomach knotted up at her words. "Be safe, Sugar. Tell the boys I said they better be good to you."

"They are. Love you, Storm. Bye."

I was relieved she didn't push for more about Madeline. Eight pairs of curious eyes were on me. It was no time to get personal. I needed to get this meeting started.

I lifted the gavel, hit it on the table once, and left it there. "These fuckin' Hunters…" I inhaled a deep breath, fisting my hands. "We need them gone before the holiday. I don't want these scumbags roaming around on the Fourth of July and making the locals uncomfortable."

Grunts echoed in the room. I made eye contact with my VP and Track. "Raul will send you out in groups of three. He and Track have put a plan together." I stared at the three members in the back of the room. Several others were missing, probably at work, and couldn't make the meeting on such short notice. "This is your opportunity to train the prospects in how we keep our territory clean." I nodded to Raul for him to take the floor.

"Don't go with guns blazing. We don't want the locals running to the Sheriff. We need to maintain our good standing here. If you catch a Hunter, call me. Or Boxer." Raul's dark eyes cut to mine for approval.

"I will be out too, so your direct contact is Raul or Boxer. I don't want this to get messy, but we'll open up the dungeon if it comes to it." I had a feeling we'd all get blood on our hands before this war was over. "Anything else?"

Glances shot from one person to another. Until finally, one spoke.

"And the woman you were with, does she get extra protection? Will we be meeting her soon?"

I narrowed my eyes at Art. Only the council and a couple of prospects knew about Madeline. But I should've known news of me staying with a woman over the weekend would spread through the club like wildfire. And I'd just told Sugar her name on the phone for all to hear. Art was a regular member and a tattoo artist. He managed Human Canvas, a tattoo parlor owned by the club, so he wasn't around much during the week. He was often the voice for the other patched members.

"No." My reply came swiftly. "She won't be coming around here."

"Jesus," Track muttered, and all eyes shot to him. I could wring his neck, but I didn't make a big deal about it because I had started this shit with Madeline.

"So you're saying she's nobody special?" Lynx asked. I knew he liked her since the day we saw her singing in The Bullet. But he was playing off Track and it fuckin' pissed me off.

"Her life is as important as the rest of the locals. Now let's get out there and rid the area of Hunters." I hit the gavel on the table, ending this meeting before it spiraled out of control.

"Track." I jerked my chin for him to stay.

Once the last member crossed the threshold, he shut the door and leaned his back against it, shoving his hands in his pockets.

I pointed my finger at him. "Don't fuckin' pull that shit during a meeting again. Your feelings are yours. Keep them to yourself. Don't bring them into church, or I'll beat your fuckin' ass. You get me, brother?"

"Yeah." He firmly held my gaze.

We might be best friends, but in church, in this club, I was his president—and he better know his fuckin' place. When we were alone, it was different. Track's concerns for Madeline were genuine. He was worried about her on my behalf. I appreciated it, but I called the shots, and he needed to roll with it.

I nodded, giving him the all-clear to leave.

I slumped in my chair, suddenly exhausted. My thoughts went to my Angel. Already, the club was treating her like she was my old lady. I had changed after she entered my life. Did shit I had never done in all the years I'd been a member of Knight's Legion. It made sense my brothers took notice and asked questions.

Now, Aunt Eve knew there was a woman. I needed to figure out what I was going to do about Madeline asap. I couldn't leave her or myself in limbo. I just didn't know what the right decision was for any of us.

CHAPTER TWENTY
MADELINE

From across the dining table, Tara flicked her sable-brown eyes my way. She'd done it dozens of times in the last couple of days. Probably waiting for me to combust from the anger building inside me.

Honestly, she had nothing to worry about. I had prepared to not hear from Storm—sort of. His bossiness and possessiveness had made me think we were starting something. Like we were more than two people fucking each other's brains out. I should've known better.

"Stop it. I'm fine." I lifted my wine glass, taking a sip.

"You're not. I'll kill him."

I waved her off as my phone rang. I held my breath, hoping Storm was finally calling. It wasn't. I answered with a small smile. "Hi, Mom…"

"Well, hello. I figured I might as well call, in the off chance you forgot my number." Mom laughed, but it didn't stop me from feeling guilty.

"I'm sorry. I've just been enjoying my summer break with Tara."

"Hi, Mrs. H," Tara stood from her chair, clearing the dinner dishes.

"Tell her I said hi back."

I turned toward Tara. "Mom says, hi."

"Tell me all about the fun you've been having. It's almost been a month since school let out. I expected a call or maybe a visit."

"Mom, I told you when I was there for Easter, I didn't think I'd be coming out this summer."

She always did this to me. Pretend like she didn't hear me or forgot, when I knew neither was true.

"I just miss you. And so does your dad."

I heard him in the background, mumbling about taking his princess, *me*, out for a sundae at Trudy's Ice Cream Parlor.

"I'd love a hot fudge sundae right now," I told her honestly.

"Oh, dear. That tells me you're sad."

I stifled a snort. "Why? It's ice cream."

"Oh honey, have you forgotten nobody knows you better than your mom? When you're sad about something, you always order hot fudge. When you're excited, it's strawberry. If you're angry, you order a banana split, extra cherries."

Wow. Mom did know me well. I got up from the dining chair and went into the living room. I dropped onto the sofa and put my feet up on the coffee table. Something told me this wasn't going to be a short call. Good thing I'd had two glasses of wine with dinner, so I was mellow.

"Mom, I was just a kid back then. I've since grown up, if you hadn't noticed."

"Oh, I've noticed, my sweet girl. I've noticed. You're an independent woman who provides for yourself and doesn't need anyone… even your parents." If I didn't know her better, I would think there was a jab in there somewhere. But Mom loved me dearly. She only wanted me to need her more.

"Mom, I do need you."

She made a shushing sound. "Tell me why you're sad? Is it about a boy?"

I groaned, rolling my eyes. "No, Mom. It's not about a *boy*." The rumbling of motorcycles drew my attention to the front window. Two bikers rode by.

I held my breath, unsure of whether to be nervous or excited.

"I can tell something is wrong. The musical lilt in your voice is missing."

Crap, she wasn't going to let this go. "I really don't want to talk about it, okay? How've you and Dad been?"

Mom sighed. "Fine, fine, fine. I'll mind my own business."

"Thank you."

The two bikers passed by again, presumably leaving the trailer park. I wasn't sure if they were Knights or Hunters. I really shouldn't care one way or the other. But I didn't want either knocking at my door.

"Your father and I are good. We just miss our kids."

"Have you heard from my globe-trotting brother recently?"

"Yes, last weekend. He's still in Europe. Said he'd try to pass through on his way to his next job."

My heart kicked up a notch. "Pass-through, meaning?"

"Minnesota, I think."

I squealed. "Really? I need to text him." I hadn't spoken to my older brother since before school let out. He worked too damn much. All he seemed to care about was his job. He'd likely deny it, but I believed our beloved Tommy had something to do with it. Tommy's death had changed us all, especially Toby.

"Been too busy to text even your brother?" The disappointment in her voice gutted me. I should've been better about staying in touch with my family, especially when I hadn't worked all month.

Damn you, Storm. I let out an exasperated breath, blaming him for screwing with my head and twisting me in knots. He'd stolen all of my attention.

Well, not anymore. I was done with Mr. Biker Prez.

"You and Dad should come for a visit. We could meet in The Cities, go to the MIA and Mall of America. Hit up some new restaurants and just wing it."

"Sounds lovely. I'll talk to him and get back to you. Bring Tara. We'd love to see her. And if there is a young man in your life, we'd love to meet him."

Young man? I almost snorted. Storm was the furthest thing from what my mom considered a "young man." I didn't think my parents would judge him harshly for being a biker with tattoos, rings on his fingers, and a snarl to his lip. But I knew they wouldn't be thrilled I was with him. They were traditional conservatives. They had accepted an MC ran their town, but they hadn't befriended any of them. They just stayed out of the way.

I should've stayed out of Storm's way. How was I so weak with him? Well, it didn't matter anymore. He dropped me like a hot potato.

Mom continued talking while I enjoyed listening to her pleasant voice. But Storm wasn't far from my thoughts, which downright irritated me.

Screw Storm. If he didn't want me, I didn't want him either.

CHAPTER TWENTY-ONE

STORM

I felt the bone crack when my right fist connected with his pointy nose. Blood gushed. The dude grunted, cowering away as I leered at him. We'd finally gotten our hands on two of the fuckin' Hunters. This one with a red river soaking his white T-shirt dared to mention Madeline and her redheaded friend being worth top dollar.

I fuckin' lost it, smashing my fist into the fucker's face before he blinked. I was hardly satisfied with one punch, so I drove my left fist into his gut, knocking the air out of him. He fell to the ground. It barely sufficed but I needed to stay in control. We weren't out to kill anyone… today, anyway. Boxer and Hero held onto the other cocky cunt. I'd introduce him to my fist next.

For the last three days, the Knights had been out in full force, divided between Bastion and Winters. This weekend was the Fourth of July, and the Hunters hadn't vacated the area. We had combed the streets, trying to capture our enemy with no results until today.

I wasn't delusional. We couldn't wipe the Hunters out of the town in two days, but we could send the fuckers a message.

Boxer, Hero, and I had seen these bastards leaving Madeline's trailer park. We kept our distance, following them to the north side of town, to The Wild Hog. The club provided security for the bar, so we strutted in and grabbed them without any incident.

Now we were in the back alley beating the shit out of them.

"Why haven't you fuckers left Knight's territory?"

The dickhead glowered and shrugged. My fist met his jaw. I heaved in a breath, fighting the urge to break his teeth. I wasn't a monster.

"I want your prez's name to set up a meeting." I could be civilized and talk to the prez. Maybe make him an offer he couldn't refuse so he'd take his crew and leave my territory. Or we'd just take them all out. It wasn't the most rational line of thinking, but I was tired of these fuckers.

"He won't see you, asshole," he muttered, spitting blood onto the asphalt. I kicked him in the side and dug the toe of my boot into his dick. He wailed on the ground like a pussy, grabbing his junk with one hand.

"Let me at him," Boxer growled. I had no problem turning the reins over to him. He was my enforcer, after all. I'd gotten out some pent-up aggression over not seeing Madeline and knowing these Hunters were scouting out women in her neighborhood. They better not so much as look at *my* woman.

I heard the rumble of bikes and knew they were my brothers. Hero had called Wolf, Lynx, and AJ for backup, in case more Hunters showed up. We weren't going to kill any of them, though I wanted to. This was about sending a message, about giving them a chance to get out of town—mostly unscathed—before we rained down hell upon each and every one of them.

These assholes were lucky I was in charge, because Boxer was itching for restitution for his sister's boutique. He was out for blood. If these motherfuckers didn't get gone, he'd get it.

"Okay, boys. Let the fun begin." I lifted my boot off the douchebag's dick, stepping back as Boxer took out his switchblade. He liked to leave his mark after an ass-beating.

Lynx stepped beside me. "Just two, eh?"

"Yeah. Neither one is talking." I kicked the moaning prick's leg.

"Looks like we'll get to have some fun beating the shit out of them." Lynx rubbed his hands together, a deranged expression on his face. He liked to strike fear into worthless pieces of shit, like the Hunter on the ground.

"We'll do more than have fun." Boxer glared at the cunt on the ground, with a menacing glint in his eyes. "That boutique you motherfuckers torched…" He seethed, "that was personal."

"It wasn't us," the dude cried as Boxer dropped a knee on his chest, digging it in.

"Don't fucking lie to me!" He pointed his blade at the Hunter's neck. Boxer's victims all received what he called *"a hickey from Ricky."* It was a large R carved into the skin. Big enough, it couldn't be missed. Ricky was what he called his switchblade.

Boxer had some issues.

The other guy struggled to get free from Hero's grasp, but it was futile. Hero's hands were like giant claws. If one got you, you were doomed.

I approached Hero, thinking I might be able to get this guy to talk. "The fire was Dirty Hunters, wasn't it?"

His eyes widened. Good.

"No need to answer. I can see the truth in your eyes. How many of you are there?" I rested my hands on my hips, clenching my jaw. I needed to calm the fuck down before I lost my shit on this guy.

"I… I don't… know." Sweat dripped down his temple. Sheer terror shined in his light blue eyes.

"Don't believe you, asshole. What is it, a dozen? Twenty? Fifty?"

We hadn't been able to get a definitive count of them, only catching a glimpse of no more than four together at one time. Without knowing where they were hiding, we had no clue what we were dealing with. We were in the dark. I fuckin' hated it. We needed to know how big of a threat they were.

"Not bigger than thir… thirty," the kid stuttered.

"Shut the fuck up," the douchebag yelled from under Boxer. Wrong move on his part.

Boxer's knee moved from his chest up to this throat. "Shut up, dickwad."

I turned back to the prospect I was questioning. "You see your friend?" I jerked my chin toward his buddy, squirming under Boxer's knee. His face was red, eyes bulging with fear. "That'll be you next. So tell me, how many are there?"

"I swear. I don't know exactly. I don't even know who the prez is. He stays hidden."

I snorted. "Sounds like a scared pussy."

The prospect shook his head. "He's a mean motherfucker. He wants Winters. Then Bastion."

"Never fuckin' happening!" I punched him in the gut, making him cough and gag. "Where does he run his prostitution ring?"

"Everywhere."

"That's a vague-ass answer." I got in his face. "What about sex trafficking? Are you fuckers holding any women?"

He trembled in Hero's grasp. "I don't know anything about it. I swear."

Boxer exhaled a frustrated breath.

"You're pretty useless, prospect," Lynx said.

Hero grunted in agreement. AJ twisted his face up as if insulted.

Fuck. I was getting nowhere with this piece of shit. It was no surprise. I never told my prospects vital information. But I had to try before I unleashed my enforcer.

I cut my gaze to Boxer. "Have at it."

I had seen his deadly grin before. I'd have to keep an eye on him to be sure he didn't kill the man.

"AJ, I want you over here with Wolf." I jerked my chin toward the prospect in front of me.

My prospect would learn the art of a proper ass beating.

As I observed my men taking their frustrations out on the Hunters, Madeline stayed at the forefront of my mind.

It didn't take my men long to beat the crap out of the Hunters. We sent them back to their prez with a message to not fuck with us and get the fuck out of our territory before it was full-blown war.

I needed to rid the town of the dirty maggots. For Madeline and I to be together, I needed to make my territory safe. Until then, I would stay away from her. I just hoped it didn't take too long, or she might not forgive me for avoiding her.

CHAPTER TWENTY-TWO

MADELINE

On the morning of the Fourth of July, I sat in a booth at Sugar Bliss with Tara, Kim, and Steph. If it hadn't been for this little gathering and the picnic at the lake later today, I might still be home wallowing in self-pity.

I hadn't heard from Storm since he left my bed Monday morning to return to his compound. I missed him like crazy.

Not only had Storm been a sex god with the endurance of a thousand men, but he'd also cracked open my heart. He'd done what no man before him could do, then he shit on it. Even so, like a fool, I wished to be with him instead of nibbling on a caramel roll.

The time we spent together wouldn't be forgotten anytime soon. Or ever. We'd stayed locked away in my room, discovering each other from head to toe and everywhere in between. We'd basically had sex, slept, showered, and ate—on repeat until his sudden departure.

We were happy and insatiable. Or so I thought.

Why hadn't he called me?

A throat cleared.

I lifted my eyes from my mug. I shouldn't be surprised by my wide-eyed friends staring at me as I sipped my latte. Tara had blabbed about my "sex-marathon" with a biker the second we'd arrived. I'd waved her off while we placed our orders, but naturally, they wouldn't be put off for long.

What did it matter now? I hadn't heard a peep from Storm, not a text or phone call after five days, even though I gave him my number before he left. I'd hoped we'd continue seeing each other. *Wishful thinking, Mads.* The president of an MC did as he damn well pleased. Took what he wanted when he wanted, then he moved along on his merry way.

God, I hated how empty I felt without him. I also hated how I let myself get swept away. How he made me remember *and* forget Kaleb. I betrayed my first love with a biker, who crushed me once he'd gotten what he wanted.

I felt like an idiot.

I wanted marriage and children. I couldn't have either with a biker. Perhaps Storm was doing me a favor after having his way with me. Like he had my best interest at heart, cutting me loose to find a man who wanted the same traditional lifestyle. Because an MC life was the furthest thing from traditional.

"Spill. It. Girl. I'm dying here," Steph whined into her mug. She was pulling out all the stops with her green puppy dog eyes, peering over the rim. So sad for her. I was immune to doe eyes, pouty lips, and crocodile tears. Most teachers were, especially kindergarten teachers like me. Still, Steph tried. Silly girl.

"What do you want me to say? We had sex. It's pretty self-explanatory." I popped my shoulders up and rolled my eyes, not wanting to talk about Storm.

"We want details." Tara jabbed me in the side with her boney elbow.

"Ouch!" I shuffled my bottom across the booth closer to the window. "What the heck?"

"I heard every noise. You two made the walls rattle. The roof nearly crashed down. Why do you think I left the house? Now I want to know what caused your screams and moans."

Steph and Kim sniggered. *Traitors.*

"Um..." I blushed, burying my face in my hands, utterly mortified. I had been loud. Louder than I'd ever been. Storm didn't give a shit either. He tortured me every chance he got, and the result was massive, out of this world orgasms. During one round, he'd made me come six times. Six. Times.

It was phenomenal.

The thought of never experiencing such pleasure again tore me asunder. Never having Storm's strong arms around me, soft lips on mine and his tender whispers in my ear gutted me.

"Come on. Tell us. It was great with the biker, right?" Tara leaned into me. "We should all find ourselves an outlaw, shouldn't we? Just tell us. If they all fuck like Storm, I want in on the action."

I nearly dropped my mug. "My God, girl. Were you listening outside my bedroom door?"

"We share a wall, Mads. A thin wall. And nobody takes an hour-long shower unless they're fucking in it." A contemplative expression appeared on her face. "Wait. How in the hell did he fit his massive frame into our puny shower?"

"When Storm is determined, nothing holds him back." It was the truth, too. Storm had me for two glorious, euphoric days. After using me, he left.

Steph and Kim stared in wonder with mouths gaping, eyes wide. I'd never felt so exposed while fully dressed before.

I was about to appease them with the shortest version of my weekend sexfest when Steph and Kim's gaze shifted off me at the sound of the jingling entrance bell.

"Oh, crap," Steph whispered. "Don't turn around. It's the bikers from the armory."

My pulse spiked.

Storm had warned me about the Dirty Hunters. I glanced out the window and searched for the prospect keeping an eye on me. I wasn't thrilled when I saw him following Tara and me this morning. Why Storm felt the need to have someone watching me didn't make sense. He was done with me.

The young guy named AJ stepped out of the hardware store across the street with his cell phone at his ear. I had a hunch he was on the phone with Storm. Not two seconds after AJ put his phone in his pocket, mine started ringing. My pulse nosedived, seeing Storm's name.

The girls looked at me with expectant expressions.

It's Storm, I mouthed. I didn't know what to do. Answer it? Ignore it?

"Answer it," Tara hissed with annoyance. She knew I was upset about him ignoring me all week.

On the fourth ring, I reluctantly answered. "Hello."

"Angel, you okay?" The gall of this man acting concerned after ghosting me. And calling me Angel? What an asshole.

"I'm fine." Lie. I was hurt, angry, and confused, but I wouldn't tell him so.

"AJ said Hunters are in the bakery, and you're still there."

"Yup. So?"

"What do you mean, so? I told you all about them."

"Yeah, you did. I'm in a public place with lots of people around. They're just buying coffee. I don't see the big deal or why you're calling me about it."

"Don't look directly at them. AJ said he saw three. Any others?"

He totally disregarded what I'd said. Jerk. Like the fool I apparently was, I peeked over my shoulder. The trio was flirting with the girl at the register.

"Just the three. They're laughing and talking with the young woman at the counter."

"Fuckers. You know why they're doing that, right? You remember what I told you?"

"I do. It makes my skin crawl. But I'm fine. You didn't need to call."

"Madeline, what's going on with you?"

"What's going on with me? Nothing. I just never expected to hear from you again." My friends' eyes widened as they silently *oohed.*

"What the fuck are you talking about?"

"Seriously? It's been five days. I've gotten nothing but radio silence from you. Whatever, I expected as much. Call off your prospect, or I'll get a restraining order. See you around."

"Don't you fuckin' hang up," he roared.

I pulled the phone away from my ear.

Tara snickered. "Shit, he sounds furious. Probably needs a little somethin', somethin'." She wiggled her eyebrows.

"Well, he's not getting anything from me." I put the phone back to my ear. "What more do you have to say, Storm? I'm busy here."

The girls snickered.

"I've been busy with shit, Madeline. I run an MC, you know?"

"You don't owe me an explanation." Not that one would be sufficient enough for ghosting me.

"Apparently, I do."

"No. You don't. But just so you know, there are forty-three thousand and two hundred seconds in twelve hours. One text saying, 'Hey, how's it going?' only takes ten seconds tops to type. You weren't busy with MC shit. You were being a dickhead and ghosting me. I'll see you around."

"Madeline! Goddammit, don't hang up!"

I sighed. "What now?"

He growled low in his throat again. I felt the vibration in my chest. He was furious, but I wasn't sure why he was doing this after getting nothing from him all week. I was afraid to hope he actually cared about me.

"Hero and Wolf are in the area. They'll be there any second with AJ. They'll escort you out if you need it." A frustrated huff filled my ear. "I want you to come to the clubhouse."

"I don't know Hero or Wolf. And I have no desire to go to your clubhouse. Besides, it's the Fourth of July. I'm with the girls. We're fine to be out in broad daylight. It's not like I'm alone."

"I want to see you, Angel."

I swallowed thick saliva, hating how I wanted to see him too. "I don't think it's a good idea."

"It's a great idea. We obviously have our wires crossed. I want to fix it." His low, gravelly voice made me clench my thighs.

I breathed into the phone like it was his mouth touching my lips. I didn't even realize I'd done it until he said, "Fuck. You're wet for me, aren't you?"

"Stop it. Be nice."

"Oh, I'll be nice, all right. When will you be here?"

"I didn't say I was coming. I have things to do." My eyes flitted to each one of my friends. As much as I wanted to see Storm, I already had plans with my girls.

"You'll be coming all right. All over my cock, Angel. What time? Won't take no for an answer."

Damn him and his dirty talk. No guy had ever talked to me the way Storm did, and I loved it. "You sure are bossy."

"Morning lovely ladies," one of the Hunter's said.

"Is one of them there?" Storm's voice raised three octaves.

I cringed. "Yes."

"Fuck! Do *not* get off the phone with me. Do you hear me, Madeline?"

"Y... yes." I gripped my cell phone tightly in my hand like it was a lifeline to Storm.

"What are you girls up to today? We're looking for some tour guides." This guy wasn't bad-looking. Tall, dark hair and eyes, tan skin like he spent his days shirtless in the sun and white, straight teeth. Steph was blushing. But Kim? She had a deep crease in her brow.

"Sorry, we're not interested," Tara said in her smart-ass voice. "Move along." My snarky friend's mouth often ran away with her.

"I'm sure I can get you interested," the biker growled.

"Breathe, Angel. I'm here." His husky voice soothed my anxiety.

I exhaled the air I hadn't realized I'd been holding in my lungs. "N... no you're not *here*..."

"You." The attractive Hunter pointed at me. Enforcer was on his patch. "It's rude to talk on the phone when you have a guest."

"Um, it's my... My..."

"Dad. Say, Dad." The edge in Storm's voice made me more nervous.

"My... my dad. It's our... our daily call." I swallowed. "I'm here, Daddy."

"Breathe, Angel. I can hear the trembling in your voice." Storm never missed a beat. This man had a way of comforting me as if it was second nature. So unlike what I'd expect from an outlaw biker.

"Tell yo daddy you need to go so I can give my speech all at once." The enforcer furrowed his brow, an expectant glint in his dark eyes.

"Daddy, I need to..."

"Do not hang up this phone, Madeline. Fuck, where are Hero and Wolf?" I heard a crash on the other line.

The entrance bell jingled, and the Hunter's expression turned grim.

"Can we help you with something?" Two *huge* men approached our booth. Both looked a little taller than Storm. These guys had muscles for miles; both had dark hair and eyes. One appeared to be Russian, maybe, while the other looked Latino. They towered over the three Hunters, looking deadly.

"You're in Knight's Legion territory. Something we can help you with?" the Latino asked. Not sure if he was Hero or Wolf.

"They there?" Storm asked.

"Mhm..."

"Not looking for any trouble, man. Just enjoying a cup of coffee," the Hunter's enforcer said.

"Let's take it outside and leave the patrons alone." The Knight doing all the talking jerked his head toward the door.

"We don't want trouble. Just talking to these nice ladies on this sunny Independence Day. Right, girls?" The Hunter smiled, showing off his pearly white teeth.

"Told you, we aren't interested," Tara said with a sneer. The Latino Knight cut his eyes to her. He didn't say anything for an intense couple of seconds.

"Sounds like *Roja* has spoken. We'll follow you boys out." He turned enough so I could catch a glimpse of the patch on his cut: Sergeant at Arms.

I looked at Tara. The SAA certainly was attractive, but Tara didn't appear to notice.

The Hunter leered at me, as if singling me out. "What about you, sweet thang. Does Roja speak for you, too?"

I had a feeling Storm was going out of his mind right now, though he was quiet. "Sorry, I—"

"Madeline, everything okay here?" The sound of Dane's voice behind me turned my blood cold.

Shit, this couldn't be happening. I didn't need my ex here on top of everything else.

"Deputy Miller, good to see you," the Sergeant at Arms said. I was super curious to know if he was Hero or Wolf. "We were just leaving with our new friends."

"And the women? Why are you at this table?" Dane asked, eyes locked on me.

My chest tightened. Storm was going to lose his shit. Lose it majorly when he found out my ex was in law enforcement.

"That your lady, Deputy?" the Hunter asked.

"No," I exclaimed. "Just an old... friend."

"Right. I get it. Friends with benefits, aye? Just what I'm looking for." The Hunter licked his bottom lip, eyeballing me.

Tara patted my knee under the table. Knowing her, it was her way of assuring me everything was okay. She could always read me when I was stressed.

"Let's go and leave the women alone." Dane and his partner Sonny blocked our table, and the bikers went to the exit.

The Knights glanced back at me. The one doing all the talking gave me a short nod. I took it to mean he'd be waiting for me.

"Jesus. That was intense," Kim said. "I nearly peed my pants. I'll be back."

"I'm coming with..." Steph got out of the booth.

With great trepidation, I returned back to Storm. "They're gone." No response. Just heavy breathing. "Storm? You there?"

"I want you here in an hour." The call ended.

My eyes burned with tears, hearing the anger in his voice.

Tara grimaced. "Shit. I heard him. He sounds pissed."

"He does." I exhaled a deep breath. "He doesn't know Dane is my ex. I mean, he knows his name is Dane, but he didn't know he's a deputy here in Winters." I had a feeling Storm might have connected the dots after Dane said my name.

"Oh, man. I thought you told him." Tara bit her bottom lip, picking at her blueberry muffin.

I sagged in my seat. "No. Stupid, I know. I was just afraid he'd want nothing to do with me."

"I'm sure it will be fine." The compassion in her voice made me more nervous. I wasn't so sure it would be okay.

"Madeline? I need a minute." Dane stood at the end of our table with his typical, *you don't have a choice* expression.

I nudged Tara to let me out, to avoid making a scene. If Dane wanted to be a jerk, he would arrest me for a lame reason. I wouldn't put it past him, so I'd talk to him just to get him off my back.

I sighed as glances shot our way from people in the bakery. "What do you want?"

He ignored me and strutted out of Sugar Bliss. Despite the gnawing in my gut, I followed him out to the sidewalk.

American flags hung from lampposts up and down the street and blew in the breeze. Confetti was strewn about from the parade earlier. I'd hoped the patriotic festivities would help bring me out of the funk I'd been in all week, but no dice. *Especially not now.*

I spotted AJ with the other two Knights. They were perched on their bikes next to the hardware store. No question they'd tell Storm about me talking to the deputy.

Dane turned abruptly on me with rage in his eyes. I recoiled, taking a step back.

"What were you doing talking to those bikers?"

"I wasn't talking to them. They stopped at our table. The girls and I were just having a late breakfast. Why are you angry with me?"

"Why do you think? I go into Sugar Bliss, and my ex-girlfriend is surrounded by a bunch of dirty bikers." He took my hand. Instantly, fear skirted up my spine. He had the same look in his ice-blue eyes he'd get when he knocked me around.

The Knights were staring at us. There was no telling what they'd do if Dane hit me. Unless a woman getting hit didn't faze them. They were one-percenters. It sure as hell never bothered Dane when he *put me in my place.*

I flitted my eyes over to the Knights, and one was on the phone.

Another appeared to be recording us. Crap, I'd bet my life Storm was getting a play-by-play right this second.

"Dane, we're not together. You can't tell me what to do." I tried to pull my hand away, but Dane's grip only tightened.

"I still care about you. Won't you give us another chance?" He kissed my hand, loosening his hold. I jerked it away. A second chance? He was out of his ever-loving mind. But more importantly, where the hell did that come from?

"No. This isn't happening. We're over. Have been for almost seven months." I took two steps back.

"I want you to stay away from them. I don't care if it's Knights or Hunters. Just stay away. They're nothing but trouble." He stepped toward me.

I put my hands up, stopping him. Did he think he could still control me? Probably. Dane believed he was above everyone because of the badge he wore. He wasn't a lousy deputy, just arrogant with a bit of a superiority complex. Crap. Why was I defending him?

"No, Dane. Stay out of my business." I turned on my heel to go back into the bakery, but he grabbed my arm. If my heart could've leaped into my throat, it would have.

"I wasn't finished talking to you," he gritted his teeth. I flashed back to a time when we were together and froze, my body trembling. He squeezed my arm. I tried not to wince from the pain. I needed to stand up to Dane and not let him bully me.

"Take your hand off me. We're finished, Deputy Miller."

"We're finished when *I* say we're finished."

"Madeline?"

Shit, I recognized the voice. It belonged to the Knight's Sergeant at Arms. The other big biker was probably with him, maybe even AJ. What were they thinking? Dane might arrest them on a trumped-up charge just to be a jerk.

"Don't be a fool, Madeline," Dane hissed in my ear. "If you're with one of these guys, it won't end well for you."

"Let go of me." I broke free from him. "Don't ever touch me again."

"Don't be stupid, Madeline." Dane pursed his lips thin. He hated when I stood up to him.

Was I just stupid? Maybe I'd been a fool for staying in Winters after finally getting out from under Dane's thumb. An idiot for getting mixed up with the president of a biker club. Either way, I owned my decisions. It was my life. Fool or not, I'd do whatever the hell I wanted.

"I'll be ready in five minutes," I muttered to the Knights as I passed them. Dane and his threats could kiss my ivory ass. He was not going to control me ever again.

Naturally, the girls tried to stop me from going with the bikers, but I knew I couldn't disobey Storm. That minor detail bothered them even more. Especially Mama Kim, who feared they wouldn't let me leave the compound once they got me inside. I tried to assure her Storm would never hurt me, but I wasn't so sure he wouldn't.

I'd been following the Latino. The other men were behind me. It felt like I was a prisoner, or maybe they were just protecting me. The way my heart raced and stomach churned, I hoped I wasn't going into a trap.

What if Storm knocked me around like Dane or forced me into being a kitten or something? My skin prickled and I gripped my steering wheel tighter.

No, I refused to believe Storm would physically hurt me. Sure, I didn't know him very well, but he wasn't a monster.

My phone startled me when it chimed. *Tara.*

"Hey."

"Where are you? The girls and I came to an agreement. We're coming after you."

I laughed nervously. "You're all crazy if you think you can

take on Storm and his brothers. They're outlaws, Tara. They have weapons."

"I'd die for you, Mads." I knew my redheaded, badass bestie would. "Give me your location."

"Promise me you won't do anything stupid. Like call the sheriff or drive out here."

Tara huffed into the phone. "How will I know you're okay?"

"I'll call or text you."

"Call. I'll need to hear your voice. I can tell when you're afraid. You stutter." Her voice softened.

"I don't... st... stutter."

"See."

"Sh... shit." I inhaled a breath, trying to calm my nerves. "I can see the compound. There's fencing around it with barbed wire and an armed guard at the gate. Fuck!"

"Give me your location!"

"We went north out of town, turned left on highway ten, drove for like five miles... I think, then turned right on another dirt road."

"Which one?"

"It didn't have a sign. There are lots of woods."

"That tells me nothing!"

The armed guard at the gate talked to the Latino, then he waved me in. The large man had a menacing scowl and a big ass rifle. Or a machine gun. Hell, I didn't know anything about guns. They all looked the same: big, long, small, black, silver....

"Mads, are you listening to me?" Tara's shrill voice scraped down my spine.

"I'm here. You'd never get through with the scary-ass biker guarding the gate." I inhaled a few more deep breaths as I parked my car next to the Latino's bike.

"Jesus, Mads. I'm fucking scared for you."

"I'll be okay." I hoped. "Storm won't hurt me. Besides, it's my own damn fault for bringing him home with me last weekend. But I'm wise to him now, and I plan to tell him off."

"Let's go," the Latino yelled, banging his knuckles on my window.

"Wish me luck."

"You're right. Storm won't hurt you. Not after what I heard going on in your bedroom."

It was only sex for goodness' sake. Honestly, sometimes Tara had a one-track mind.

"I'll call you in a little bit. Bye." I tucked my phone into my purse and sat there, hoping my racing heart would slow down. I didn't need to go into cardiac arrest and die on an MC's compound. My mother would flip her shit, losing another child.

The three bikers stared at me with their arms crossed. The prospect, AJ, didn't look half as menacing as the other two. Maybe he would help me if I got into trouble.

Probably not.

AJ's loyalties were to Storm and the club. I was on my own.

Shit, shit, shit. All I could do was pray Storm wouldn't hurt me, and I'd have all my fingers to enter the pin on my phone to call Tara. Or I guess I could use my nose if they chopped my digits off for some insane reason...

CHAPTER TWENTY-THREE

STORM

The fucker kissed her hand. He touched her. Deputy fuckin' Miller. *I'll kill him.*

Sure, Madeline looked pissed and pulled out of his grasp, but they looked like they knew each other. Didn't take long to put two and two together. She never once mentioned her ex, Dane, was in law enforcement.

Why didn't she tell me? She wasn't a stupid woman. She had to know how important this kind of information would be to me.

I slammed my hand down on the bar, seething. Why the fuck didn't she tell me?

"You need to calm down. She'll be in here shortly." Track eyed me from his stool. I hadn't taken my eyes off the main gate's monitor. I didn't want to miss Madeline arriving with her escorts, Hero, Wolf, and AJ.

"Calm down? Her ex is fuckin' Deputy Miller. My archenemy." As if I needed this complication.

It had been a shit week, already. Another of the club's businesses was vandalized yesterday. No doubt it was payback from the Hunters after what we had done to their men, breaking a few ribs and one of the dude's arms. I was sure Boxer's "Hickey from Ricky" didn't go over well either.

I'd been cleaning up mess after mess, not having a spare minute to call Madeline.

Not true.

I needed time to think.

Madeline had fucked with my head last weekend when we were together, and I needed to get myself straight. I had purposely not called or texted. A dick-move, for sure. She'd sounded more than a little pissed about it, too. I expected as much. She was my fiery little minx.

It was what it was, and I couldn't change a damn thing. All I could do was talk to her and figure this shit out. I wanted her with every cell in my body. But she deserved better than me. She also distracted me. I needed to stay focused with the Hunters wandering around and trying to invade my territory.

But after one weekend of fuckin' her senseless and loving every second of it, something changed in me. I needed her. Fuck. I never needed anyone before Angel.

"Try to remember how much you like her. I'm sure there's a good reason why she didn't say anything."

I tilted my head toward Track. "It's a betrayal." Even though I wanted her, I was furious with her. It felt deceptive, like she was keeping secrets. I didn't tolerate secrets. Not from my brothers. Not from my woman.

"Would it have made a difference?" Track snorted, as if trying to get a rise out of me.

Of course, like a dipshit, I took the bait. "If I'd known the truth, I wouldn't have hooked up with her."

"Hooked up? That's what you're calling it after spending the weekend with her? You never *sleep* with a woman. You just fuck 'em. What about all the hell you put us through when you came back from the lake? Moping around, biting off our heads at the littlest thing?" Track shook his head, lifting his beer to his mouth. "She's fucked you up, man."

"She hasn't."

"Just admitted it. You have it bad for her. And what you're angry about is knowing who'd been fucking her before you. Deputy Miller, the little prick. He's been up your ass for years trying to take down the club. Now you find out he's been with your woman. It sucks, man. It really does. I'd probably go ape shit myself, but you can't. Do you want to risk losing her?"

"No," I grunted.

Fuckin' Track. He called it. I hated the deputy. He'd arrested me at least a dozen times over the years. Never for anything serious. Always just to show he was in control. I should've taken the motherfucker out long ago.

But I didn't kill for sport, only in self-defense or when absolutely necessary. Even so, Boxer took care of most of it. I already had enough blood on my hands and did everything possible to avoid more.

"Didn't think so. Miller will probably try to take her from you. Don't push her away, or you might push her back into the prick's arms."

Never gonna happen. The asshole treated Madeline like shit. Now that I knew *he* was the one that messed with her so bad, she would never go back to him, and I'd make damn sure she didn't.

Madeline's car appeared on the monitor. I inhaled a deep breath, finished off the whiskey I'd been staring at, and waited for her. Track was right. I needed to calm down.

I'd been a crazy cuss dealing with the Dirty Hunters. Stressed about Madeline, missing the fuck out of her. I'd planned to call her over the weekend. It was stupid. I shouldn't have put it off and invited her to the party tonight. We didn't make a big deal about the Fourth of July. No fireworks or anything. A simple club party was enough for the guys around here. But she should've been invited long before the drama this morning.

"Heard your woman arrived." Lynx entered the bar, smirking. "Finally, got her out here to meet us, did ya?"

"Not now." Track leveled his gaze at Lynx.

Lynx eyes cut to Track's. "What? Something happened while I was balancing the books?"

"Miller is her ex," I told him straight up because I didn't hide important shit from my brothers.

Lynx gaped. "Deputy Miller?"

"Yeah." I watched the monitor, feeling the muscles in my shoulders turn hard as steel.

"Fuuuck. And she hadn't told you?" The surprise in Lynx's voice increased my fury. I should've known about Miller being Madeline's ex.

"Nope."

"Damn, Prez. No wonder you look ready to kill. But come on, this is Madeline. Your saucy little woman and—" Lynx wiggled his eyebrows like Groucho Marx. Sometimes I couldn't deal with his antics.

"She's not my fuckin' woman," I yelled, pushing off my stool. It crashed onto the floor. "Just someone I fucked, all right?" I blew and in a big, disastrous way. The words flew out of my mouth as I lost my cool. Reacted to Lynx's taunting. But dammit! Why didn't she tell me about Miller? Deputy fuckin' Miller! This kind of shit was a deal breaker.

"Oh, man…" Track whispered, lifting his beer to his lips, tilting his head toward the door.

And I knew then, Madeline had heard me.

I turned my head to the entrance of the bar. Madeline and I stared at each other for a long second. Nothing I said now would matter. Not with this fireball. I knew a massive ass-chewing was heading my way. She just better not do it in front of my brothers.

"I'm here. What do you want?" She crossed her arms over her chest, a scary expression on her beautiful face. But I didn't miss the slight tremble rolling through her body. She was afraid, but trying to hide it.

Hero and Wolf stepped behind the bar and out of the way. Smart guys.

"How about a quick fuck?" She scanned the bar. "Right here with an audience. Isn't that how you guys like to do things? Out in the open?"

Her goddamn smart mouth fired me up and turned me on every fuckin' time. I drank Madeline in. Her lithe, curvy body was cloaked in a red and white polka dot sundress with thin straps. It fell mid-thigh. She had on her brown boots with the stitched cross on the front. Her dark, silky hair fell in loose waves over her sexy shoulders, her makeup light and natural. Seeing her on the video did not do her justice. She was stunning, even with the bitter scowl on her face.

"Lost for words?" She tapped the toe of her boot, getting angrier. "Where do you want me? On my knees? Laid out on the bar, spread eagle? How about I just strip right here." She turned toward AJ. "Put something titillating on so I can do a striptease."

Now she crossed the line.

"Will you just shut the fuck up for one goddamn minute, woman!" I scratched the side of my head, willing myself to get a grip.

Of course, she didn't listen.

"I know you brought me here because of Dane. Let's just get this over with. I betrayed you and should be punished. But it's not really a big deal because you were just fucking me and cut me loose—"

I tilted my head at her, feeling like I was about to explode. "The fuck you say?"

She held up a hand, stopping me. Damn, stubborn woman. "No worries. It's what I expected. It's why I didn't open up to you about my private life. Or tell you Dane was a deputy in Winters. Let me assure you, I know nothing about your club's dealings or any of your brothers. I'd never say anything to that son of a bitch." She inhaled a deep breath, eyes glossy but resolute. "Gentleman. It's been... interesting. Happy Independence Day. Stay safe." She spun on her heels and bolted, leaving me speechless and livid.

What the fuck just happened?

"You gonna just let her leave?" Track asked. "She's fucking awesome, by the way."

"A little too mouthy for my taste," Wolf muttered.

Lynx and Hero laughed. *Assholes.*

"Son of a bitch." I stormed after Madeline, catching her wrist just as she exited the double entrance doors. "That mouth of yours always gets you into trouble, Angel." I spun her around and pushed her up against the wall. My breath caught in my throat, seeing tears rolling down her face.

"Let me go." She turned her face away, as if embarrassed, and tried to wiggle out of my grasp.

"You're mine, Angel. Not giving you up."

"Bullshit. You don't own me." Her baby blues flashed and the disgust in them put a severe ache in my chest. I never wanted her to hate me.

"I. Heard. You."

"I was angry and talking out of my ass."

She shook her head. "Every time you're angry, you gonna talk out your ass? You gonna make it sound like I don't mean anything to you just so you look big and bad in front of your brothers? Because if so, Storm, I'm out. I am so freaking out. I don't need that kind of shit in my life again."

Again.

I had a feeling she was referring to Miller. I wanted to wrap my hand around his long, thin neck and squeeze the life out of him for hurting her. When I saw her so broken at her place, I already wanted to kill him. Well, now I wanted him gone—yesterday. I didn't know the details of what he did, but I would find out. Then I'd make the motherfucker pay.

I ran the pads of my thumbs under her eyes, wiping away her tears, and kissed her nose. She didn't fight me. I was damn grateful, too. Lowering my voice, I said, "I'm sorry for being an ass. But you should've told me about Miller."

"When was I supposed to tell you? We've hardly spent any time together. At the lake, you took off. I never thought I'd see you again. Then last weekend was a whirlwind of sex. Amazing sex,"—she bit her bottom lip, blushing the prettiest shade of pink—"but when Storm? When you left Monday morning, I expected to hear from you, but it's been five days and not one call or text. You're such an asshole." She shook her head. "When was I supposed to tell you?"

She was exactly right. It appeared we needed to do more talking and less sex. Another time, though. First, I wanted her to officially meet my brothers.

"You're right, baby." I pressed my body against hers, brushing my hand over her hip and up to her waist.

"I am?" Her pretty mouth popped open in surprise. I went in for the kill, kissing her like I'd been lost in the desert, dying of thirst, and only she could replenish me.

Her tongue curled with mine, hands gliding up my abs, over my chest, and to my neck. Her nails did their little thing at my nape. I shivered and turned hard as granite.

I pulled away, cradling her face in my large hands, and stared into her baby eyes.

"You're the first woman in my life I've slept with. Not talking sex. We slept together, cuddling and spooning. I've never done that with women before. You mean something to me. I care about you, and when I knew Hunters were in the same building as you and I couldn't protect you myself, I lost it, baby. I fuckin' lost it."

Her pretty eyes softened and filled with understanding. "And then, Dane appeared."

"I've hated him for years."

"I'm not surprised. I can't stand him either."

I crushed my lips to hers again. When she kissed me back just as eagerly, my mind was made up. I was never letting her go. I felt like shit for not calling her. I'd known what I wanted, and it was her, but I'd been too damn afraid to admit it.

"I want you to meet my brothers. Officially," I said against her mouth, nibbling and licking her lips. "You okay with that?"

"Yes, if you're sure. No more games, Storm. No more ghosting me. I won't be so forgiving the next time."

Damn this woman was fierce. I'd clearly met my match.

"There won't be a next time. I wasn't playing games. I want you."

She considered me a long, intense second. "What will you do with me afterward?" The flirty lilt in her voice made my spine tingle. There were about a dozen different things I wanted to do.

I dropped my face to the curve of her neck, pecking light kisses on her skin. I breathed in her soft scent and mumbled, "Take you to my bed."

"To sleep?"

"Baby, you know better than that… to fuck."

"Maybe we should talk first."

"We'll talk after we've fucked."

She giggled. "So, bossy."

I hugged her tightly, exhaling a sigh of relief. Madeline was mine. All mine.

CHAPTER TWENTY-FOUR

MADELINE

Storm's brothers were decent and didn't ogle me too much. Well, Lynx and Hero did a little. Wolf, the guy Storm called "Russian giant," had given me a short nod, then hung back. Well, as much as a ginormous man could, standing taller than all the other guys in the room. He was a giant for sure. The SAA was Hero.

I remembered Track and Lynx from The Bullet the night I met Strom. Lynx talked more than the other guys. He was the club's treasurer and managed The Bullet.

Track studied me a lot with what felt like a critical eye. He was introduced as Storm's best friend and road captain. I was most concerned about Track liking me.

It was easy to see these guys respected Storm, even when joking around like brothers. Storm wasn't much of a jokester. Especially when they flirted and complimented me on my "toned legs and sexy boots." I liked his possessiveness.

Storm kissed below my ear. "You ready to go, baby?" He'd been standing behind me the entire time with his arms wrapped around my waist. I loved every second of it, too. "I want you all to myself."

"Yeah, I'm ready." I tilted my head up, and he pressed his lips to mine.

"Who do we have here?" a woman asked.

Storm stiffened and ended the kiss.

I turned my head toward the voice. The blonde sashayed farther into the bar, wearing *tiny* denim bootie shorts and an American flag printed tube top, exposing her midriff. She glared at Storm as if she'd caught him cheating on her.

Was she his go-to kitten? Well, if so, not anymore.

I plastered a bright, friendly smile onto my face. "Hi, I'm Madeline." I tried to move forward to shake her hand, but Storm wouldn't release me. His grip tightened around my stomach, and his lips dropped to my neck. What the hell? "Storm… stop," I whispered, but of course, he didn't listen.

"Carla, Storm's kitten." The woman introduced herself. She pushed her hip out and set her hand on it. Her eyes raked over my body, sizing me up like I was doing to her.

Shit. This woman was his go-to. She wasn't ugly by any means. A little taller than me, bigger breasts, but they didn't look real. Then again, what did I know? She was attractive. I could see why Storm would be with her.

Jealousy bloomed in my chest.

My body went straight as a board when her violet-colored eyes connected with mine. Violet? Was it even a natural eye color? This kitten, this Carla-chick, sneered like she wanted to claw my eyes out. I wasn't a catfighting kind of girl, but mess with *my* man, and my nails would come out.

"Not true," Storm bit back in a commanding voice. "Kittens belong to all the patched members."

Carla huffed. "But I'm your favorite."

"I have the only woman I want, right here." He kissed my neck again. I adored this man even more for making me feel secure. "Let's go, baby."

"Great meeting you, Madeline," Lynx said with a friendly wave. Track, Hero, and Wolf gave me a nod, and AJ smiled.

"See ya guys later." I waved as Storm tucked me into his side.

Carla's face turned red, and her nostrils flared. I might feel bad for her if she'd been with Storm recently. But according to him, he hadn't been with her in over six months. The woman needed to move on because I had no plans of giving this man up.

"Handle that," Storm hissed, but I wasn't sure what he meant or who he was speaking to. It didn't matter, I was going to be alone with him, and I couldn't wait.

We went up a flight of stairs and down a long hallway to the very end. Storm took a ring of keys out of his pocket and unlocked the door.

"After you, Angel." He jerked his chin for me to enter.

What does the bedroom of an MC president look like? What little I knew about Storm, he was a no-nonsense man, always wearing jeans, T-shirts, boots, and his cut.

I never expected a pristine, well-put-together bedroom. Directly in front of me was a king-sized bed flanked by floor-to-ceiling windows. Between them was a herringbone pattern made from what I guessed was reclaimed wood. It was so stunning, it could be a piece of art.

Gray linens dressed the bed. There was a weathered black chest of drawers and a matching set of nightstands. The room wasn't huge, but it was a lot bigger than mine. There was even a leather club chair and ottoman with a floor lamp in a corner opposite the bed. Hardwood floors, a vaulted ceiling, and a large oriental rug completed the room.

"Wow, I don't know what to say." My eyes flitted around the space.

"Hopefully, that's a good thing." He closed the door and locked it.

"But don't be too impressed. This used to be my Uncle Matt and Aunt Eve's room. When she moved out, it became mine. I just bought new furniture."

He'd told me his uncle was the original president and died of cancer. I could tell Storm respected his uncle a lot. I hoped to meet his aunt and cousins sometime soon.

"Does the maid come daily to keep, all this"—I waved my hand in front of me—"clean and tidy."

"Nah, I don't let anyone in my room. Just you baby..." He circled my waist with his hands and tugged me up against him. "Shit... You freaked me the fuck out earlier." His mouth was on mine. He couldn't seem to get enough of my lips.

Freaked him out? Why? I'd ask him to clarify, but this kiss turned my brain to goo and my bones to jelly.

Storm inhaled me as if I were all the air he would ever need. Part of me hoped I didn't imagine it. The other part kept wondering how I'd fit into his MC life.

While plundering his tongue into my mouth, clashing it into mine, he backed me up until my legs hit the bed. He pulled back, staring into my eyes. Both of us heavily breathing.

"When those Hunters were near you, and I wasn't there to protect you..." He dropped his head, shaking it. "I'd only ever felt so helpless one other time in my life. I'd done everything possible to never experience such weakness and vulnerability again. You make me feel both."

I couldn't believe it. This cocky, powerful, and scary man was revealing a piece of himself to me. I didn't know what to make of it. All I knew was I would treasure this moment, always.

"Storm, I—"

He placed a finger on my lips. "No. Not a word. You need to listen to me. Listen carefully."

I nodded, brushing my hands up his chest, wanting to soothe him.

The anger I had dwelling in me all week and the jealousy I felt after meeting Carla were pushed aside. What Storm was telling me was more important than anything else.

"I have enemies. They want to take down my club. Destroy me. If they know how much you mean to me, you'd be the link to my destruction." He sighed, covering my hands with his. "If we're going to be together, you can't act hastily. You have to stay alert to your surroundings, and you *must* listen to me."

There was no way to hide the way my body trembled at his words. Fear radiated through me. At the same time, a warmth bloomed in my chest. I mattered to him. I made him weak and vulnerable. Hearing all this stunned me, making me feel important.

"I'm sorry I didn't call or text. I just needed time to think things through."

"Like whether to be with me or not." I needed clarification. I needed to know why he hadn't called.

"Angel, there's no question I want to be with you. But being with me could put you in danger, and I sure as hell don't want that."

"I have a right to choose too, ya know? And I want to be with you, Storm—more than anything. When I didn't hear from you, I thought you were done with me. Figured you'd gotten what you wanted and tossed me away."

"Shit, baby. I never wanted you to feel that way." He reeled me into his strong arms and held me close, kissing my temple over and over.

"We have a lot to learn about each other."

"We do, but first, let's reconnect." His stormy gray eyes shimmered like platinum.

"Okay, we'll talk after you make me come all over your dick."

He groaned in my hair. "Love it when you talk dirty."

I giggled.

"Now, strip. No music, I want you to sing the song from the night

I first saw you."

"What? Sing? Nuh-uh." I shook my head, laughing.

"Okay, fine. Be that way." He twirled me around, bent me over the side of his bed, and lifted my dress. His hand rubbed up the back of my thigh to my thong, and he pulled it down until it was wiggled free of my boots. "Don't wanna sing for me? You'll only get my fingers." One plunged into my hot, wet opening.

"What?" I fisted his comforter. Another finger joined the first. His breath on my ear made me shiver with need.

"You heard me. No cock for you, Angel."

Bastard!

His fingers slipped in and out, getting slick with my cream. It wasn't enough; I needed more. I needed his dick. "Fine. I'll sing."

"Good girl," he said with amusement in his voice.

"You play dirty. Just remember one thing, handsome. Paybacks are a bitch."

His fingers fell away, and he put them to his mouth and licked them clean. The sight of his eyes slowly closing, like he was savoring the taste of me, turned me molten with desire. I lifted off the bed and pushed him back.

I started to sing "Before He Cheats" by Carrie Underwood. It'd been my jam months before I'd caught Dane in the act. I'd listened to the song thousands of times, absorbing the lyrics and rhythm into my flesh and blood. I'd promised myself no man would ever cheat on me again.

As I sang, I danced around Storm, gyrating my ass into his thigh, shimmying my shoulders as I lowered one strap, then the other. The heat in his eyes gave me the confidence to belt out the song like I knew I could. I was on point, hitting every note perfectly.

Back home, when I was in the church choir, the director had told me I was the brunette version of Carrie Underwood. It was the biggest compliment I'd ever gotten for my singing.

When I left for college, I sang in a jazz band on campus and at various bars and coffeehouses on amateur nights. Unfortunately, it was my voice Dane had noticed one night at a bar near my university. He'd bought me a drink after my performance, and I took him home. And so began the worst two years of my life. A big part of why I wanted nothing to do with Storm the night we met had to do with Dane. But that all changed. Every piece of me wanted every part of him.

At the end of the song, I pushed Storm onto the bed and let my dress fall to the floor. I stepped out of it, completely naked, save for my boots.

I cradled Storm's face and captured his bottom lip between my teeth. "Don't you cheat on me…"

He swept me off my feet faster than I could say, *ever* and tossed me on the bed. Desire rushed through me as I bounced, watching as he literally ripped off his shirt. God, he was magnificent. He tugged off his boots and had his pants tossed aside just as fast.

Storm pounced on me. The thick crown of his cock entered me. A powerful thrust came next. I yelped his name as he fucked me, hard. Drilling into me without regard for how loud I was or if anyone was around.

"Fuck, Angel. You're everything. I'll never cheat on you. I promise."

We kissed, wildly touching each other. Chasing our orgasms as if our lives depended on it. We bucked harder and faster. The sound of our skin slapping was all I heard.

Storm put his hand between us and found my ball of nerves. "Come for me. Let me feel you come on my dick." He rubbed and flicked my clit.

I shot off like a rocket. My cries of ecstasy pushed Storm to go off next.

"Fuuuck Angel. Fuck, you feel so damn good, milking my cock." He groaned, his body tensing through his release until he collapsed on me.

We held each other, touching and kissing as the hours passed. It was heaven.

I ditched my friends to stay the night with Storm. Tara was relieved to hear I was alive and didn't give me crap.

Storm didn't want to go to the club's party. I assured him it would be okay if we went but had gruffly said no. Neither of us cared about the Fourth of July when we had our own fireworks show in his bed.

Sometime after seven, a prospect delivered food to Storm's room. We had sex several more times while music vibrated the floor beneath us. I eventually fell asleep in *my* man's arms, deliriously happy and sexually satisfied.

It was the best Independence Day of my life.

CHAPTER TWENTY-FIVE

STORM

This morning Madeline and I washed each other in my oversized walk-in shower. It was fuckin' fantastic. She'd lowered to her knees on the tile floor, a dazzling smile on her gorgeous face. My girl loved the hell outta my dick. I'd nearly crumpled onto the floor in front of her.

Her mouth was wickedly talented. I'd made sure she knew it too, so she'd get dipshit Miller's words out of her head. I wanted to beat him to a pulp for making Madeline feel inadequate. Because she wasn't, she was every man's dream come true. I'd meant it when I told her she could suck my dick anytime.

"I need more on than your T-shirt." Madeline's pink cheeks were freaking adorable. She rarely blushed, but when she did, my chest tightened.

Whenever she was near, I couldn't keep my eyes off her. There wasn't anything about her I didn't like. I especially liked her long silky brown hair and her cute aqua blue toenails. She seemed to love the color blue.

"Angel, you're gorgeous. We're just going downstairs for breakfast. I thought you were hungry."

"I'm starving. But what will the others say when they see me in only your shirt? When will your aunt and cousins be back from their road trip? I can't meet them looking like this." She tugged on my shirt.

I knew she wanted to make a good impression with my Aunt Eve and the boys, but she didn't need to worry. I was confident they would love her.

"Not for another week. They decided to stay in DC for the Fourth of July." I was glad too. With the shit going on here, I preferred they stayed away as long as possible.

"Oh. That's nice." She rolled her toes under.

I smirked, raking my eyes over her, and licked my lips. I wanted her again. Right then.

"The hungry look in your eyes is what I'm talking about. I don't even have panties on." The blush in her cheeks deepened.

I reeled her into my arms and dropped a kiss on her forehead. "I promise, the guys will leave you alone. They know better. But it's not like they've never seen a naked woman before." I copped a feel of her ass cheek. Yeah, I definitely wanted her again.

"I'm not sex on a stick. I'm not a kitten, Storm, and I don't want to be treated like one." She shoved my chest. I could tell she was getting worked up, so I needed to quickly defuse her.

"Baby, they'd never treat you like a kitten. They know you're mine."

"They do?"

"Yeah, baby. Bringing you up to my bed and ditching the party sealed it. You're mine. They won't disrespect you. They know I'd beat the shit out of them if they did."

"Wow. But still—"

"My shirt covers more of your body than the pretty little dress you had on yesterday."

She twisted her lips, looking down at herself, then flashed a brilliant smile.

"You are so right. I'm swimming in this shirt." She laughed. "Okay, let's go."

"That's my girl." I took her hand and led her to the kitchen.

The clubhouse would be busy, which was perfect for parading my girl around.

And she looked damn fine in my favorite Ozzy Osborne tee. Ozzy was hitchhiking to hell. I rarely wore it, always afraid I'd ruin it. Uncle Matt had given it to me on my twenty-first birthday. All these years later, it was priceless to me. I loved it. I loved it even more on Madeline. Fuck, I was hard just looking at her in it.

"Morning, Prez," Track greeted us with a smirk. His brows shot up, seeing Madeline in my coveted T-shirt. "Morning darlin'. You're looking mighty fine with Ozzy on your chest."

"Good morning to you, too. This old thing, I just threw it on." She playfully waved him off. Damn, my woman knew how to handle herself with my brothers. She just kept getting better.

Track chuckled. "Well, you've improved it."

"I agree." I pressed my lips to her temple. "Coffee, baby?"

"Please. Just a little creamer."

I jerked my chin to a barstool at the giant island. She took a seat two down from Track.

As the president of the club, I didn't serve anyone. I was always served. It was just how it was in my world. An outsider wouldn't understand it. So when the eyebrows of some of my brothers shot up, I was sure they wondered if I lost my fuckin' mind offering Madeline a cup of coffee.

I poured two mugs while more guys filed in and lingered near the island with curious eyes. Most looked groggy after partying last night. I was surprised there weren't any kittens hanging around. The boys must have worn their asses out, so much they left after preparing breakfast.

"Oh, you're still around…"

Well, one kitten was here. I cringed, hearing Carla's salty voice. Damn Lynx was supposed to have straightened her out. I slowly glanced over my shoulder at Madeline. She didn't seem fazed. Rather than rush to her defense, I hung back and observed.

If Madeline was going to be my old lady, she needed to learn how to deal with the kittens. The club whores knew their place here and accepted it, but they acted like they owned the cocks in the club. They had no claim to any of us, but there was a pecking order and Carla was at the top. They claimed ownership over the men when a new girl entered the kittens domain. Like Carla was doing now.

The way Carla acted yesterday with Madeline wouldn't be allowed, but it was better to let the women deal with each other in situations like this. Madeline needed to show Carla and all the other kittens who was boss if she was my woman. My queen.

If it got out of hand, I'd step in and shut it the fuck down. Especially since I hadn't warned Madeline.

"I am. Did you just get here? I hope you got lucky last night." The smartass tone in Madeline's voice made me chuckle.

Carla huffed. "Yeah, well, at least I'm dressed for the day." The stupid woman never could think up a quick comeback. But she knew how to be mean and nasty. Not sure why I let her stick around, other than she was an expert cock sucker.

I glanced over my shoulder again just as Madeline shrugged.

"We stayed in bed having sex this morning and planned to have more after breakfast. Getting dressed for the day seemed… *pointless*." Madeline tilted her head with a sassy expression.

Carla scowled and several deep chuckles filled the room. I knew my woman could handle herself.

"That's right, baby." I place a mug in front of her. "What would you like to eat?"

Carla screwed up her face. Again, my brothers looked at me like I'd just grown a pussy on my forehead. Fuck it. I didn't care. I'd watched my Uncle Matt serve Aunt Eve plenty of times.

"Whatever you're having." Madeline lifted her chin, flashing me a radiant smile.

I couldn't resist capturing her lips in front of everyone. She didn't hesitate to join in. In fact, she moaned against my mouth, driving me wild. I knew it was all for show, because of Carla. It pleased me how she didn't let a kitten get to her.

Throats cleared. I noticed Track shifting on his stool.

"Fuck, Prez," Lynx bellowed as he entered.

Madeline pulled away, face flushed, and smiled wider. "Good morning, Lynx."

"I should say so gorgeous. You're looking well-rested and glowing." He gave her a slow wink.

"Glowing, maybe. Well-rested?" She snorted, thumbing my way. "With him? No. He's like the Energizer Bunny. He just keeps going and going and going. I'll need a vacation just to catch up on sleep."

The guys roared with laughter. I loved how they all seemed to like her. A couple of prospects were in the back, eyes twinkling. My chest puffed up with pride. *My woman.* Damn, I loved the sound of it. She was winning over the guys left and right.

Boxer guffawed. "Fuck, Prez. Kept her up all night, did you?"

"Don't let my little Angel fool you." I crossed the kitchen with two plates filled with scrambled eggs, bacon, sausage, and biscuits. I set a plate in front of Madeline and took the spot next to her. "This woman has an insatiable appetite." I cupped the back of her head and crushed my lips to hers again. Who needed food? I was ready to take her back to bed and feast on her.

"Well... Who do we have here?" Tina sang. Justin's daughter giggled softly.

I ended the kiss. Might as well make introductions now. "Morning Tina." I nodded.

Raul and Justin entered next.

"Since most of the important people are here, except for Sugar and the twins, I'll introduce this lovely lady to all of you."

Tina smiled. "This is exciting."

"Angel, this here is Raul, my VP, and his old lady, Tina. They're married and have two kids." Tina was Raul's second wife, but I didn't want to mention it in front of so many people. We all loved Tina. Most of us had never known Raul's first wife Jessica, Track's mom. She was killed in a driveby in front of the clubhouse almost twenty years ago. Her murder was why the whole property was gated and we kept an armed guard at the entrance.

"It's nice to meet you both. I'm Madeline," she said with a wave. "Where are your kids?"

Tina stepped around the island to get closer to Madeline. "At summer camp. Raymond is eleven, and Valerie is eight and a half."

Emilee, Justin's daughter followed Tina with curious eyes observing Angel. Emilee was the shy type. She and Tina were very close.

"Oh, elementary school age. I'm a kindergarten teacher at Heritage in Winters." Madeline's whole demeanor changed in an instant. "Are there any other kids in the club?"

The guys frowned. None of us ever wanted kids. We were one-percenters. We all lived and died for the club. Christ, were things going to change with Madeline around?

"Sadly no. I keep telling these guys to get busy having the next generation, but then their balls go into hiding." Tina laughed as some guys grumbled. "You must like kids if you're a teacher."

"I adore them. Especially the young ones. They need the most nurturing and cuddles being away from their mommas."

Damn, she really did love kids. I wouldn't think about it right now, though. There were too many people around, and Carla was shooting daggers at my girl.

"Hi, I'm Emilee." She extended her hand, and Madeline accepted it with a smile.

"I'm pleased to meet you, Emilee. And you are… an old lady? Kitten?"

"Oh, hell, no." Justin stepped forward. Madeline's eyes went wide. "This pretty girl is my daughter. Not an old lady or kitten. Christ, I'd have a heart attack if she was. I'm the club's secretary. This guy here treating you good?" Justin jerked his chin my way.

"Well, he has a bit of a temper, but I'm sure you're all aware of that." Madeline smiled up at me. "I think I can handle him."

Raul winked, sidling up to Tina's side. "From what I've heard, I think you're right. If not, come see me, his VP, and I'll take care of him."

"I'm Boxer, the enforcer around here. Tell me…" He leaned into Madeline, elbows on the island, his face mere inches from hers. "You do some voodoo shit to catch him? This guy has never brought a woman around, let alone let her wear his prized Ozzy shirt and sleep in his bed. I want to know your secret, *honey*."

"Hey. Don't go honeying her, Box," I barked.

He raised his hands. "Didn't mean any harm. I can just tell this pretty lady has a special touch."

Madeline rubbed my thigh in a calming way. "Well, Boxer, I might have a special touch. No voodoo shit, just good old-fashioned charm."

Justin's daughter laughed. I could tell she was intrigued by Madeline. She'd grown up within the club and not around many old ladies, just kittens, which Justin didn't want her getting close to. Sugar and Tina had been the only mother-figures to Emilee after Justin's wife, Laura, died years ago after a valiant battle with breast cancer.

Then there was Jill, Boxer's sister. She'd been Wolf's old lady for about a year or so. I was sure Jill would like Madeline. Hell, everyone seemed to like Angel. Except Carla. She continued to glare at her, and I'd about had enough of it.

"Good old-fashioned charm. I like it." Boxer threw a wink Madeline's way.

"She has a special touch, all right." I pulled Madeline close. "Eat up, baby. Your food is getting cold."

Carla huffed, rolling her eyes.

"Where the hell did Lynx go?" I glanced at Raul, then cut my eyes to Carla.

"The Bullet," Raul replied.

If he'd talked to Carla, she wasn't listening. I was tired of her bullshit and had been for months now. She needed to go.

"Madeline, will you be sticking around or at the party tonight?" Emilee asked. "I'd love to talk to you about teaching. I'll be declaring my major in the spring. I'm considering Early Childhood Ed. I don't think I'd be good with older kids."

"I'm better with the little ones myself." Madeline smiled, then lifted her mug to her lips.

"Then you'll be here tonight?" Emilee asked again, a hopeful smile on her face. "Maybe we could talk before the party."

"She'll be here," I answered for Madeline. I had a feeling she didn't know how to respond.

I scarfed my food like I'd been trained to do in the Marines. After ten minutes of listening to idle chit-chat, I'd had enough. "You ready to go?" I whispered at the shell of Madeline's ear.

"Yes." She slipped off the stool, holding the hem of the T-shirt down, then reached for her plate.

I stopped her. "Carla's got it." I cut my eyes to the bitchy kitten and took Madeline's hand, leading her out.

"It was great meeting all of you! See you this evening." She waved and smiled.

Shouts of *see ya* and *bye* followed us out.

Back in my room, Madeline turned toward me, went up on her tiptoes, hooking her arms around my neck. "They're all great. I look forward to talking to Emilee tonight."

"I could tell they all liked you, too."

"Yeah, except for Carla... your kitten."

"Don't do that, Angel. She means nothing to me." I didn't want to have this conversation, but I knew we'd eventually need to.

"But she was your go-to. What made you keep going back to her? How long were you with her?"

I pulled out of her arms, and she pouted. Suddenly I felt ill. My stomach was tight and churning. I sat on the corner of the bed, bracing my elbows on my knees. I clasped my hands together and stared at them.

Madeline stayed back and didn't say anything, but I felt her eyes on me.

I ignored her questions and asked one which mattered most to me. "Did you love Dane?" I lifted my head to see her expression.

"Wow, that came out of nowhere." She tugged the hem of my shirt down, shifting from one foot to the other. She was nervous. It put me on edge.

"Just answer the question." I gritted my teeth.

"No. I cared about Dane. I cared a lot about him until he started treating me like crap and cheated."

"Really? Have you been in love before?"

Her eyes darted around the room. She still hadn't moved closer to me. Why was she acting nervous?

"Yes."

Fuck. Not what I wanted to hear.

"Have you? Been in love with someone?"

"No. Never."

"Then what was Carla to you?" Her arms wrapped around her

stomach like she was protecting herself from me. My damn chest ached somethin' fierce. I couldn't handle it if she pulled away from me.

I leveled my gaze on hers, so she'd know I was serious. "An easy, familiar fuck. Nothing else." I watched her fidget with her fingers a moment. "Do you still love him?"

She inhaled a breath and looked off to the side.

"Look at me, Angel. I need to see your eyes."

"What attracted you to Carla? How long were you with her?"

"I wasn't with her," I snapped harsher than I meant to. "I fucked her, or she sucked me off when I needed it. A year maybe. Before her and after, it was just random kittens, none of which are still around."

"But you kept Carla around."

"I shouldn't have. She's getting difficult. Possessive."

"Well yeah, she's possessive. Anyone can see she cares about you. She probably loves you. She wants to claw my eyes out, if you hadn't noticed."

"I noticed. Carla won't touch you, though. You handled her well."

"I didn't handle her, but I will if needed."

"I believe you could. Tell me about *him*." Her hesitancy was scaring the shit out of me. I already hated this guy.

"There's not much to tell. He was my brother's best friend, kind of like part of the family and a lot older than me. It'd never happen between us. I'm sure he never thought of me beyond his friend's kid sister. But he was more to me." She came to me and dropped onto her knees between my legs.

We stared into each other's eyes for several seconds. I wanted to hear more. I wanted to know what was so special about this guy who'd won her heart. I worried he might still own it.

"What else? Do you still love him?"

"I don't know if you ever stop loving a fantasy. He was my dream guy. Kind of like a celebrity."

"Except he was in your life for real. Like part of the family, you said."

"Yes. And I haven't seen him in over a decade. He moved away when I was young. Haven't seen him since. But a little girl's dreams can live on for a long time, y'know." She shrugged a shoulder, but there was sadness in her eyes, dulling their brightness, and it gutted me.

"You still love him."

She sighed but didn't deny it. This fuckin' conversation was pissing me the hell off.

"Did he keep you from loving Dane?" Shit, I really hated this dream guy. The thing about a fantasy, it was perfect and couldn't be destroyed. I wanted more than anything to knock this guy off the pedestal Madeline had him on.

"No. Dane did it all on his own. I always thought when the right guy came along, he'd break through the walls I'd built around my heart. Dane didn't come close."

"Maybe your walls are impenetrable." Fuck me. No fuckin' way would I be second to some perfect dream guy. Shit, I hated feeling jealousy spur in my chest.

"I thought the same until you." Her eyes were glossy now. "I know it sounds crazy. I mean, we've only known each other a month, but the time we've spent together…" She shook her head, cheeks blushing. "I don't want to be apart from you. Somehow, you've gotten under my skin. I don't know how, but you did."

"I feel the same way." I lowered my mouth to hers, our lips a breath away. She'd just given me hope. "I don't want to compete with a fantasy. If you're with me, you gotta let him go."

She nodded, blinking back tears. "I know. I want you Storm— only you. But you need to know if I ever caught Carla hanging on you or found out you fucked her or she gave you head…" She inhaled a deep breath, eyes locked on mine. "I'll be gone. I won't stick around for an explanation or an apology. Understand?" Her words were calm and direct. "And that goes for any other woman, not just Carla."

God almighty, she was fierce. I was glad she wouldn't put up with any bullshit. Deputy fuckin' Miller had done a number on her. I might not know the half of it, but I could tell it had to have been awful. One of these days, I'd find out what exactly he'd done to her, then I'd teach him a painful lesson.

"You're all I want, Angel. You don't need to worry about Carla or any other woman."

She climbed onto my lap and softly kissed my lips. "Good. Now take me to bed. I need to go home to get ready for your party tonight. How many are you expecting? Can I bake something?"

"You don't need to trouble yourself. There will only be a couple dozen people here, and the food is covered." I twisted around with her, putting her on the bed, devouring her mouth.

I wasn't going to fuck Madeline. I wanted to make love to her and drive her fantasy guy out of her heart forever. There was no room for him if I was around, and I had no plans to go anywhere, so he fuckin' needed to get gone.

CHAPTER TWENTY-SIX

MADELINE

Raul's birthday party was… entertaining. Unlike anything I'd ever experienced before. The classic rock tunes my dad listened to when I was young blared through the speakers: The Rolling Stones, Lynyrd Skynyrd, Eagles, and of course, Ozzy Osborne. It was cool how so many of these guys appeared to enjoy the music. Most were in their early twenties to early thirties. The prospects were at least twenty-one. Storm had told me Raul and Justin were the veterans in the club.

Some guys played pool while others sat around drinking and shooting the shit. It was fun to see them kicking back and relaxing. Others were hardcore making out with kittens, bumping and grinding. Even under the dim lighting of the bar, I could tell some were getting BJs, not fifteen feet away from me. It was an arousing sight.

My face was hot as my eyes flitted around the room, taking it all in. The bold, unapologetic behavior surrounding me was like nothing I'd ever seen before. Not even college parties were like this. The kittens were nearly naked, parading themselves around in thongs and matching bras.

This was Storm's life.

I tried to not be jealous anytime a kitten gazed at him with longing. I warred with my wild imagination to not picture her lips around his long, thick cock.

It wasn't easy.

Would I be able to overlook the life he led? I prayed to God I could.

"Your cheeks are red, baby." Storm bit my earlobe hard enough, my pussy throbbed with need. His hand crept under my dress, moving higher and higher up my inner thigh.

"Storm…" I exhaled, heart racing with anticipation of what he might do. I distracted myself by turning my head away from him. This damn man knew just how to work me up, every single time.

A long bar was on the northside of the room, pool tables were on the southside. Neon signs glowed in colors of red, blue, green, and gold on every wall. Most were beer logos. The ones I could read from here said *Ride or Die, Fuck Off, The Reaper is Coming, Kitten Pussy Rocks*.

Yeah, that last one turned my stomach.

Tables were clustered with the council's on the east side. It was empty while we were at a corner table with several of Storm's brothers. Apparently, women weren't allowed at the table.

I'd been perched on Storm's lap since we sat down. He wouldn't allow me to sit in a chair. Yep, my man was bossy and unrelenting about some things. I was okay with it, though. From on his lap, I had a perfect view of the entire bar.

Track and Hero were to our right, both drunk. Lynx was across from us with a kitten on his lap, Amber. She was a pretty little thing. Shorter than me by a couple of inches, so maybe five foot two. She looked itty-bitty next to Lynx's massive frame. She had light brown hair and green eyes and looked *young*. Storm assured me all the kittens were at least twenty, so I left it alone.

"I saw you watching Grizz getting blown by Libby. Did it turn you on, Angel?" His fingers grazed over my pantiless pussy. It wasn't my choice to go commando; *the prez* ordered me to.

What the prez wanted he got. Admittedly, it was dirty and erotic to be sitting here with his hand between my legs, and no one seemed to care. Thank God I wore a knee-length sundress.

Well, except Carla. The woman hadn't taken her eyes off us since we got here. I wished she'd just accept Storm's decision and leave us alone.

"It did turn me on. You gonna do something about it, Prez?"

He growled into my ear. "Finger fuck you."

I gasped. "You wouldn't." The words stupidly flew out of my mouth. Storm would likely take it as a challenge, which was the furthest thing from my mind. I was in a different world, a world I never imagined being part of, and strangely, I was okay—more than okay with Storm by my side.

"Watch me." He capped the back of my head and smashed his mouth to mine as two fingers penetrated me. We groaned into each other's mouth and kissed wildly. His thumb rubbed my clit as his tongue lashed with mine. Storm had absolutely no shame. He did as he damn well pleased, even finger fuck me in a room full of people.

I felt eyes on me and blinked mine open. Lynx was grinning as he gave me one of his slow winks.

I might die from embarrassment. I stiffened, trying to retract my head, but Storm wouldn't release me. He rubbed me even more, plundering his tongue in my mouth and growing hard as fuck under me.

These men were Storm's brothers. They probably had an idea of what was happening. I was confident they did. I doubted they'd call him out for playing with my pussy. Shit, they'd probably seen him fuck kittens before. The very thought should make me feel icky. But it didn't. I knew how Storm was with me. From what he told me about the other women he'd been with, he only fucked them from behind. Never in a bed and only against walls or on tables. He rarely kissed or talked to them.

Somehow, I believed him.

A throat cleared. I glanced at Track and Hero. They seemed to have noticed what was going on over here. Of course, Carla was watching too. I couldn't screw around with Storm while eyes were on us. I just couldn't. If he wanted me, then he needed to take me upstairs.

I pushed against his chest and broke our liplock. I was totally aroused and clenching around his fingers. "Not here."

"Fuck, Angel. I need inside you."

"But it's only after ten, isn't it too early to leave?" I hadn't even gotten a chance to meet Wolf's old lady, Jill since they hadn't arrived.

"We leave when we want to. And I want you *now*," he growled into my ear and took my hand, putting it on his firm erection.

I shivered and glanced around. "Okay, then. Let's go." I stroked his chest and pecked his lips.

My dirty man removed his hand from under my dress and stuck his two fingers into his mouth. "Fuckin' delicious," he rasped into my ear.

I couldn't resist smiling when I noticed Carla's jaw hit the floor. She never got Storm's tongue on her. He told me he hadn't given a woman oral pleasure since he was in the marines.

Carla really needed to give it up. No way in hell was I letting go of Storm. He was *mine*.

"Shit Prez, never seen you like this before," Hero hollered and clapped loudly.

Could I crawl under the table?

"No joke." Track whooped, raising his hand in the air. He was nearly wasted. "Guessing you two are heading upstairs."

"Yeah. I'll see you motherfuckers tomorrow." Storm smiled like a kid in the candy store after being told he could have *anything* he wanted.

Track nodded. "Good night, *Angel*." He had a smirk on his face.

"Yeah, sweet dreams, *Angel*," Hero chimed next.

The next thing I knew, every guy in the room was calling me Angel and wishing me good night. Storm led the way out, his arms possessively around me.

Honesty, I loved the attention. There wasn't anything better than being accepted by my man's brothers.

I waved to Tina and Raul at the bar. We were almost scot-free when I heard, *"God, I hate that cunt..."*

My eyebrows shot up, hearing Carla's voice. No question she was talking about me. I blew it off, she didn't deserve a second of my time, but Storm reacted. He left my side so fast I hardly knew what was happening.

"What did you call my woman?" he yelled, gripping her face in his hand and pushing her against the wall. The rage in his eyes was lethal. No one else seemed fazed. "Answer me, goddammit!"

"Storm... don't do this, please." I slowly reached for his forearm. "She's just bitter. Come on, baby. Let's go."

The shock on Carla's face was palpable. She clearly hadn't expected him to go after her. Lynx stepped beside me and was surprisingly calm, a contrast to my violently trembling core. Watching a woman get handled this way was a first for me, although I'd experienced worse with Dane a couple of times. It was just different seeing it done to someone else. I needed to trust Storm wouldn't hurt her. He was only defending me. God, I hoped he wouldn't hurt her.

"Prez, I'll take care of this bitch," Lynx said in a tight voice. Everyone in the bar was watching us. I didn't think they could hear anything with the music still playing. They probably knew whatever was going on had to be significant, given the murderous expression on

Storm's face.

"I thought I told you to straighten her out," Storm yelled in Lynx's face. "I don't want this bitch around if she doesn't know her place. You get me?"

"It's handled."

Storm turned back to Carla. "Don't you ever go near my woman, touch her or talk to her or glare your fuckin' fake purple eyes at her; understand?"

"Yes, Storm," Carla whimpered, bobbing her head.

I took Storm's hand, tugging until his focus was on me. His other hand cradled the side of my face, and he kissed me. No words were spoken as we left.

Once we were in Storm's bedroom with the door locked, he paced the room like a ferocious lion. He stalked across the floor, hands in his hair, back and forth, from one side of the room to the other. I wasn't sure what to do.

My man had quite a temper. The little display downstairs probably wasn't even close to what he was capable of, when enraged. I wanted to calm him down. Get his mind off that stupid woman. She likely called me a cunt to ruin our night together. I wasn't going to let her win.

I went to Storm's bed, sat down, and removed my boots. I carried them over to the dresser and set them down beside it. All the while, Storm glanced at me as he paced, nostrils flared and breathing heavy.

I shimmied my dress up and over my head, then folded it. Goose bumps covered my body, feeling Storm's burning gaze. I placed the dress atop the dresser.

I wasn't wearing a bra, so I was completely naked.

Storm didn't say a word. Like most men, I assumed he didn't want to talk about what happened downstairs. Honestly, I didn't want to either. Carla was a horrible woman who seemed to want to cause trouble.

Without looking at Storm, I went into the bathroom and turned on the shower. When it was just the right temperature, I opened the glass door and stepped inside.

The steam fogged up the glass as I waited for Storm under the showerhead, hoping he would join me. If he didn't, I'd feel like an idiot. I brushed my hair off my face, letting the water soak through it, then squeezed out the excess.

I closed my eyes, sending up a short prayer. God answered me quickly.

The door opened, and Storm stepped in, eyes narrowed and dark, lips pressed in a thin line. I switched places with him, putting him under the waterfall shower head. He shut his eyes and exhaled a long breath.

"What do you need?" I skimmed my hands up his firm chest, over the tops of his sculpted shoulders, and down his inked arms. We stared into each other's eyes as my hands continued gliding over his wet, smooth skin.

"On your knees," he commanded in a deep baritone voice.

I pushed him against the tile wall and lowered myself before him. His dick was semi-hard, thick, and beautiful.

I gripped his shaft with one hand and collected his balls in the other, rolling them between my fingers.

"Jesus…" he hissed as I took him into my mouth. "Fuck, baby…"

I licked the salty precum off his slit, swirling my tongue around the rim. A loud groan eddied from his lips. I pumped his cock while sucking and playing with his balls. I would do whatever Storm needed.

Pleasing him was all I wanted.

Storm's silky cock pulsed against my tongue. It filled my mouth completely when fully erect, stretching me—just as it did my opening when he entered me for the first time.

I wanted Storm to take his frustrations out on me. I wanted him to lose himself in *me* and let go of his stresses. I knew about the vandalized businesses, the fire at Wolf's old lady's boutique, and Storm's concern for me. More alarmingly, women in the area were at risk of being taken against their will and sold into sex trafficking. It all weighed heavily on Storm.

Carla's remark had pushed him over the edge. Storm attacked her on my behalf. Now I would save him from falling. I would pull him away from the ledge and help him regain control so he wouldn't break.

He was mine, and I would protect him.

I sucked harder, taking him farther into my mouth. I gagged a little when he hit the back of my throat, but recovered quickly.

"Shit," he growled, placing his hands on the sides of my head. "Shit, Angel. Your mouth is heavenly."

I released his thick cock and looked up. "Whatever you need, take it from me. I'm here for you. Do with me as you wish."

Storm blinked several times as if processing what I'd said. Then he bent at the waist and kissed me, biting my lower lip.

I whimpered and clenched down low.

There was a noticeable shift in his mood. He slowed down, his eyes boring into mine while his thumb ran over my cheek. His lips softly caressed mine as if saying *thank you* in advance.

When he broke away, he tipped my chin up. I opened wide, letting him guide his rock-hard cock into my mouth. He swiveled his hips, thrusting forward, then pulled back. He repeated the action over and over, rotating his hips, pushing forward, and pulling back... Each time he went deeper, hitting the back of my throat.

Storm squeezed my head between his hands and plunged his pulsing cock to the hilt. He wasn't like this with me often, but I enjoyed being owned. Possessed by my sexy man. Storm showed the world his hard edges, like he didn't have a soul, but he was soft and tender with me. I was thoroughly turned on by his feral side.

I closed my eyes, feeling the sting of tears. They weren't from pain. Something shifted inside me. An all-powerful emotion I hadn't felt before bloomed in my chest.

"Eyes on me, Angel. Eyes on me," he rasped.

I locked my gaze on his dark stormy depths. His nostrils weren't flared anymore, and his jaw relaxed. "You okay?"

I nodded.

"You're so fuckin' beautiful with my cock in your mouth. So beautiful." He drove in forcefully. I clenched my thighs together, trying to ease the ache. "You're perfect." Another hard thrust. "My Angel." His hips bucked forward, and he squeezed my head harder. He wasn't hurting me, though. God, I loved his power and control. "My Angel..." His face screwed up, his pace picking up. His head went back as he plundered my mouth, owning it with every deep thrust he unleashed on me.

I had to hold onto his thighs so I didn't fall. Storm fucked my mouth for all he was worth, grunting and hissing. Controlling me. Dominating me.

"Fuuuck, Angel!" He shattered, choking me with his cock and roaring like a mighty king. His primal sounds bounced off the tile walls as ropes of his cum shot down my throat.

I winced from the pain of his hands, holding me in place with a fierce grip.

I breathed through my nose, soothing the overwhelming pressure of having him so deep in my throat.

Storm heaved as I watched the stress in his body swirl down the drain. We stared into each other's eyes. His were clear, less stormy. The tension marring his handsome face was gone. His hands relaxed around my head and glided to my face, where he tenderly caressed my cheeks. I'd swear he saw straight into my soul and heard the thoughts whirling in my head.

Tears pooled in my eyes when the all-powerful emotion I felt earlier returned. I wanted to be the person Storm needed. I'd walk through the gates of hell with him. Fight alongside him and his club against the enemy trying to destroy my man.

A fierce love swelled in my chest, staring into Storm's unclouded eyes.

Tonight, I'd given myself to him, to use however he needed. To take his anger and frustrations out on me so I could get him to the other side of it. To the side of peace and tranquility, love and affection. I knew this calm would be short-lived, but I would embrace it just the same.

Being here with Storm was where I was meant to be. He needed *me* to help process and manage the worry threatening to tear him down. He needed *me* to be his safe haven.

I loved every bit of what we'd just done.

I loved *him*.

Storm helped me to my feet and washed me. He brushed his lips across my back, making me tremble, my needy clit pulsing as I thirsted for him.

As I went to wash him in return, Storm turned the water off. "Let me take care of you now, Angel." He stepped out of the shower, holding my hand. I followed, letting him dry us both off. His strong arms carried me to his bed. Nobody ever made me feel so adored and cherished.

Some indiscernible rock song played below the floor. Storm set me tenderly on the bed and killed the lights. He crawled over me, settling himself between my legs.

"So damn beautiful. Sweet..." He dropped a light kiss on my lips. "And fierce." Another kiss on my jaw. "So damn strong and understanding." He kissed down the bend of my neck. "You're everything I never knew I needed, Angel."

Emotions bubbled into my chest. That all-powerful emotion I felt earlier. It had a name: love. "Storm—"

He claimed my lips and eased his cock inside me. He moved at a slow, intentional pace. Making love to me. Everything about this was night and day different from what just happened in the shower.

It was like he knew what I needed just as I'd known about him.

He lifted my thigh, penetrating me deeper, rubbing against my clit with each thrust. My orgasm formed, building in strength as this intense man made emotional, passionate love to me.

Every kiss, every touch was like a promise—a promise of forever. Storm poured into me, without hesitation. Our hearts and souls fell into sync, becoming one—just as our bodies were.

"Come for me, Angel," he whispered at the shell of my ear.

I cried his name, pricking his shoulders with my nails, tightening around him as I launched into oblivion. He followed me off the ledge, groaning my name.

Once we calmed, we were wrapped in each other's arms, completely sated. I was sure a cosmic event occurred between us.

Storm must've felt the monumental moment. "Together, we're an impenetrable force."

He was right. Nothing and no one could break us when we were together.

CHAPTER TWENTY-SEVEN

MADELINE

Thump. Thump. Thump.

The pounding on the door jerked Storm's body beneath mine. His arms around me squeezed with anaconda strength. My eyes flashed open. His once calm heartbeat under my head leaped into a heart-stopping gallop.

"Storm!" More banging on the door. "It's The Bullet!" I recognized the voice; it was Track's.

"Shit," he hissed. "Baby, I gotta get up." He released me, and I lifted off his chest so he could get out of bed.

My heart raced, wondering what was going on. I turned toward the digital clock on the nightstand; 1:39 a.m. We'd only been asleep a little more than an hour.

In the nude, he unlocked the door and opened it. "What happened?"

"Hunters, they got two of our servers. Nancy and some new girl, Ava. They're pretty messed up." Track sounded furious, talking a mile a minute.

Storm growled, the muscles in his back coiling. "Fuck! Where was Ire?"

I just met Ire yesterday in passing before the party when he was on his way to work. He was the head bouncer at The Bullet. His road name suited him perfectly as he appeared to hate the world.

Sitting up in bed, I pressed my back against the wall and pulled the sheet up to my neck. Track couldn't see me. The door was only cracked open. Storm's backside was quite the sight from where I sat—thick thighs, muscular, round ass, trim waist leading up to a broad muscly back.

I wanted him again. God, I never tired of this man.

"They knocked him out with a lead pipe. He was unconscious when Art found him. I called Patch." Track's voice faded into a whisper. I strained to hear what he was saying.

"Motherfuckers," Storm hissed and punched the wall. "Fuck."

I jerked in the bed, utterly unnerved.

"Boxer went over. He'll bring the women and Ire here."

Bring them here? Shouldn't they go to a hospital? If Ire was unconscious, he needed to go to the ER. He was almost the size of Wolf, the Russian giant. The Hunter must have struck him hard to knock out someone his size.

I cringed at the thought of a pipe hitting Ire's head. My stomach churned. I needed to stop thinking about the metal hitting his skull.

"Good. I'll get dressed. Meet you in my office in five."

"Okay."

The door closed. Storm turned toward me with a grim expression. I tugged the sheet taut against my breasts as he stalked toward the bed.

"Shouldn't they go to the hospital? Ire was unconscious. Jesus, Storm, that's serious."

He sat next to me and tugged me onto his lap, sheet, and all. He kissed the top of my head and held his lips in place. "No baby. We don't want the sheriff involved. The hospital would file a report. We have a doctor, Patch. He'll fix them up here."

This was insanity. I took Storm's right hand to examine his knuckles where he'd hit the wall, then kissed them. Thankfully, they were intact.

"Is there anything I can do?" I pressed my face in the crook of his neck, breathing him in. I had a feeling I wouldn't see him for a while.

He tipped my chin up and stared into my eyes. "I just need you to stay here in bed while I deal with this situation." He dropped a kiss on my lips.

"But I can help. I *want* to help. I can assist with the women."

"Tina will be there. She's familiar with this kind of shit." Storm's eyes flitted over my face as if memorizing every detail from my eyes to my lips.

My chest tightened something fierce.

"Well, if I'm going to be with you, shouldn't I get familiar too?" I didn't think I'd ever get used to the violent part of the MC life. But the more Storm told me, I would do everything I could to not freak out. I chose to be with him, so I needed to *toughen the fuck up*, as Storm would probably say.

"You will, Angel, but let's ease you into it."

I pouted, but didn't give him shit about it. I didn't want to add to his stress. "Okay. I'll stay put, but if you need me, come get me."

"I will." Storm cuddled me close and kissed me for a minute, then tucked me back into bed. Before he left, he made me promise not to leave the room and to text him if I needed anything.

What else could I do but agree? This was his club. He was the president. His brothers didn't challenge his authority, neither would I.

Five hours later, the sun was awake, and so was I. I had nodded off and on. Tossed and turned, and paced the room. I felt like I was losing my mind, sick with worry for Storm. There wasn't a damn thing I could do about it.

Something didn't sit right with me. When Track had whispered, I knew it was so I wouldn't hear. Had someone been killed? I shook the thought out of my head, not wanting to imagine what could've happened.

How did I get to this place? Of loving an outlaw biker in such a short amount of time? My heart had been permanently closed off to men. Sure, I had short-term boyfriends in high school and dated in college. But I kept myself mostly closed off because I was pining over a boy I'd never have.

Then my one serious relationship with Dane didn't last longer than two years. He had screwed with my head from the beginning, but I was too damn blind and stupid to recognize it. After I moved in with him, the physical abuse began and I stuck it out for a while until I finally got out.

I never believed I would love a man the way I had Kaleb. Nor had I planned to get involved with someone so soon after Dane.

But Storm changed everything.

This incredibly sexy, hot-tempered, determined, and strong— so damn strong man came at me with tornadic speed and hurricane strength. He blew into my life and sent me into a whirlwind love affair. The epic kind love stories were made of. With highs so high, they touched the heavens and lows so low it was hell.

Storm might not ever love me the way I loved him. He might not ever say the four-letter word or ask me to marry him. I could honestly see him denying himself true happiness and undying love the way he talked about his demons. Or believing I deserved better than him. But when we were together, he loved me fiercely despite himself.

I replayed his deep voice in my head, whispering, *Together, we're an impenetrable force.* Yes, we were.

Somehow, Storm had bypassed my ironclad heart and went

straight for my soul. And I fell in love with him. Our sizzling passion and intense emotions were like nothing I'd ever experienced before. Certainly not with Kaleb. He'd only been a teenager back when I gave him my heart, and I was only a kid.

But now I was a grown woman, and Storm was a man. He knew how to love me and pleasure me. Kaleb wouldn't have been able to do half of what Storm could.

Putting it simply, I loved Storm.

I needed him. And only wanted him.

I had to let Kaleb go. Release him into the wind to blow away and out of my life forever.

Storm deserved all of me. There was no room in my heart for Kaleb anymore. He'd owned it long enough.

CHAPTER TWENTY-EIGHT

STORM

I looked each one of my men in the eyes, fury radiating off them, filling the room to a suffocating degree. We'd just reconvened for church after spending the last couple of hours searching for Hunters.

The fuckers had beaten one of the girls because they declined to work for them and raped the other. Both assaults were "a little lesson" to teach other women what would happen if anyone refused a Hunter.

This shit was out of control. I didn't want to imagine what might've happened if Art hadn't arrived. Nancy had said when the sound of the motorcycle was heard, the Hunters ran.

I was losing control in my own goddamned territory.

"I can't fucking take this bullshit anymore," Boxer yelled. "They destroyed Jill's boutique. Now Ire and the women. I want fucking blood." He and Ire were close. They trained at the gym and entered underground MMA events together. For Boxer, it was a sport. For Ire, it was his chance to beat the crap out of someone. He never lost a match.

I nodded. "You'll get your blood, brother." We all fucking wanted revenge, but I needed to keep a level head so my brothers would too.

It wasn't easy for a volatile man like me to stay calm. For the last several hours, I'd been running on adrenaline. When I saw the women's condition, I nearly lost my shit. It could've been Madeline they got. Fuck, the very thought threatened to unravel me. But I'd held it together, swallowing down bile to not show weakness in front of my brothers and the women.

I nodded at Raul to take over.

He returned a nod and exhaled. "This was a warning. We took two of their men and roughed them up. They retaliated and one-upped us."

"Fucking pussies," Boxer roared. "Beating up two women, raping one of them, it's fucking low. They're a bunch of animals. I should've cut off their guys' dicks." He was at the end of his rope. I'd never seen him like this before. Not even when we were in the marines getting shot at in Afghanistan. Seeing Ire before the meeting didn't help.

Patch had said Ire would need to take it easy for a minimum of one week, two would be better, but Ire had told him he'd be fine after a nap. Crazy son of a bitch. I ordered him to not leave his room until further notice.

"I agree, son. That's not how we roll. The Dirty Hunters don't give a fuck about women, only themselves. They're a young club with no home and weak members. They have to hide because they know we will pick off their herd one by one." Raul clasped his hands together on the table, jaw ticking.

"What now, Prez?" Track's calm voice got my attention. He was the peacekeeper during times of duress, somehow keeping the guys levelheaded.

"Right now, I want you all to eat, shower, and rest. Call a kitten if you need some lovin'." I sure needed to hold my Angel. "Then, we meet back here at noon." I banged the gavel on the table. "Go do what you need to do."

Chairs scraped against the floor as they were pushed back, and my brothers filed out. I raised my hand to Raul, Track, and Boxer for them to wait. Once the others were gone, Boxer shut the door.

I cleared my throat as I stood. "I'm going to pay Sheriff Hendricks a little visit. Track, you're with me. We'll go later after church."

"What about the guys?" Raul asked.

"I want you and Boxer to divvy them up to do a sweep of Winters and the surrounding area. The Dirty Fuckers only creep into Bastion at night. We need more manpower, so I'm calling in a marker with the Fallen Soldiers." The Soldiers were a small MC in Iowa. They owed us big from three years ago. "Now they can help us rid our territory of Hunters like we helped rid theirs of gangbangers."

The three of them nodded.

"Let's go eat." I stalked into the kitchen, where breakfast was in full swing. Eyes flitted my way as I loaded up a plate with enough food to feed Madeline and me. I piled it high with French toast and sausage, drizzled syrup, and then filled two travel mugs with coffee. I ignored my brothers. They didn't need to worry I'd explode. Not when I had the calm to my storm waiting upstairs for me.

Tina put her hand on my shoulder. "Try to get some rest. It was a long night." She smiled softly, setting a fork on the plate, and patted my arm. "Let Angel take care of you."

Take care of me? I'd never had a woman to take care of me before. Never wanted to need one, but I needed Madeline more than air in my lungs.

"Thanks, Tina." I made my way out, then barked at my brothers, "Don't be late for church. Noon."

Grunts echoed in acknowledgment.

Madeline was on her stomach, facing the door with her cell phone in hand when I'd entered the room. Her baby blues were filled with concern when they met mine.

"Storm." She was off the bed before I kicked the door shut. "I've been so worried." She took the cups from my hand and set them on the dresser.

"Sorry to leave you alone for so long." I set the plate on the bed and took her into my arms. *My sweet Angel.* I held her close with my lips on the top of her head, breathing her in and letting her essence soothe me.

"No, I understand." Her arms wrapped around my waist, squeezing me tight. "Are the women okay? How's Ire's head? Is there anything I can do?" She peered up, waiting for my reply.

Talking about what happened was the last thing I wanted to do. I only wanted to be with my girl. Absorb her light before I went back into the dark world. It was going to get ugly around here. Madeline kept the savage part of me at bay. I liked not feeling unhinged or ready to erupt in a volcanic blast. And after what happened to Ire and the women, I was hanging by a thread.

I took her hand and collected the plate. "Grab the coffee, baby."

"Okay."

I stretched out on the bed with my back to the pillows along the wall. Madeline set the cups on the nightstand and scooted in next to me.

I forked a bite of French toast and fed it to her. "Let's eat before it gets cold."

She smiled as she chewed. "It's delicious."

I shoveled a monster bite into my mouth. "It is," I mumbled.

We ate in silence, me feeding Madeline and her accepting what I gave her with loving eyes locked on me. She never pushed to talk. It made me appreciate her all the more, because I couldn't tell her club business.

Once the plate was empty and our coffee cups drained, we snuggled in bed. I'd kicked off my boots but refrained from removing my clothes. Madeline was wearing my Ozzy T-shirt again. She was the most alluring woman I'd ever known. Her long hair was braided loosely, and her face was free of makeup. She was gorgeous in her natural state. I was one lucky fuck to call her mine.

"I know you've got a lot going on, so I thought I'd head home."

The muscles in my shoulders tensed. "Absolutely not."

"Storm, there's nothing for me to do here but be in the way. At home, I could clean the house and get some laundry done."

"You're not leaving the clubhouse, Angel. This isn't up for discussion."

She furrowed her brow, gazing up at me. "Storm—"

My lips were on hers, kissing her until we were gasping for air. Breaking away, I clutched the side of her head and pressed it to my chest. She could probably feel my racing heart.

The words shot from my mouth. "I won't be able to focus if you're gone. The Hunters could go by your place again. They could get you." I inhaled a deep breath so I'd stay calm. "I need you here where I can protect you. Understand?" I left no room for argument. No fuckin' way would I let her off of the compound. Not after what happened to the women.

"I understand, but I do have a life, ya know." She rubbed her hand over my chest. Her tenderness comforted me, but I knew she didn't like being told what to do.

I wasn't ready to tell her one of the women was raped. I would, eventually. But Jesus, I felt guilty as hell for not getting those fuckers out of our area. I could barely contain my fury. I couldn't tell Madeline what happened in the state I was in.

"You're on summer break. What else do you have going on?"

She sighed. "Nothing until Wednesday. I'm supposed to meet my friends at Sugar Bliss. We were going to hang out, do a little shopping, maybe catch a movie."

"Okay. I'll go with you."

She tossed her head back, laughing. "You're going to go with me? Mr. Biker Prez is going to have coffee and pastries with a group of women and go shopping?" She giggled some more. I loved hearing the amusement in her voice. The musical sound was a balm to my aching chest. "You're out of your mind."

"Hey, I'm down with hanging out with you and your girlfriends. I'm confident in myself. Shopping doesn't scare me."

She rolled her eyes with a big smile on her face. "God, you're incorrigible."

"Then it's settled."

"Not so fast, Prez. If you think it's not safe for me to be at home, what about Tara? They know she lives there too."

Shit. I hadn't thought about the redhead.

"Can she stay with one of your friends for a while? Just until we get the Hunters out of Winters?"

"I suppose she could, but is this really necessary?"

"Yes. When you see Nancy and Ava later today, you'll understand."

She noticeably stiffened. "That bad, huh?"

"Yeah, baby, it's bad." I pressed my lips to her head, my innards twisting into a knot. It would kill me if anything happened to my beautiful woman. "Let's take a nap. I'm exhausted."

"Okay…" She turned to her side so I could spoon her.

I exhaled, wrapping myself around her warm body and burying my face in her neck. My eyes closed, and I was out.

I hit the gavel once, bringing the meeting to order. I leveled my gaze on every man. This was my executive council and several select patched members at my table—eleven in all. Not one of them looked happy to be in church *again*. Nor should they.

In the five years I'd been president of Knight's Legion, not once had I called church the day after a club party.

"Raul, what you got?" I called out my VP. I left it up to him and Boxer to put a plan together for the men. I trusted they would pair them up properly.

"We're doing this smart. You hear me," Raul barked. "Three patched, one prospect. I want you armed and your fuckin' trackers on your goddamn phones. Grizz checked. One of you motherfuckers had yours off."

"What the fuck you just say?" I stood from my chair, hands on the table. "Who?" I narrowed my gaze to Raul.

"Lynx."

Lynx threw his hands up. "My phone broke, just replaced it. Forgot to turn it on. Sorry."

I glared at him, then turned toward Raul."Continue."

He cleared his throat. "We've only been able to identify six men who we believe are Hunters." Raul looked at Grizzly. The 75-inch flat-screen on the wall turned on, and images appeared of some ugly-ass fuckers.

"Two of these bastards are the ones the prez and Boxer messed up at The Wild Hog. They mostly travel in groups of three. The security cams around The Bullet captured partial images of four of these bastards." Another image appeared. "Their enforcer and a prospect took down Ire. He never saw them coming when they got him from behind. Two more prospects got the girls."

Boxer growled and pounded his fist on the table.

"Play the footage," Raul told Grizzly.

"Motherfucker," Boxer hissed and dropped his gaze. Several others did the same to avoid watching the enforcer assaulting Ava.

I diverted my gaze, biting down on my back molars. My fuckin' blood boiled. From the angle of the camera, we could only see his back with his pants down. It was clear what he was doing to the girl as she struggled. But the enforcer was three times her size. Raping innocent women was probably how he spent his free time. The other assholes were beating up Nancy, punching and kicking her on the ground. I couldn't see their full faces. They weren't wearing cuts like the enforcer. With the video footage and the recon we had from Raul and Boxer, it was enough to confirm the attackers were Hunters. I didn't need any more proof.

"I want to pluck these cunts off one by one. We'll start with the four cunts on the screen." I leveled my gaze on Boxer. "Be ready."

"Already am, Prez." His nostrils only flared when boxing or when he thirsted for blood.

"I want their nest found. Someone's helping them. I want whoever it is found too. Now get your asses out there and bring me some fuckin' Hunters!" I slammed the gavel on the table, calling this meeting adjourned.

Grunts echoed as the men filed out.

"Track, get our prospect so we can meet with Hendricks." I jerked my chin toward the door.

"On it."

I cut my eyes to Raul. "I'll be in touch."

"Got it."

I was pissed at myself for being lax with the Hunters when they first rolled into our territory. Not all nomads were terrible. We'd had a few groups pass through, over the years. My Uncle Matt had always been slow to react.

Madeline had distracted me. I hadn't kept a close enough eye on these assholes. I let my club down and Winters Township. It's my fault Ava was raped. Nothing I did would ease her pain. I needed to drive these sons of bitches out of Knight's territory once and for all.

I stood beside Sheriff Hendricks at the edge of Wennberg Pound. It was our rendezvous spot when we discussed shit we didn't want anyone to hear. It was secluded, and on Knight's Legion property, half a mile behind the compound. I'd just finished telling him about the attacks. His face was red and his nostrils were flared.

"This goddamn shit has got to stop. I thought you were handling them?" He scrubbed his hand over his face.

"They're pushing back. Obviously. It's time we moved onto more convincing tactics." My gut twisted knowing what was to come. I wasn't a pussy by no means. I'd killed my share of violent, soulless men. Didn't mean I enjoyed ending a life.

He cut his gaze to me. "Eve will be home with the boys soon. I don't want her getting tangled up in this shit. Matt promised me she'd be safe."

"I plan to uphold his word. You think I like what's happening? I have Madeline to think about now."

"Madeline?"

I groaned, cracking my neck.

"You have a girlfriend?"

"An old lady."

"Unbelievable. Matt must be grinning his stupid, cocky grin right now. He always said the right woman would tie you down, but I never believed him."

I snorted. "He was too damn arrogant for his own good."

"Amen brother." The sheriff saluted the sky. Hendricks respected my uncle and loved him like a son, despite being the president of an outlaw biker club.

"If the club doesn't handle the Hunters our way, it could get uglier than two women being assaulted." I didn't forget about Ire. He didn't look so good when I'd checked on him before leaving the clubhouse. With Hendricks, I needed to appeal to his fatherly side. Aunt Eve was all he had left in the world.

"Try to keep it in Bastion. I don't have jurisdiction in Winters. Sheriff Bush and Deputy Miller won't turn a blind eye."

I fisted my hands hearing deputy fuckin' Miller's name. "I know. Why do you think it's taken us so long to contain them. They stay in

Winters. Someone is helping them."

"I'll ask around. Do what needs to be done and keep my girl…
and yours safe."

Hell yeah I'll keep my girl safe.

I gave the sheriff a short nod and glanced over my shoulder at
Track. It was on. The Hunters better run out of Minnesota because the
Knight's Legion was coming for them.

CHAPTER TWENTY-NINE

MADELINE

I tried to make myself helpful around the clubhouse while Storm was off doing whatever it was the president of an MC did. We'd napped for a couple of hours, then he made love to me before going to church. *Church.* When I'd looked at him strangely, he'd chuckled and rephrased his statement, "A meeting."

Church was an hour ago, and I had yet to see him. I knew he was in the building, which gave me a little comfort.

Tina, Raul's old lady, was busy preparing several pans of tater tot hotdish for dinner. She'd said it was the men's favorite comfort food.

"So, what are you putting in the hotdish?" I was chopping veggies and fruit while we chatted.

Tina snorted. "Everything but the kitchen sink."

I peered into the pans. "No mixed vegetables?"

"No ma'am. The men in the club only like green beans in it."

"Huh, maybe that's why yours looks tastier than others I've tried. It smells better too."

"I add my own special mix of spices to it." She winked. "Tater tot hotdish is a staple around here. You really can't mess it up."

"I've seen some pretty nasty ones." I wrinkled my nose. I didn't care for casseroles, *hotdish*, or tater tots. "So, how many are we feeding?" I assembled slices of cantaloupe on an aluminum tray.

"Twenty to thirty, maybe more." The speed she moved around the kitchen, you'd think it was her own. Well, I guess in a way it was, since she was an old lady.

"Wow. I'll cut up some more melons."

Tina smiled warmly. She was a pretty woman with sandy blonde hair, olive-green eyes, and about my height. Storm had told me Tina was thirty-eight, but she looked much younger. She had another daughter who was twenty. Storm had said Tina's daughter wasn't with her, but not by choice. He didn't want to tell me why, saying it was Tina's story to tell. The look in his stormy eyes told me it wasn't good. I just hoped Tina would one day feel comfortable and safe with me to share about her daughter.

"So, you and Storm… Is it serious?" She smirked as if her plan worked when I stilled.

"I um, well, um…" I sighed, setting the knife down and turning toward her. "I've only known him for a short time."

"Yes, but are you serious about him? There's no time limit on feelings."

"Can this stay between you and me? I mean, I know your loyalties are to Raul, Storm, and the club, but can this be just between us girls?"

Tina bounced over excitedly and took my hands in hers. "Yes. I need another ol' lady around here to gab and bitch with when my man is driving me nuts. I can't complain to Sugar. It only makes her miss Matt. And I'd rather not get close to the kittens."

"Why not?" I was curious about her thoughts on the kittens.

"Ugh… The kittens are okay, a little catty sometimes. No pun intended." Tina snorted. "They're here for a purpose, one we don't get a say in, if you know what I mean."

"Sex?"

"Yup, that'd be it." Tina made a face like she didn't like it and I was right with her. "I don't like how they slink around like they rule the roost. Not all of them are awful, but you've met Carla."

I inhaled a deep breath. "Yes, I have. Storm assured me there was nothing between them, but she was his favorite, and he didn't share her."

"Hon, as far as I could tell, he only fucked her. He'd take her into the bathroom or over a table or against the wall. He was never alone with her for longer than five minutes."

I gaped. "Did he do it in front of everyone?"

Tina nodded with a frown. "Yes. He didn't care because she didn't mean anything to him. Not like you."

"Oh my gosh. I can't imagine having sex out in the open."

Tina shrugged. "It's what a kitten is here for. They have a job to do. None of them are ever meant to be an ol' lady. I mean, they could, I guess. If one of the guys fell in love. But our guys are too damn possessive and don't like to share."

"Like Storm."

"Mhm. For him, it was about control and showing the others, he was the king. But kittens belong to the club, to the patched members. Most of the women want to be with all the guys, not just one. A few have gotten clingy, like Carla. They don't usually stick around long if they get possessive with the men."

"I hate seeing Carla around."

"I know how you feel. It was the same for me when I first got here. Raul was a mean, dirty fucker." Her voice trailed off. She left me hanging on her every word, hoping she'd tell me more. "I once caught him with his pants down fucking a kitten when we were getting to know each other. He was such a bastard back then. Ruthless. He had his reasons. But let me tell you, that kitten was gone once I became his ol' lady. And I've had him by the balls ever since."

"Wow. He fucked a kitten while he was with you?" I couldn't believe she'd be with him if he was screwing someone else.

Tina frowned. "I was kind of messed up back when we first got together." She shrugged her shoulders. "Raul was too. I guess we were made for each other with all the shit we'd been through. Once he claimed me, he didn't fuck anyone else."

"I wouldn't stand for Storm screwing a kitten or any other girl." I fisted my hands at my sides. No man would ever cheat on me again.

"Well, you'll have more power than Sugar and me to deal with the club whores."

I lifted my gaze to Tina's. "I will?"

"Oh honey, you'll be the prez's ol' lady. You will reign as the queen." Tina winked. "You'll have all the control over the kittens. Just don't get rid of all of them. Some are pretty sweet."

I considered Tina's words and knew Carla would be gone in a flash. I hadn't had a problem with the others. "I thought some of the guys had ol' ladies, like Wolf?" Subject change. I wanted to stop talking about Carla.

"Oh sure, Jill. Wolf's woman is great, but she hardly comes around. Before the fire, she worked her ass off seven days a week at her boutique. Boxer is her brother. I don't know if you knew that."

"I didn't."

"They're pretty close. He sent Jill to visit her bestie in Seattle while the club cleaned up the mess in her shop. Since she got back, I haven't seen much of her." Tina bit her lower lip and narrowed her eyes. "You got me off track with my question. You're slick."

"I'm with five-year-olds all day. Deflection is required to survive."

Tina laughed. "I bet. So. Tell me how you feel about Storm. Because girl, I've never seen the prez like this. And I've been around since before he was sent to us. He's crazy about you."

"What do you mean sent to you?"

"There's my girl." Storm made a beeline for me the moment he stepped into the room. He cradled my face in his big, calloused hands and kissed me in front of Tina like she wasn't just a few feet away. "Missed you, baby. Doing okay?"

I bobbed my head as his nose touched mine. He dropped another kiss on my lips.

"I'm fine. What about you?"

"Better now." He wrapped me in his arms, holding me close. "How ya doing, Tina?"

She wiggled her eyebrows. "Great. Getting to know Madeline better."

He looked down at me, a curl in the corner of his lips. "Good. I don't want her alone."

"I'll take care of her." Tina smiled, getting back to making the hotdish.

Storm turned away from Tina and lowered his voice. "We're heading out for a while. I just wanted to see you before I left."

"How long will you be gone?" I grabbed onto the gray T-shirt under his cut.

"Not sure, baby. Don't leave the clubhouse. I've got prospects guarding the entrance and back doors. Dodge is at the gate."

"I'll be here." My stomach flipped with unease. He was leaving, and I hardly felt comfortable with him here. Without him, I'd feel like an outsider.

Track strutted in, jerking his chin at Storm. "Ready?"

"Yeah." Storm kissed me again. I held his shirt tighter in my grasp, not wanting to let him go. "I'll be back." He gently pulled away, and I released him.

"You better."

He lightly pinched my chin before he kissed me one more time.

"Take care of my girl, Tina."

"I will. You guys stay safe."

I watched Storm leave, suddenly feeling cold. The glances passing between him, Track, and Tina put me on edge. Tina telling them "to stay safe" made me nauseous.

Where were they going? What would they be doing?

"He'll be okay." Tina capped my shoulder, giving it a gentle squeeze. "The guys will protect him."

"So, he'll need protecting?" I twisted my hands together and flicked my eyes in the direction Storm went. Was I ready for this? Being involved with an outlaw? I knew I wanted to be with Storm, so I guessed I needed to be prepared for anything. Still, it didn't mean I had to like it or not be afraid.

Tina smiled sympathetically. "Most days, danger lurks around the club. It'd been quiet for a long time. Then the Dirty Hunters rolled into the area, wanting what wasn't theirs. The club needs to protect its territory, or other clubs might *invade*. The Knights can't look weak. They need to handle the Hunters."

"You sound like it's just another ordinary day around here."

"I guess it is. They're just doing what needs to be done." Tina grabbed a plate off the shelf and filled it with fruit and some cookies. Next, she went to the large commercial grade fridge and took out two bottles of water. "Let's take a little afternoon snack to Ava and Nancy."

"Sure." I forced a smile, taking the bottles from her.

I had yet to see the women. I was nervous. Storm had told me they were pretty roughed up. What that looked like, I wasn't sure. Nor was I ready to see them. But I was with Storm, and I needed to toughen up and be more like Tina.

"This hallway leads down to the dorm rooms in the basement. There are fourteen. Only half are occupied full-time. Some of the patched members own homes, and so do most of the exec council members."

"Oh, really?"

"Yeah. Living at the clubhouse isn't really family-friendly. But the construction going on in the back is a family wing."

"Family wing?"

"Mhm. Storm wanted to have it ready when some of the guys have a family, like Wolf and Jill. There've been whispers about them getting married." She smiled wide. "The new building will be nice for when we're on lockdown, and members and their families stay on the compound. It'll be more comfortable for children. Like my own, which I'd rather them not witness a kitten sucking off Uncle Lynx." She rolled her eyes.

Uncle Lynx, so cute.

"No, I don't imagine they need to see such activities. The new wing sounds terrific. And it was Storm's idea?"

"Yup. He takes good care of his brothers and their families."

It was clear Tina was fond of Storm and cared about him. So far, everyone here was great. Save for Carla. I'd only met two other kittens: Amber and Libby. I was glad most hadn't been with Storm. It disgusted me enough seeing Carla, his preferred kitten, mewling about.

Tina stopped at a door where a guy I hadn't seen before casually leaned against the wall. "Hey, Copper. How are they doing?"

"Haven't heard a peep out of them. Who do we have here?" His eyes raked over me as he scratched his jaw. He looked young like AJ, just beefier and a ginger.

"Down boy, she's Storm's woman."

"Oh shit." He pulled his eyes off me. "Sorry, um…"

"Madeline." I smiled, stifling a laugh. I appreciated how being called Storm's woman made all the men stand at attention and treat me with respect.

He nodded, and Tina laughed, tapping her knuckles on the door. "Yeah?"

"It's Tina and Madeline. Thought you two might like a snack."

There was a clicking sound—a deadbolt, I assumed. The door opened. "Come in."

The room wasn't dark enough to hide the black and blue bruises and swelling on both women's faces. I did everything possible not to gasp, cry, or stare.

Jesus, these poor women.

"Thanks, dear. Is there anything either of you need?" Tina set the plate on the nightstand. She reached back and took the bottles from me, placing them beside the dish.

"No, we're okay. Thanks." The blonde peered around at me.

"She's Madeline," Tina said before the woman could ask. "She's Storm's girl."

"What? Seriously?" She studied me. "Weren't you at The Bullet last month singing karaoke? You look familiar."

"Yes." I recognized her too. She'd flirted with Storm.

"I didn't know you could sing." Tina's eyes twinkled.

"She sings really good. I'm Nancy, by the way. Congratulations on catching Storm. You've done what we've all dreamed of doing."

"Um… thanks?" *Awkward.* "I wasn't trying to catch him."

"Probably why you caught him. You know, a man likes a challenge. And those little dresses and boots are quite a look too. How long have you been together?" Her gaze skirted up and down my body.

I shifted from one foot to the other, fisting a bit of my skirt. I didn't have anything else to wear here, and I didn't want to run around in only Storm's T-shirt.

"Not long. A couple of weeks, maybe. We're just dating." Was it *only* a couple of weeks? It felt longer like we'd always been together.

Tina giggled, tossing her head back. "You're not dating. Do you think you'd be here right now if you were? No, sweetie, you're his. We all see how crazy he is about you."

She had no idea how happy she just made me. I knew how I felt and thought I knew how Storm felt, judging by how he treated me, but

I had no clue how anyone else saw us.

"Where is the prez?" Nancy asked.

"Out," Tina replied plainly. "How are you doing, Ava, dear?"

She was curled onto her side with the covers drawn up to her neck. She hadn't spoken once. "I want to go home." She appeared worse off than Nancy. But it wasn't the two black eyes or busted lip that made me feel different toward her. It was the haunted, empty look in her eyes. The attack must have been more terrifying for her. God, my heart hurt for these women.

"Soon, dear. You let Copper out in the hallway know if you ladies need anything. I'll be back later with dinner unless you'd like to eat in the kitchen?"

Ava shook her head.

"Thanks, but we'll stay here. We aren't ready to show our messed-up faces." Nancy winced as she touched her cheek.

My stomach churned, eyes ping-ponging between the women. What the Hunters did to them was horrific. I could only imagine what they'd do to the Knights if they got their hands on one. Emotion caught in my throat. I was so damn worried about Storm.

"Okay, get some rest." Tina put her hand on my back, guiding me to the door. Making our way back to the kitchen, she turned to me. "You look a little pale. Are you okay?"

"I didn't sleep well after Storm left in the middle of the night. I think I'll go up to his room and rest a little."

"That sounds like a good idea. Dinner won't be for a few more hours."

"Thanks, Tina."

When I was alone in Storm's room, I took my boots off and climbed under his covers, snuggling with his pillow. I inhaled hints of his aftershave and leather, closing my eyes.

Fear got the better of me as tears slipped out the corners of my eyes. I sent up a silent prayer for him and his brothers to be okay.

For Storm to come back to me.
In one piece.

CHAPTER THIRTY

STORM

On the outskirts of town, the club owned a hunting cabin in the woods. Below the small structure was a basement where we conducted interrogations. The scum brought here never saw the light of day again. We couldn't risk the captive telling anyone about "the dungeon." Hell, only the council and a few select patched members knew it existed.

It really was a dungeon made of concrete. Chains were attached to the wall, holding our prisoner. A meat hanger hung from the ceiling, strong enough to hold three-hundred pounds. There was a drain in the floor and a garden hose connected to a wall spigot, for easy cleanup. A red mechanics cart on wheels held Boxer's *toys*.

In the last decade, we'd only used this place three times. With the Dirty Hunters refusing to get out of town and causing problems, I had a feeling we'd spend more time here than I cared to.

Boxer was ready to get to work. Wolf was by his side. One thing I respected more than anything about Boxer was the level of control he maintained. The man held his shit together better than anyone I knew. He might have raged the day Jill's boutique was torched or earlier over Ire getting hurt, but he never went off half-cocked.

When Boxer tortured a prisoner, it was intentional and calculated. This was why he was the club's enforcer. I could trust him. The little maggot who was about to meet Boxer's wrath was one of the boys on the video, beating the shit out of Nancy. He also held Ava down while the enforcer raped her. He deserved everything Boxer would do to him.

"Ready," Boxer grunted.

I nodded to get on with it just as my phone vibrated. I'd texted Madeline half an hour ago and hadn't gotten a response. I needed to know she was okay. Otherwise, I wouldn't be able to focus on the blindfolded scumbag chained to the wall. So, I'd texted Tina after my patience waned.

Tina: She's probably napping. Went up to your room over an hour ago.

Of course, napping. Madeline said earlier she didn't sleep much after I'd left to deal with the attack.

I breathed a sigh of relief.

Storm: K. Thx.

I tucked my phone back into my pocket, joining the others, and crossed my arms over my chest. Boxer held his hunting knife. He'd just cut off the dude's clothes, leaving him shaking in tighty-whities. I didn't know they still made those ugly shits.

For dramatic effect, Boxer cut off the blindfold with his knife. He always tried to scare the shit out of everyone so they'd talk. He didn't really enjoy torturing or ending a life. But the person brought down here was the scum of the earth and deserved what they got.

We didn't harm innocents.

"Okay, asshole. This is how it's going to go down. I ask the question. You give the answer. I think you're lying. I remove a finger."

Boxer took out his favorite red-handled pliers from the cart. The ones with the jagged teeth. A wicked smile ghosted across his lips as he admired his toy.

The prospect's eyes widened. He didn't look very old. It was a shame his young life would be cut short. And I meant literally cut short. Once Boxer was through with him, his club would get a few pieces of him back. Getting mixed up with vile Dirty Hunters came at a high price for this dude—his life.

"I don't know nothin'!" the boy yelled before Boxer even touched him.

"Already lying." Boxer shook his head. "Let's start with an easy question. What's your president's name?"

"Don't know."

"I figured you'd say that."

Without another word, the dude's pinky was snapped off. His screams were like nails on a chalkboard. His body shook as he stared at the little bit of blood trickling onto the cement.

This was only the beginning. He didn't need to endure so much pain. A bullet in the head was the humane thing to do. We'd gladly put him out of his misery if he'd just answer our questions. I hoped he wouldn't make this worse on himself.

"Next question. Where's your nest?"

The guy shook his head as he sobbed. Boxer remained unfazed, but fuck, I hated this kind of shit.

"Answer me, goddammit!" Boxer didn't wait for a reply and snapped off his thumb. His wails raked down my spine, piercing my eardrum. Stupid kid. He wasn't making this easy...

My enforcer set the pliers down in a bucket, then pulled out another knife. A boning knife. The one he cleaned fish with. I knew where this was going.

"All fucking summer you Dirty Fuckers have monopolized my time." He leered at the sobbing kid. "Preventing me from my favorite pastime… fishing. Do you have any idea how much that pisses me off?"

The kid shook his head, drool dripped down his chin.

"No. Of course you don't. Because you don't give a fuck about anyone else, but yourself. Not the women you hurt or my brother's skull you smashed with a lead pipe." Boxer inhaled a deep breath. "You ever been fishing?"

"N… no."

"You're missing out. Sitting on a boat, breathing in the fresh air, just you and nature. And the fish. It calms my nerves. Keeps me sane. But I haven't been out on the lake. I haven't caught one fucking fish." Boxer admired his knife. "Do you like walleye, son?"

"Ne… never… ha.. had it."

Fuck, my stomach roiled knowing where Boxer was going with this.

"You're missing out." Boxer smiled wickedly. "I love to grill mine with some butter, lemon and fresh herbs." He scowled. "Haven't gotten the pleasure all summer because of *you*." He ran the knife along the dude's stomach. "Gutting a fish is cathartic, y'know. It calms the itch in me to hurt someone. Were you ever abused when you were a boy?"

Jesus. Boxer never talked about his childhood. I glanced at Wolf. He appeared thoroughly engrossed.

The dickhead shook his head. "Please…"

"Please what? Don't take my fury out on you? Gut you like a fish? Please what? Show you *mercy*?"

The dude cried like a baby. And slobbering like one too.

"Did Ava beg your enforcer to not rape her?" Boxer hissed as he slowly sliced into the guy's flesh, but not deep enough to cut him totally open. The prick struggled along the wall. A blood-curdling scream filled the room. His chains clanged against the cement as he tried to break free. The fool. "I want your president's name and where you fuckers are hiding." Boxer gritted his teeth, steeling himself. "Or I will make your last hour on this earth hell."

"I don't know!" The prospects snapped his eyes shut before he looked at the open wound on his stomach. Blood flowed like a rushing stream, soiling his white briefs.

"Okay, motherfucker, you asked for it..." Boxer went to his cart and pulled out the lye. He shook the container, getting the dude's attention. "We use this to help dispose of worthless fuckers like you. It's also used for lutefisk in these parts. Ever heard of it?" Boxer was once again calm, but with a menacing expression. "Lots of Norwegians live in Minnesota and they like their lutefisk. Personally, I don't like *jellied fish*."

Our prisoner thrashed as he watched Boxer open the jar. It didn't have to be like this. All he had to do was give us information. But I could see he was loyal to his club... his prez. It was too bad, too.

"I won't talk! Just kill me!"

Boxer shook his head with a disappointed expression. "I thought as much. This is going to hurt..." He sprinkled some lye into the open gash on the dude's stomach.

I might throw up...

Thirty minutes later, the dumbass finally stopped screaming. To the very end of his life, he didn't give us shit for our questions. All he told us was the Hunters had outside help. We didn't know who was helping them, where they were hiding, or the prez's name.

It fuckin' pissed me off. We got nowhere with this dickhead. Lucky for him, Boxer didn't waste time torturing a worthless piece of shit just for the hell of it. Once my enforcer knew he wasn't getting anywhere, he rushed toward the finish line—to the end of life part.

"What a waste of my fucking energy," Boxer muttered, cleaning his tools. Wolf was washing the floor after bagging up the body parts we'd somehow deliver to a Hunter.

I hiked an eyebrow. "But you enjoyed blowing off some steam, didn't you?"

Boxer issued me a wry smile. "Fuck yeah, I did."

I scratched the back of my head, shaking it. Boxer was something else. A mean son of a bitch. Loyal and protective of his club. He might like to inflict pain, but he only killed when absolutely necessary.

I hated the stench of death. Blood and tears. When a person's life ended because of stupid ass choices.

I lived with the consequences of my unforgivable actions. Tortured daily because I was a selfish asshole.

For the last twelve years, I'd wished it was me who'd died. Not the boy. No matter how many times I stared the Reaper in the face, wanting to die, he passed me by. The torture of living with blood on my hands. The memories of what I'd done were the worst kind of pain.

I didn't deserve to have a kind, loving, fuckin' remarkable, beautiful woman in my life. But I wouldn't give my Angel up for anything. I'd work my fingers to the bones to deserve her. To be a better man.

My phone vibrated in my pocket. The guys stopped what they were doing with expectant looks.

"It's Track," I told them, answering the call. "Yeah?"

"We got us another lone Hunter."

"Another prospect?"

"Nope. He's wearing a patch."

I exhaled in relief. "Bring him to the cabin." I eyed Boxer. "Prepare for your next Dirty Fucker."

Boxer and Wolf smiled.

"You should go home and rest," Track muttered into the phone.

"No time to rest, brother. This is where I need to be." Why the fuck would Track think I'd be anywhere else?

Track sighed as if frustrated with me. "What about Angel?"

"She's fine. Tina is looking after her."

"But she needs—"

"Enough," I gritted out. Fuckin' Track. "Better she learns now how things are. The club is my priority. I'm the president. This is my job."

"I get it. Just don't forget about her."

"No chance." I ended the call. The last thing I needed was Track up my ass about Madeline. Everything I was doing was to make the area safe for her. This shit was personal. My woman's safety was at stake. Of course, I couldn't say that to anyone. I would've done all this even if Madeline wasn't in the picture. However, she motivated to a new level.

"How long before they get here?"

I turned around to face Boxer. "Half hour, maybe."

"It'll probably be a long night..."

Sonofabitch. I could read between the lines. Like Track, Boxer was thinking of Madeline. They needed to stop. I couldn't have her distracting the whole club.

"We work until it's done. No matter how long it takes. Understand?" I cut my eyes to Wolf. "I need a smoke."

"In the top drawer of my cart." Boxer jerked his chin to his red toy box. "Got some joints in there too."

"Perfect."

A little weed would go a long way in taking my mind off Angel. After all was said and done, I hoped she didn't dump my ass. MC life wasn't for the faint of heart. It might be too much for Madeline. Hell, at times it was too much for me. I wouldn't stop her from leaving if she couldn't handle it. It would destroy me, but I'd let Angel go.

It was almost eleven when the guys and I returned to the clubhouse. I needed a drink before I took my woman to bed. She was seated at the bar with her usual rum and coke and Tina beside her.

I strolled up behind her, snaking my hands around her waist, and dropping my lips on her neck.

"Ah!" She twisted halfway around. "Oh, God. Storm."

I raised an irritated brow. "Why did you startle? Has someone messed with you?"

She hooked an arm around my neck, pulling me toward her. "No one has bothered me. Kiss me." She puckered her luscious lips.

"Missed you, Angel." Our lips connected and I moaned, delighting in her tongue. Kissing her was everything.

I reluctantly pulled back, feeling a stirring in my pants. "Let me get a drink and we'll go upstairs."

"Perfect." She curled into my side.

"What can I get you, Prez," Copper asked.

"Whiskey and IPA." I turned to my girl, burying my hand in her long, silky hair. She fluttered her baby blues. "How are you?"

"Okay. Just here with Tina."

I nodded to Tina. "Raul should be here any second. He was behind me coming in."

"He texted he'd be late." Tina sipped her drink.

Copper set my drinks in front of me. I tossed back the shot and relished the burn.

I gazed into Madeline's expectant eyes. "Let's go."

She smiled, grabbing her drink. "I'll see you tomorrow Tina."

"Bye, hon. See ya, Storm."

"Later, Tina." I glanced around the bar at my brothers as we left. They were doing their thing, drinking and shit. Not me though. After the night I had, I needed quiet and my woman.

I locked the bedroom door, exhaling.

"Want me to start the shower for you." Madeline smiled, stroking my chest.

"In a minute." I took her hand, leading her to the bed. Taking her drink, I set it on the dresser with mine. Earlier today she asked about going to her house to pack a bag. I put her off, telling her I'd take her tomorrow. Of course she didn't understand the severity of the situation with Nancy and Ava. It was time I told her.

"Is something wrong?" Concern marred her beautiful face as she sat.

I kissed her hand and dropped to my knees, between hers. "I want to tell you about what happened to Nancy and Ava."

"They were beaten at The Bullet."

"Yes, they were. But that's not all."

She shifted on the bed, eyes locked on mine. "Wh… what else happened?" Her eyes teared up, as if she knew.

I kissed her hand again, rubbing my thumb over it. "There's no way to soften this, baby. You need to understand how dangerous shit has gotten around here. So you don't go off on your own."

"Just tell me." She swallowed, holding my gaze.

"The Hunter's SAA, he's responsible for the safety and security of his club. He's the same guy at Sugar Bliss on the Fourth of July, remember him?"

She nodded, biting her bottom lip.

"He raped Ava."

The color drained from Angel's face. She gripped her stomach, taking deep breaths. Try as she might to hold back her tears, she lost the battle. My girl had a tender heart. She didn't need to be strong for me. I adored her vulnerability.

She shook her head, tears rolling down her cheeks. "No, Storm."

I wrapped my arms around her. "I know baby. I know."

"Jesus, that poor woman." Her body shook against mine. It cut me deep, seeing her breaking this way.

Madeline shouldn't be involved in this shit. No woman should but my Angel? Fuck, I hated knowing she had a target on her back because of me. It could have been her they assaulted.

I held her for a spell, rubbing her back and assuring her she was safe.

"Want your drink?" I asked when she calmed. I sure needed mine. Fuck that was hard.

"Mhm." She sniffled, wiping her fingers under her eyes.

I plucked a few tissues out of the box on the nightstand and handed them to her.

"Thank you." She blew her nose and dried her eyes. "I want you to get those fuckers out of our town. Whatever it takes."

My eyebrows shot up at the lethal tone in her voice. "Yes, Angel. We'll get those fuckers." I gave her the cup.

She gulped it, then stood. "How about that shower?"

"Anything you want." I was in awe of this phenomenal woman.

No question Madeline could handle anything my world threw her way.

CHAPTER THIRTY-ONE

MADELINE

"What can I get you, beautiful?"

I lifted my eyes to Copper behind the bar. He was the official clubhouse bartender when he wasn't tending at The Bullet in the evenings. During the day, he guarded Ava and Nancy's room until AJ switched with him. We'd been getting to know each other a little each day. He was one of the few people around to talk to.

"Rum and coke, please." I forced a smile, not wanting to act like a pouty baby, though I felt like one.

"Comin' right up." Copper had a great smile—full lips, straight teeth. Most of the men around here didn't smile much. Brooding or pissed off seemed to be the everyday look of a Knight's biker. Each time I saw Copper, he appeared happy.

He looked like a hockey player with his ginger hair hanging over his forehead and flowing to the side. I'd attended a few games in college and Copper was built like a goalie.

"What're you up to tonight?" He set my drink in front of me.

I shrugged, looking around the room. Aside from the music playing and a table of kittens gabbing, the place was quiet... For the second night in a row.

"Not much at all." I took a large gulp of my drink. "Why aren't you off with the others?"

"Someone needs to stick around to guard the women and serve them drinks." He waggled his eyebrows, his eyes sparkling like emeralds.

"Lucky you."

"I'd say so." He crouched down, resting his forearms on the bar, staring at me. "What's wrong, beautiful?"

That was twice he called me beautiful in less than a couple of minutes. Storm would be furious if he heard him.

I studied his arms. They were muscly and tattoo-free. Copper was clean-cut and charming for a man wanting to get patched into an outlaw biker club. It made me curious about his story.

"Should you be flirting with the prez's woman?" a deep male voice asked.

I turned my head to the left. Raul and Tina were standing at the end of the bar. Raul's dark eyes were narrowed at Copper.

"Just talking to her." Copper backed away from the bar with a nervous glint in his green eyes.

Raul took a stool next to Tina. "Two drafts."

"When did you get back?" I perked up. If the VP was here, my man should be too. "Is Storm back?"

"No. He's finishing up some stuff. Should be back in a couple of hours."

"A couple of hours?" I glanced at the clock hanging on the mirror behind the bar. "It's after nine. I wanted to go home to grab a few things. Storm said he'd take me. I have nothing here."

Not to mention tonight would be the third night I haven't taken my birth control. Storm would just have to use a condom, which he'd hate, but it was his own fault for putting me on lockdown with the rest of his club. Could have packed a bag if I'd been planning to stay this long.

"I can take her home." Copper placed two beers in front of Raul and Tina.

"No," Raul muttered.

"Please. If Storm is keeping me here, I need some of my things. I'm going out of my mind. I don't have my laptop or even a book to read. My makeup is at home and other *personal* items." I looked at Tina for reinforcement.

"What could it hurt?" Tina cooed to Raul.

"We won't go anywhere else, just to my house and back. It shouldn't take more than an hour, tops."

"Storm wants you to stay here." Raul shot me a stern look.

"Well, then he should've taken me to get an overnight bag. This is ridiculous." I grabbed my phone off the bar and dialed Storm. "I'm calling him now."

Raul groaned, drinking down his beer.

It rang and rang. I hadn't bothered Storm once, knowing he was busy and stressed. But honestly, the one time I called, he should answer.

"This is utter bullshit." I set my phone down in front of me.

"I'm sure Tina has some clothes you can borrow."

I narrowed my eyes at Raul. "I want my own shit." I took a gulp of my drink. "Well, I'll tell you this, Storm will have to wrap up his dick, or he isn't getting between my legs."

Raul choked on his beer. *Good.* "Fuck. What's that supposed to mean?"

"If you must know, it means I don't have my birth control here. I don't think Storm wants a kid right now." I glanced at Copper, who was smiling.

"Fine," Raul growled. "Take her, and be quick about it." He pointed his finger at the ginger across from me.

"Thank you. I'll just run up and grab my purse."

"So bartending is a step up from cleaning toilets and washing the execs' bikes? How long were you doing the menial shit?" I yelled from behind Copper. We were on our way back to the compound. Riding on another man's bike felt oddly like a betrayal, which was dumb. Maybe because my arms were wrapped around his waist the way I held onto Storm, only looser. But I had to hold onto him, so I wouldn't fall off the bike.

"Too damn long. I'm hoping to get patched in soon," Copper yelled back.

"Did you always want to be in an MC?"

He laughed as we turned onto the dirt road leading to the entrance gate. "No, babe. A biker wasn't what I wanted to be when I was a little kid."

I considered him for a moment. He didn't seem to be hiding behind a brick wall like many of the others. I appreciated his candor. He made me feel comfortable going to get my things and hadn't stopped talking since.

Copper continued through to his parking spot after Dodge let us pass. Once he turned the engine off, he twisted partly around to help me with my helmet.

"So why?" I adjusted my backpack straps. I had limited space for carrying stuff, so I'd dug out my old college backpack. Finding it had delayed us. The one-hour I'd told Raul had turned into an hour and a half.

"I grew up in foster homes. Never really had a family." He shrugged with a lopsided grin, making my heart hurt for him. "When I get patched, the Knights will be my family. I'll have a crap ton of brothers."

"You'll get patched." I smiled at the hopefulness in his green eyes and put my hand on his arm, giving it a gentle squeeze. "So, what's your real name? I don't imagine it's Copper."

His cheeks turned pink. "Nah, Copper is my very unoriginal road name." He ruffled his hair. "My name's Cole Davis."

"Well, Cole, thank you for taking me to my place. It was fun getting away from the compound for a little while."

"No problem, babe."

"Angel?"

I whipped my head toward Storm's gruff voice. His stormy eyes were locked on me as he stalked toward us. Cole stiffened.

I flung my leg back to dismount off the bike. "Hi, when did you get back?"

Storm didn't answer. He tugged me into his arms and captured my lips in an intense kiss.

God, I'd missed him. It would be easy to get lost in him but we weren't alone. I patted his chest and pushed gently, feeling awkward for kissing like a horny teenager in front of Cole.

"Storm," I whispered against his mouth, trying to pull back. I hadn't even gotten the rest of my stuff out of Cole's saddlebag.

"Missed the fuck out of you, Angel." He glared at Copper. "Prospect."

"Hey, Prez." He removed my small tote from his saddlebag and handed it to Storm.

"Thanks for the ride, Cole. I appreciate it."

"Anytime."

Storm growled. "Let's go, Angel." He slipped my backpack off my shoulder and carried it in one hand, his other pressed to my lower back.

We entered the clubhouse and went straight for the stairs leading up to his room. Anger rolled off him like the lava rising over the edge of a volcano on the verge of exploding. With every stomp of his boots, my gut clenched tighter. I sensed his vexation had everything to do with me… and probably Cole.

CHAPTER THIRTY-TWO

STORM

"Storm? Wha… what's wrong?" She sounded nervous. She should be. Hell, even scared.

I bolted the lock and tossed her bags onto the club chair. It took everything in me to not lose my shit on her—*everything*. I rolled my fingers, making a tight fist. This shit, her being gone when I'd returned, seeing her on the back of Copper's bike, her calling him Cole, it all threw me over the edge after the foul mood I'd already been in.

Was it too fuckin' much to ask for her to stay put? After getting absolutely nowhere with another Hunter and disposing of him, I'd wanted to come home to my woman. *My* goddamn woman. Fuck. This day was going to get a lot worse. Fuck!

"I told you to stay here. You gave me your word." I ground my teeth and tried to hold it together because I knew if I blew up at Madeline, she'd fight back and might walk out my door. I couldn't lose her. Not like this. I cared too damn much for her.

I needed her.

"And you said you'd take me to my house so I could grab a few things."

"You know I'm dealing with all kinds of shit after the attack. Important shit."

"And you know I *only* have the clothes on my back. I've been wearing this damn dress for three days now. And the same pair of panties." But I also knew she washed them every night before we went to bed. They were dry by morning.

"You were supposed to stay put. Instead, I get here, and you're gone. And on Copper's goddamn bike too! What the fuck, Madeline? On another dude's bike?" I seethed at this betrayal. She might as well have fucked him, too. "You're *my* goddamn woman!" My voice was getting louder, but she didn't appear fazed.

"Well, I couldn't take my car because the key was missing. Know anything about that?" She crossed her arms over her chest and tapped her boot. Shit, she was getting pissed.

"Yeah, I took it off your key chain just in case you decided to leave. Looks like I was right."

"Don't be a jerk. I needed clothes. Deodorant. My birth control pills! I've missed a couple days this cycle. You'll need to suit up for the next seven days because of it."

Holy hell. I shoulda thought about that. Me? Wear a condom? She had my attention.

"Not happening. I've had you bare. I refuse to wrap it up."

"Then you won't be getting between my legs. The pill needs to be taken daily at the same time each day. Otherwise, I could get pregnant."

"Would it be so bad?" I couldn't believe I just said that, but would it? Us having a baby together sounded spectacular to me. I was shocked she could diffuse my rage with a simple concept.

She laughed as if I were out of my mind. "You can't be serious?"

"Serious as a heart attack." I stalked across the room, reeling her into my arms. "I know how I feel about you. If we made a baby together, I wouldn't be upset. I'd be thrilled." All the anger barreling through me evaporated. Shit like this never happened before, but with Madeline, it happened all the time.

"But… We… Storm…"

I cradled the sides of her face in my hands and kissed her softly. Damn, this woman made me weak. The thought of her pregnant with my child? It made me light up inside. A baby? Our baby? I'd only known her a little over a month, and I couldn't imagine my life without her.

She moaned against my mouth as I traced my tongue along her bottom lip.

I gathered the hem of her dress into my hands. "Arms up."

She lifted them on command, and I had it off her lush body, tossing it aside. I knelt in front of her, placing feather-light kisses across her chest and down to her stomach.

Her moans made me hard as fuck.

A baby.

I peppered more kisses over her belly, imagining my baby tucked inside. *My* baby in *my* woman. *Mine.* My chest swelled as I loved on her stomach.

Her fingers played with the hair on my head, brushing through it tenderly and melting away every bit of tension in my body.

A breathy sigh filled my ears. "Storm…" My name on her lips undid me, but it wasn't my name. Not my real name. I wanted to hear her call me by my birth name just as she had that little fucker Copper. *Cole.*

Since becoming a member of Knight's Legion MC, only my road name had been used. I sure as hell wouldn't tell a kitten or any other woman what my real name was. It was too personal, intimate. But I wanted it on my Angel's lips and only hers.

"Kaleb." I dotted more kisses across her skin, filling my hands with the silky flesh of her hips.

"What?" Her voice cracked, hands stopping in my hair, body turning rigid.

All the color seemed to drain from her face as if she saw a ghost.

"My name, Angel. It's Kaleb. I'm giving it to you, only you. When I heard you call Copper, Cole, it made me insane." Insanely jealous, but I wouldn't admit it to her. "Stick to his road name, and from now on, call me Kaleb when we're alone."

"I... I..."

I smirked. "What's the matter? Don't like my name?"

She blinked her glossy blue eyes. "Kaleb... I love the name." She swallowed thickly as her fingers started to move again in my hair. "Kaleb," she whispered my name. "Kaleb..."

The way she said my name felt like a healing balm to my soul. All the darkness inside me disappeared. A sense of promise and hope for a future filled with love and family with Madeline replaced it.

"Sit." She did, looking a little shocked, or maybe she was thoroughly turned on. I hoped for the latter. I removed her boots and socks, tossing them over with the dress.

She arched her eyebrow. "If we're having sex, you'll need a condom." Welp, maybe she wasn't so out of her mind for me like I thought.

"You're so damn beautiful." I pushed her onto the bed, ignoring her, and covered her body with mine.

"I mean it, Storm... *Kaleb.*" Chills shot down my spine, hearing her say my name. "I'm not ready for a baby. How can you be? Given what's going on with the Hunters." She had a point. Those dirty bastards hadn't entered my mind once since being here with Madeline.

"I'd never let anything happen to you or our child." I nibbled along her jawline—*our child.* "My club will protect both of you. They'd die for you, for both of you. Just as I would."

"Oh, God, don't say that."

"It's the truth. I'd die for both of you." To some, this might sound like crazy talk. I'd only known Madeline a short time, but I'd had her in my bed the last several days, woken up to her, made love to her, and paraded her around my club as my old lady. My queen. These weren't decisions I made lightly. In the depths of my soul, I knew Madeline was the one, and I didn't want to waste a second with her.

Tomorrow wasn't promised. I knew it better than anyone.

"But… But I'm a traditional kind of girl. The kind of girl who dates a guy then gets engaged, then has a wedding. The baby comes after everything else." She tugged my shirt up. I pulled it off, tossing it with her dress.

"I claimed you as my woman. Everyone here knows it. It's the same as marriage. Just gotta get my mark on you and your leather jacket, showing you belong to me."

"What do you mean, your mark on me?"

"Tattoo."

"Um, no." She shook her head, body going rigid again. "If you hadn't noticed, I'm ink-free."

"Oh, I noticed." I knew her body better than my own. I'd memorized every inch of it from her tiny little pinky toe up to the small scar at the hairline on the right side of her forehead. She'd told me the other night a branch had given it to her when she was twelve. Her body was a masterpiece, pure and pristine. But… "It doesn't have to be a big tattoo. It can be hidden." I kissed down the valley between her breasts, skimming my hands up and down her sides.

She exhaled an aroused breath. "Then what's the point if no one will see it?"

I lifted my head and stared into her glimmering eyes. "I'll know it's there." But I'd prefer it to be visible to the world.

"You're serious?"

"Yes." I resumed kissing her at the same time I slipped her panties down. Her back bowed as I continued my journey south.

She moaned. "Oh, wow… Kaleb, I missed you… so much…"

I cracked a smile as I stood at her feet and removed my boots and jeans.

"Missed you too, baby. Get into the middle of the bed for me."

"Condom."

"No."

She crossed her legs. "We're not doing this without a condom."

"Spread your legs for me, Angel."

"No."

I growled as I climbed on the bed.

"No," she repeated.

I hated hearing that goddamn two-letter word. "Spread your legs so I can eat your goddamn pussy… *please*."

Hesitantly, she did as commanded. "But if you think—"

"I fuckin' heard you the other times. I'm not deaf!" I dove in, sticking my tongue into her entrance. I wasn't gentle or slow. I devoured her pussy like a rabid animal. Swiping broad strokes across her heat and in between her folds, circling her clit with my tongue. I was starving for her.

And it pissed me off to no end how she was forcing me to wear a fuckin' condom.

"I'm sorry," she whispered, lightly touching my head.

"I'll never get enough of you," I murmured into her pussy, pissed she was making me slap on the latex so I could be inside her.

I sucked and bit on her clit. Each time her thighs squeezed my head. I wanted to hear her beg for my cock. Beg me to fuck her. She would, too. I could get her so desperate for more, and then what?

"Yes… Kaleb, yes!" She held my head in place, taking from me what she wanted as her orgasm hit. I loved making her come this way. Never tired of it.

"You're like the sweetest dessert." I lightly licked her, waiting for her to pull me up. Teasing and manipulation weren't beneath me. But with Madeline? My Angel?

Shit, I couldn't do that to her. I'd fuckin' wrap up my dick. Hopefully, she would hate it just as much as me and never make me wear another condom again.

"I need you. Please, I need you so much," she whimpered.

"Gimme a minute, Angel." I climbed off the bed and went into the bathroom to get a condom. While in there, I rolled it on, hissing at the feel of it. It made me think of the women I'd fucked. The meaningless sex I'd had. The life I'd lived before I'd met the woman I'd come to adore and cherish. I was falling hard and fast in love with Madeline.

We were more. So much more.

We were forever.

"What are you doing?"

"Suiting the fuck up," I grumbled, returning to the bed.

She pouted. "I'm sorry, baby."

I grunted.

"Take me from behind." She flipped onto her stomach and lifted her pert ass in the air. It was one of my favorite positions, but I'd prefer to feel my woman bare more.

Damn, I felt like a whiny-ass child, wanting to throw a tantrum until she gave into me and let me have my way.

"Come on, handsome." She wagged her bottom.

"This isn't going to be gentle. I'm sexually frustrated and irritated."

"I know, baby, I know. I want it. I can take it." She looked back over her shoulder, a guilty smile on her pretty face.

I got behind her, ran my fingers across her wet pussy. She was always sopping wet for me.

Gripping her hips, I thrust forward, and Madeline yelped. I tunneled in and out of her tight little pussy at a steady, frantic pace. Our skin slapped together as I tried to get myself there, but it wasn't the same. I couldn't feel her warmth, her wetness. It all felt fuckin' artificial, numbing my emotions like before her.

I hissed, driving harder into Madeline, giving her and my balls a beating.

"Oh, mercy! I... Oh... Storm!"

"Kaleb," I growled and slapped her ass. She yelped again. "Call me, Kaleb, dammit!" I smacked her ivory flesh, harder this time.

She cried out, pushing back into me. "Yes, Kaleb! You feel so amazing, just like I knew you would."

Her words made me pause, but I was getting close and ignored them.

She moaned, fisting the comforter. God, I loved seeing her like this. It did me in every time. I keyed into the sounds she was making, forgetting what I was feeling or more like *not* feeling because of the fuckin' latex barrier between us.

Madeline mewed, arching her back. "Harder..."

"Holy hell, Angel. I'll fuck you into oblivion if that's what you want."

"Yes... Fuck me harder. Fuck me, Kaleb! Own me, Kaleb!"

I grabbed onto her long ponytail, wrapping it around my hand. Tugging her head back, I crushed my mouth to hers, kissing her fiercely while I jackhammered my hips mercilessly, going balls deep each time until we both went off.

Her sweet pussy clamped around my dick like a vice, sucking the life out of it. When Madeline screamed, it set me off. I came so damn hard, groaning from deep inside.

After she collapsed on the bed, I went down on top of her, both of us gasping for air. I rolled off Madeline, pulling her to me, and held her possessively. *Mine.*

"That was out of this world." She snuggled closer, lips on the bend of my neck. "So good, Kaleb."

"It was all right..." One thought entered my mind at this moment.

I'd do whatever it took to never wear another condom ever again.

"Just give me a little more time about a baby."

"How much time?" I brushed languid strokes up and down her back.

"Until after the Hunters aren't a threat."

I had no idea how long it would take to rid the area of them, but I saw her point. "Fine. But once they're gone, we're revisiting the topic of a baby."

Her head popped up. She had the brightest smile I'd ever seen on her.

"Deal. In the meantime, you show me how a baby and I would fit into your MC life. I know how I feel about you, *Kaleb*. I've never felt this way for anyone, and having a baby with you doesn't scare me. In fact, it makes me feel all warm and fuzzy inside."

I pressed my lips to her forehead, right over the tiny scar, and inhaled her sweet essence. Madeline was becoming everything to me. *Everything*. I never dreamed a broody, selfish bastard like me would ever have a woman who was my world. Fuck, this was a strange and terrifying territory to be in. But I wanted it all with my Angel.

"I'll show you how amazing our life will be and how a baby will fit into it." My heart grew ten times larger at hearing my own words.

She squealed so damn cute. It made me feel warm and fuzzy inside.

"So, what about the tattoo?" I lifted her chin so I could see her dazzling blue eyes. My chest tightened, staring into her glittering depths.

"It's a huge commitment."

"It is. And one I want to make to you. Let's go tomorrow." The words flew from my mouth faster than I could stop them. I knew Angel would say no. I just hoped I didn't freak her out.

"Tomorrow?" Her eyes went wide. "Too soon."

"In a week?" I countered. Damn, pushy much?

"A month. A month from today, I'll get it if we're still crazy about each other." She stroked my cheek.

"I'm more than crazy about you, Angel." *I'm in love with you.* But I couldn't bring myself to give her the words yet. Maybe waiting a month was a good idea. "I'll give you a month."

"Thank you, Kaleb…" She pecked a soft kiss on my lips. Damn, I liked hearing her say my name. "So, will Sugar be here tomorrow?"

I was okay with the subject change. I didn't want to pressure her… too much. I rolled out of bed to free my dick from the latex. "Yes. You'll finally get to meet her and the boys. She's going to love you."

Madeline furrowed her brow as I entered the bathroom. "I hope so. I can tell her opinion matters most to you."

"It does. But I'm not worried and you shouldn't be either," I hollered, disposing of the vile, suffocating wrap. I took a piss, then washed my hands. Madeline had stopped talking, but she picked up where we left off as soon as I exited the bathroom.

"How do you think she'll take the news of the attack and all the crap with the Hunters?"

I slipped back into bed and tugged her into my arms. "Not well. She'll be furious with me for not telling her, but she'll get over it."

"Mr. Overconfident, you don't fool me. I can feel your body tensing under me. Two women were attacked, one raped." She shuttered against me, but I knew it wasn't fear that made her body shake. It was anger. "No woman would take it lightly. I just don't want her going off on you. I might have to say something."

I smirked. My girl was a spitfire for sure.

Together we were a fierce, impenetrable force. She fit me and seemed to know what I needed. I never believed in soulmates before, but I did now. Madeline was meant to be my queen.

"Sugar won't give me shit. Well, not in front of you or anyone else. She's reasonable."

She lifted her head, smiling. "Do you think I can bake cookies tomorrow? Sort of like an offering, a gift to her and the boys. It might help keep the tension down."

I arched my brow. "You want to bribe them with cookies?" *Yep, right there, my soulmate.*

She poked me in the side. "Not bribe. Just…" She thought for a moment. "Shit, I am trying to bribe them. Look what being around you is doing to me."

I let out a hearty chuckle, squeezing the shit out of my girl. "Baby, you bake all the cookies you want. Make a shopping list. I'll send a prospect out to get what you need."

"What's your favorite cookie?"

"I don't like sugary treats. So forget about bribing me with them."

A wicked glint sparked in her eyes. "The only thing I need to bribe you with is between my legs."

A growl rumbled in my throat. "Angel, don't ever use your pussy as a bargaining chip or weapon against me. It won't end well for your ass." I slapped her bottom. She didn't yelp or jump.

"You sound awfully possessive, Kaleb."

I put her on her back, covering her body with mine. "You're mine. All of you."

She kissed her finger, then pressed it to my lips. "And you're mine."

"Better believe it." I was about to drive my cock into her when she managed to close her goddamn legs.

She arched her brow like I was one of her students. "Condom."

"Fuckin' hell." I rolled off her and stomped back to the bathroom, bringing the box to our nightstand. "I'm not okay with this, Angel."

"I know, baby… Just six more days…"

CHAPTER THIRTY-THREE

MADELINE

Each time I heard footsteps, I held my breath, anticipating Sugar's arrival. Storm had been texting with Maddox all day. I was totally freaking out. Storm's aunt was the most prominent person in his life. I needed to make a good impression because if she didn't like me, I feared she might convince Storm to dump me. It was probably foolish thinking, but I couldn't help but worry.

Or stop eating loaded oatmeal cookies and chocolate chip cookies.

All afternoon people were in and out of the kitchen while I was baking. It was a nice distraction. I ate up their compliments as they devoured my baked treats. Rough and tough bikers might deny having a sweet tooth, but several of the Knights moaned after their first bite of my oatmeal cookies. Ire was one of them. He'd promptly grabbed a few, following his vocal display, and disappeared. He didn't look fully recovered, but it was good to see him out of his room—if only for a few minutes.

Storm had been hovering over me all day. It'd been quiet regarding the Hunters, so he stuck to me like glue. I loved having him around. He didn't help me bake but he sampled a few cookies… and my lips...often.

"Their ETA is thirty."

"Oh God." I inhaled, reaching for another cookie.

Storm wrapped his hand around my wrist and tugged me onto his lap. "Angel, she's going to love you. Stop stressing. No more cookies."

"Don't tell me what I can and cannot eat." I bit off half the cookie and chewed in his face.

"Tomorrow you'll gripe about eating too many and probably bitch me out for not stopping you. So no more."

Dammit, he was right—as always. I put the other half of my cookie to his lips. "Eat it."

He opened his mouth and took my finger with the cookie. I stirred down low, feeling his slick tongue.

"Let me take you upstairs and distract you." He wiggled his brows.

"Is Sugar here yet?"

I turned toward Tina's voice. "No." I deflated against Strom's chest. I was about to let him take my mind off Sugar.

Tina leaned against the island. "What's wrong, honey?"

"She's freaking out about meeting Sugar." He rubbed his thumb on my inner thigh in a teasing fashion. The stinker.

"Oh." Tina sat on the stool beside me and rubbed my back. "She's going to love you."

"I told her as much, but she refuses to listen to me." Storm pinched my ass.

I jerked in his lap, narrowing my eyes. "You'll pay later for screwing with me, big guy."

His gray orbs glittered with amusement. I faced Tina. "If she's nice to my face and tells you she hates me when I'm not around, you gotta tell me." I covered Storm's mouth as he growled in frustration. "I mean it Tina. We confide in each other, tell each other everything, don't let me down."

Storm forced my hand down.

Tina tilted her head, a sweet smile on her pretty face. "Honey, I won't hide anything from you. But I really believe she's going to love you."

"What do you mean you confide in each other?" His gravelly voice rumbled down my spine.

Oh shit. Me and my big mouth. I slowly peered up at Storm. "Girl stuff. That's all."

Storm dropped a firm kiss on my lips. "Yeah, right."

A wolf whistle pierced through the air before Storm could make me tell him what Tina and I had been confiding in each other. The loud sound made me jerk on his lap. "What was—"

"There he is! My boy." A gorgeous, petite blonde appeared in the doorway of the kitchen. She smiled brightly, eyes locked on Storm.

Two tall, dark-haired guys appeared with huge grins. They resembled Storm, a little. In the eye. They were handsome and clean-shaven.

A weird pang settled in my stomach. These boys reminded me of someone else I couldn't quite place. The connection made my stomach hurt worse.

Kaleb... I still couldn't believe it was Storm's birth name. What were the chances I'd fall in love with two guys named Kaleb?

"Hey, Sugar. You're early." Storm rubbed my back in a soothing motion, pulling me out of my thoughts.

One of the guys laughed. "She told me to lie about how close we were."

"I wanted to surprise you, is all." She shrugged on her way toward Storm, took his cheeks in her hands and kissed them. "I missed you." Her eyes cut to mine. I saw caution in them. "And this is…"

"Madeline, my girl." His arm tightened around me like he knew I needed to feel secure.

Sugar slowly raised an eyebrow. "Your girl, as in…"

"My old lady. I've claimed her." The unwavering tone in his voice made me shiver. I'd heard it when he spoke to his brothers and the prospects. It meant: *Don't question me.*

I couldn't look at Sugar. Didn't want to see her reaction. Claiming a woman was a huge deal for Storm, one he didn't take lightly. I imagined his aunt might be a little more than critical with me.

"Well, Madeline, it's nice to meet you." She reached her hand out and I shook it.

"It's a pleasure. And these are your sons, Maddox and Markey?" My eyes flitted over to them. My goodness they were good-looking guys.

"They sure are." She smiled fondly at her boys, then went around Storm, throwing her arms around Tina. "Girl, I've missed you."

"Who baked?" Maddox took a chocolate chip cookie off the plate. Markey grabbed oatmeal.

I couldn't stop looking at them. The pang in my stomach grew.

"Angel did." Storm kissed my cheek. "To butter you all up."

I elbowed him. *Brat.* "I love to bake."

"These are fantastic." Maddox reached for another. "So what's been going on around here? When we drove through town, there was an eerie feeling."

Storm stiffened. "Yeah, we've had a little trouble with that nomad gang who arrived Memorial weekend."

Sugar's hazel-green eyes widened. "What?" She looked furious. "What kind of trouble? And why in the hell didn't you tell me?"

CHAPTER THIRTY-FOUR

STORM

Fuck. I didn't want to do this. Not now. Sugar had only been home for two minutes. But I knew she wouldn't let it go, so I might as well bring her and the boys up to speed.

"Let's take this into the bar. I need a drink." I slid Madeline off my lap and took her hand. Sugar and the boys followed. On my way out of the kitchen, I hollered for Raul, and whoever else was around to join us.

We all got our drink of choice. I gave Sugar and the boys the lowdown. Only the basics, nothing specific to the club. Just enough so they'd be aware of their surroundings and to steer clear of the Dirty Hunters. She didn't say a word the whole time, but I was sure she had plenty to say.

Through it all, I held Madeline's hand. My woman kept me grounded. She was a treasure. My God, how had I found her?

"So they've been quiet the last twenty-four hours. I hope they got the message and left town. Either way, there's been groups of Knights combing the streets here in Bastion and Winters."

Sugar sighed. "Jesus. And Ire and the women are okay?"

"Yes. Mostly." I thought about their status. Ava was having a hard time, understandably. Ire wasn't back to normal yet. He'd wanted to know what happened to the women but I hadn't told him about Ava. He took his job seriously. When he found out what happened to her, Ire would lose his mind.

Sugar relaxed in her chair, crossing her arms over her chest. "I can't believe my dad didn't say anything the three times I talked to him."

I leveled my gaze on Sugar. "I asked him not to. You and the boys needed time alone together. And you were safe. Nothing else mattered to me."

"You're right. We did need this road trip. It was what Matt wanted." Sugar looked at her sons with a small smile. She loved her boys dearly, including me. No question, she was feisty and stubborn, but she was as sweet as her nickname my uncle Matt gave her.

I nodded, knowing as much. Once the boys graduated high school, I was sponsoring Maddox to be a prospect. He'd be the youngest, but I had every confidence he would earn the privilege. He was a lot like his old man and would make a fine addition to the club. Markey hadn't shown the same interest and had talked about going to college.

"We're getting the area under control, Sugar. It's just been rough because these assholes seem to be ghosts. They have outside help." Raul lifted his bottle to his lips. "Fucking pisses me off, too." He guzzled his beer.

Sugar turned toward Madeline and me. "I'd love some alone time with your girl. Would you be okay with that?"

"Absolutely."

Sugar stood. "You too, Tina." She looked at the kittens in the corner. "Where's Carla?"

Madeline lifted off my lap and squared her shoulders. "I haven't made her feel welcome. She's rude and acts like she owns my man. I won't stand for it." She cupped the side of my face and gave me a chaste kiss.

A flicker of respect sparked in Sugar's eyes. "Well, I like you already, honey. Come on." She took my woman by the hand and winked at me on the way out.

Angel would be just fine with Sugar. Next month I would put my mark on her. More than ever, I needed to get the Hunters out of the area so Madeline and I could start the baby-making process. I wanted nothing more than her pregnant with my child.

CHAPTER THIRTY-FIVE

MADELINE

We were in the kitchen at one of the two round tables eating cookies and drinking milk. I was grateful for this private moment with Sugar and Tina.

"Do you love him?" Sugar squeezed my hand as she stared into my eyes. "Don't be afraid to say no, if it's how you feel. I just want to know where you are with my boy. I only want the best for him and I can see how much he cares about you. It does my heart good too. He's never been like this with a woman."

"Like what?" My heart raced a little. I wasn't sure if it was nervousness or excitement. When it came to Kaleb, I forever felt flutters in my heart. A gentle tightening in my chest. A stirring in my soul. It all made me antsy and giddy. Nervous and excited.

"Tender and protective. Smitten and in love."

My cheeks warmed and my eyes teared up because I saw everything she saw. "I do love him, but we haven't told each other yet. I guess I'm waiting for the right moment."

Tina stared at me knowingly. "Like when she gets his mark." She bobbed her, wiggling her eyebrows. Crazy woman. The sun cascading in from the window created a halo around her head, turning her sandy blonde hair nearly translucent. Her olive-green eyes were full of amusement.

I smiled at Tina. I'd told her I was waiting to declare my love for Storm until next month, but it wasn't the whole truth.

"Getting a tattoo scares me. Needles terrify me. I want to be sure we'll last." I fidgeted with my nail as Sugar held my gaze.

"You've been hurt before, haven't you?" The understanding in Sugar's voice put a lump in my throat.

"Yes." Dammit. I didn't mean for the conversation to go in this direction. It wasn't a pleasant one. I rarely spoke of Dane. But when asked point-blank, I couldn't lie to these women.

"Tell me." Sugar's eyes remained locked on mine.

I inhaled a deep breath. I hadn't told Storm what I'd been through with Dane. Not all of it. Something told me he wouldn't be upset if I shared it with his aunt and Tina.

"My ex is Deputy Dane Miller."

Sugar's eyes bulged and her hand covered her mouth. "Oh, shit."

My innards twisted into a knot the size of Lake Harriet. "Yeah. When Storm found out it wasn't pretty."

Sugar's shocked expression softened. "I can imagine, but you're still here."

I bobbed my head in agreement. Storm could have kicked my ass to the curb. Especially after the way he found out. I would've been sad for sure. More than sad, heartbroken.

"I assure you, my devotion is to Storm. I would never betray him. I know what it feels like..." I inhaled a deep breath. "Dane used to slap me around and called me pathetic and incompetent for just about everything. I haven't told Storm any of this. He knows about Dane cheating on me and probably has some idea about the verbal abuse but

I haven't told him Dane hit me."

Sugar's brows knitted together the way my mom did hers. "Why haven't you?"

"I'm afraid of what Storm might do. It's over. I got out. It's not worth rehashing." I'd put that part of my life behind me. The past needed to stay out of my present. My future with Kaleb was all that mattered to me.

Sugar patted my hand. "You're a caring woman for trying to protect Storm. But honey, don't get in his way of avenging you. Storm won't cross the line, trust me."

"But there's more…" My voice trailed as I warred with whether to tell these ladies everything. I believed I could trust them, but I wasn't a fool. Their loyalties would always be to Storm and the club, first and foremost.

"You can trust us, Angel." Sugar squeezed my hand, eyes flicking toward Tina. "Us ol' ladies need to have each other's backs just as much as the men take care of their brothers." Sugar

"Yeah, honey. I've been in your shoes with an abusive boyfriend. I got out too, but it cost me, my daughter. Raul and the club will take care of my ex when the time is right and get my daughter back. As you might imagine, Raul is out for blood. I'm not about to stand in his way." This was the first time Tina opened up about her past. I had felt like we were similar on some level. It appeared it wasn't my imagination. I wanted to know more about her, but now wasn't the time.

The words flew out of my mouth. "Dane forced me to have sex when I didn't want to. If I was sick or tired, he didn't care. If I complained or told him no, he knocked me around. It wasn't until the fourth time I had finally learned the pattern."

Tina's eyes teared up and I had the distinct feeling she experienced the same with her boyfriend.

"He forced you to have sex?" Sugar asked in a lethal voice.

My heart raced, fearing she'd tell Storm. "I let him get what he needed so he'd leave me alone."

"Jesus, Mary and Joseph." Sugar covered her mouth with her hand.

"Oh, honey." Tina blinked back tears. I saw it in her olive-green eyes; she knew my pain. She'd gone through the same.

I swallowed thick saliva, trying to control my own emotions. If Kaleb caught me crying, he'd freak out. But I couldn't help feeling raw and exposed. Dane forced sex on me. So many of my wounds hadn't healed. Tara and Steph didn't even know. Nobody knew.

"Please don't tell Storm. You know how he feels about sexual assault. He'll go ballistic." I turned to one, then the other as my stomach churned.

They nodded with worried expressions. I wasn't sure if they'd keep this to themselves though. What if I'd just made a colossal mistake?

"Dane's out of my life. Storm would never let him hurt me now. Nothing else matters." And I meant every word. What Storm and I had was beautiful and passionate. He treated me like a queen. Whatever happened in the past, I wanted it to stay there.

"Okay, Angel. Your secret's safe with us. You have my word." Sugar reached over and hugged me. "You have my blessing to be with Storm. Not like you need it." She snorted. "My nephew does as he damn well pleases."

"He does. But your blessing means the world to me." I hugged her back.

"I love having another ol' lady in our small group." Tina hugged me from the other side. "Welcome to the ol' ladies club, honey."

"Thank you. I'm happy to be here."

We pulled away and grabbed a cookie.

I loved the camaraderie I felt with Tina and Sugar. It was different from what I had with Tara and Steph, and Mama Kim. Intenser, much like what the men in the club displayed. Danger lurked around the club as Tina once told me. When most people were oblivious to the hidden evils or chose to ignore them, like with the Dirty Hunters, we were in the middle of it all. The locals didn't know about Ava and Nancy's assault at The Bullet. They had no idea how hard the club was working to rid the area of those vile men.

Having a group of women in the club, fellow ol' ladies to rely on was priceless. Except there was one I hadn't gotten an opportunity to get to know on a personal level.

"I wish Jill was around more." I'd only seen her twice, and both times were in passing.

Tina frowned, eying Sugar. "Yeah, Jill's always kept a safe distance from the club. I think it's the way Boxer prefers it. He's super protective of his sister. The same with her ol man, Wolf."

"Have any of the other guys shown any interest in a woman while I've been gone?" Sugar broke a piece off her cookie and popped it into her mouth. "Mmm, so good."

I mulled over Sugar's question and Hero entered my mind. The day at Sugar Bliss, I was sure Tara had caught his eye. Maybe not, though. He hadn't seen her since, so it probably wasn't worth mentioning.

"Nothing I've noticed. They've been busy with the Hunters."

We continued chatting and getting to know each other better. Eventually, Storm came and took me upstairs.

He shut the door and locked it behind me.

"How's my girl?" His arms went around my waist and he gazed into my eyes.

"I'm perfect." I ran the tips of my fingers through his beard. "Sugar is wonderful."

"And you were worried she wouldn't like you." He brushed his nose against mine. "I got her wink of approval."

"Did you?" I cradled the back of his neck and pulled his head toward me.

"Yeah. It's all good from here on out." His lips ghosted over mine.

"And in one month, we'll be official."

"In my heart, we already are." His mouth descended on mine and I was swallowed up in his arms..

My heart was in the same place as Storm's… *Kaleb's*. He was mine and I was his.

I was the happiest I had been since the summer at Lake Waleska when I had drooled over my brother's best friend. Except what I had with Storm was real love, not a childhood crush.

Storm was my forever.

CHAPTER THIRTY-SIX

MADELINE

Today was a big day. One month had passed, and this afternoon I was getting inked. Or "marked" as Storm put it. It was symbolic to him and his club to show I belonged to him.

For me, it meant forever. I was ready. Ready to be Storm's... forever.

We were a perfect match in our daily lives and in bed. While Storm did his job as president of Knight's Legion, I stayed at the clubhouse and learned the ins and outs from Sugar and Tina. I had become very close to them.

Sugar helped me read Storm's moods and Tina helped me deal with Carla.

"This is so good, baby." Storm groaned as he chewed on a giant bite of a caramel roll.

I giggled. Storm said the same thing every time he tried something new at Sugar Bliss. He had a sweet tooth, though he'd never admit it, believing sweets made him a weak pussy. He could be so cocky and judgy sometimes.

Steph and Kim gawked at him while Tara couldn't keep her eyes off Hero. He was sitting with Track in the booth behind ours. The same scene had played out each time I met up with the girls for our weekly breakfast. With all that was happening, Storm refused to go out without protection.

I couldn't believe August had arrived. Storm and I were closer than ever. Although, neither of us had said the L-word. Anyone would have to be blind not to see that we were deeply in love.

"I know. It's one of my favorites." I wiped a bit of icing off his beard with a napkin. If we had been alone, I would have licked it off.

"We should take some back to the clubhouse for Sugar and the boys." He wiggled his dark eyebrows. His eyes sparkled like platinum. This was the happiest I'd seen him, maybe ever.

"How long will she be staying at the clubhouse?" Tara asked in an annoyed tone. "She's been there for a month. School will be starting in a few weeks."

Oh, man. I didn't want to have this conversation with everyone around.

Storm had made no bones about it. He wanted me to move in with him. I'd put it off because it was a huge deal and commitment. I'd already lived with a man, and it didn't last. But then, Storm was nothing like Dane.

I loved *my Kaleb*. My stomach tightened as I stared at him. It happened regularly. I hadn't gotten over the shock of Storm's birth name being Kaleb. I thought it was a sick joke from God, but then I took it as a sign that despite his dangerous lifestyle, this outlaw biker was the man I was meant to be with.

"Indefinitely," Storm replied with a full mouth.

"What?" Tara turned to me. "Is he screwing with me? Are you moving in with him for real? Even after what happened with Dane."

Storm's hand dropped onto the table, rattling the coffee cups and plates. I covered it with mine and brushed my thumb over it. Anytime I tried to calm or soothe Storm, it worked. I apparently had the magic touch, or so he'd told me at least a dozen times.

I flicked my gaze to Tara's. "Let's not do this here. I'll swing by the house afterward, and we'll talk."

"As if it would do any good. You've already made your mind up. Haven't you?"

All eyes were on me. *Shit.*

I had made my decision. I wanted to move in with Storm. No, I already had moved in.

In the beginning, I stayed with him because the club was on lockdown, and Storm wanted me safe. The Knights hadn't fully contained the Hunters or driven them out of the area. Storm didn't want me out of his sight. I knew it was about more than my safety. Neither of us wanted to be apart.

The numbers of Dirty Hunters were dwindling. Storm and his brothers had cracked down and weren't being so nice about it. I didn't know how they were handling things, nor did I want to.

"Yes. I'm moving in with him."

"Well, this is just great!" Tara exclaimed, but it wasn't with glee. The sarcasm in her tone and the bitter scowl on her face said otherwise. "I should've known this would happen after more and more of your closet emptied. Guess I was in denial."

"I'll still pay my portion of the rent and electricity."

"No. I'll pay it," Storm cut in.

"I can't let you pay my bills." Holy crap! This man constantly surprised me.

"We'll discuss it at home, Angel." There was the unyielding tone I was familiar with. Storm wasn't a total pushover or controlled by his dick as Sugar once said. When his mind was made up, it was impossible to change it. I sensed this was one of those times.

Tara snorted. "Home? You really want your *home* to be on a

compound with dozens of greasy bikers?"

"Hey! Watch it, *Roja*," Hero barked, getting to his feet. "You don't know shit about us, but I'd be happy to give you the low down tonight."

Tara rolled her eyes. "In your dreams, *Hero*. Like what kind of road name is that anyway?"

He cracked a cocky smile. "Tonight, I'll show you what it means."

These two bantered all the time. Hero wanted Tara. Storm had confirmed it, but Tara? She was a stubborn redhead. She might openly stare at Hero and drool, but she'd hated on Storm and his crew because he'd "stolen me away" from her—her words, not mine.

Tara wanted Hero as much as he wanted her. She was just playing hard to get, and taking her sweet time holding a grudge against the boys.

"Oh! The club's having a party Friday night." I squeezed Storm's hand and he issued me a nod of approval. "Come to it. See how the other side lives."

"Not me," Kim replied quickly. "I mean, I'm sure you're all swell, but I'll be with my boys." Last week at breakfast Kim had mentioned spending the weekend with her boys before they returned to college.

"I'm down for a party." Steph popped her shoulders, always eager to try something new.

"Well, Tara? How about it?" I watched her eyes flit toward Hero. He'd returned to his and Track's booth.

"I'll consider it."

Stubborn redhead.

I hated needles. The buzz of the tattoo gun reminded me of the one place I despised most and avoided at all cost, beyond my annual visit—the dentist. Yes, I only went once a year.

Storm and I entered Human Canvas, a KLMC owned tattoo parlor in Bastion. This was my first time here. The whining of the guns made the hairs on my arms flare.

"Hey Storm!" A woman at the counter smiled too wide for my liking. Her arms and neck were covered in an array of colored ink. She had a small heart-shaped teardrop below the corner of her eye. Her hair was chin-length on one side, shaved on the other, and was the color of blue raspberry Laffy Taffy. "Saw your name in the books. What're you getting inked?"

Was I invisible? The woman made no attempt to acknowledge me. *Rude.*

"My woman," Storm replied through gritted teeth.

Every time a woman's face lit up like a freaking floodlight, I couldn't help but wonder if he'd screwed her.

"Oh…" Yup, she seemed disappointed by his reply. *Great.* "Well, Art will be with you shortly."

Storm grunted, pressing his hand to my lower back to guide me to a sofa along the wall. He sat and pulled me onto his lap.

"Breathe, Angel. It'll all be all right." He knew my fears and promised to hold my hand. But I was sure I'd need more than his hand to get me through this.

"I doubt it. At least at the dentist, I get Novocaine."

"Here, you can have tequila or whiskey." He winked, gripping the back of my neck and kneading it.

I exhaled a sigh in response to his soothing ministrations. "If I was pregnant, I couldn't have either."

His eyes cut to mine. "You trying to tell me something, Angel?"

Dammit. I should've known better than to mention the P-word and especially not the B-word. *Pregnant* and *baby* were off-limits.

Storm was wound tighter than a drum with getting the Hunters out of his territory. He wanted the area safe for me, his MC family, and the locals. My poor man carried an unbelievably heavy weight on his shoulders.

But knowing I wouldn't consider having a baby until it was safe took his stress to a whole new level. And I'd just given him false hope. *Crap.*

I cradled his face in my hands and pecked his warm lips. "No, I wasn't trying to tell you anything. I'm sorry. That was insensitive of me." I kissed his lips lightly.

The disappointment in his stormy eyes crushed me.

"It's all good, Angel. The area isn't safe yet." He wrapped me in his hulking arms, swallowing me up, and gave me a real kiss. The kind that made me wet and gasping for air.

The area isn't safe yet repeated in my head. My heart hurt. He was doing everything imaginable to rid Bastion and Winters of the dirty maggots. I wanted him to succeed so we could move forward in our relationship.

He pulled away, ending his delicious kiss. "When we're done here, we'll go home and practice our baby-making skills."

"Yay, something to look forward to." I clapped, wiggling my ass on him to lighten the mood.

He chuckled and squeezed me.

I wanted to tell him I loved him, so he knew we would know I was in this for the long haul. I hoped he believed it. But I didn't want to whisper *"I love you"* for the first time in a tattoo parlor.

Instead, I kissed him as passionately as possible, pressing my breasts into his chest. When he groaned into my mouth, his large hand cupping my butt, I felt a little better about my stupid remark.

"Prez, you need a private room?" A voice bellowed with laughter.

I reared back. Art was grinning like a fool. How all these men found each other and became brothers was one of life's greatest mysteries. They were all tall, muscly, tatted, ruggedly handsome, and oozed sex appeal. But mostly, if you had them on your side, as

Storm did, they were willing to take a bullet for you. They were loyal, dependable, and not afraid to die.

Mercy, their grit astounded me.

As the prez's old lady, they would protect me with their life too. I still hadn't fully wrapped my brain around it.

"You got one free?" Storm quipped.

"For my prez, absolutely."

I laughed, shaking my head. "Please, don't give him ideas." Knowing Storm, he'd take me into a back room and have his way with me before I got branded with his mark. Hell, I was surprised he hadn't already, up against the brick wall in the alley behind the shop.

"Aw, come on, baby..." His mouth dropped to my neck, teeth nipping at the tendon along the bend. Dang it, I was dripping wet.

"Christ, never seen you like this before, Storm," the receptionist said, frustration in her voice.

Art chuckled. "Because he hasn't been. But Angel here is special." He clucked his tongue. "Don't you forget it."

"Yeah, whatever," she muttered, rolling her eyes.

Storm lifted his head and turned toward the woman. He didn't say anything, and I dared not look at his face.

"Sorry, Storm," the tart receptionist said in a softer voice.

He grunted.

"Come on, let's take you back. I'll be doing the honors, Miss Madeline. Espada's booked solid working on a pair of titties that would rival Dolly Parton's." Art licked his bottom lip as if he'd love to sample them.

"Damn, man, really?" Storm sounded intrigued.

I elbowed him hard. He didn't flinch.

"Baby, yours are perfect." He reached for me.

I pushed his hands away. "Shut up, you big jerk. It's a mortal sin to talk about another woman in front of your girl."

"Angel," he said in a warning tone, letting his alpha out for pushing him away. I knew his game. He didn't scare me. If he thought it was okay to talk like that, I'd have to show him how it felt.

"You know, Art. I'm fine with you inking me. I like your work," I said in a sweet, flirty voice for a little payback.

Storm growled low. *Good.*

"Oh yeah? Been admiring it?" Art wiggled his brows.

"Every night…" My voice trailed when I wanted to say *when Storm and I have sex.* Art usually did all of my man's ink. It was phenomenal. My cheeks heated, probably turning red as we went down the hallway. I was getting a smaller version of Storm's tattoo on the back of my neck. He wanted blue stormy cumulonimbus clouds with hints of my eye color peppered through it. His was all in black. In the middle of mine, it would say "Property of Storm." And in a smaller font point, KLMC.

But now… "You know, I think I want the tat on my left tit. Think you could handle it, Art?"

"Goddammit, Angel!" Storm reeled me in, so I was flush with his body. He grabbed the sides of my face firmly between his large hands and put his forehead to mine. "It won't happen again."

"Are you sure?" I stared him hard in the eyes. I wouldn't take any shit. "If you're talking about other women and their body parts or what you might like to do to them, I'm going to think you don't want me anymore. Then I'll—"

He gritted his teeth. "Don't say it. Don't. I don't want any other woman. Only you."

"But you said—"

He cut me off with an intense kiss. "Won't happen again, baby."

I gazed lovingly into Storm's eyes and said, "Looks like the back of the neck it is, Art. Where's the tequila?"

Storm hugged me, and I felt it—crazy, fierce love. We were okay, but I didn't keep my mouth shut when stuff bothered me. Not after everything I went through with Dane. I spoke my mind and didn't care who else heard me. Storm encouraged me to not be afraid to tell him when he'd crossed the line or upset me so he could fix it.

Damn, I loved him.

"All right, Angel. Let's get started."

I grabbed a handful of Storm's T-shirt. My heart jackhammered against my ribs.

He lifted my chin with his thumb, leveling his eyes to mine. "I'm here, baby. It'll all be okay. I'll be holding you."

I knew he would. I was so glad he showed me how I'd lean into him with my forehead braced on his chest. I doubted most people needed someone literally holding them while getting a tattoo, but I needed Storm. He was my comfort and wouldn't let anything happen to me. I trusted him with my life.

Now, I would have his mark on me, showing I was his property.

Property. It may sound extreme and degrading to some, but not to me. To my man and his club, it was the same as taking a marriage vow. Maybe even more so because a divorce could end the marriage. The tattoo was permanent. Unless I went through the painstaking process of getting it removed.

But I'd never remove it because Storm... *Kaleb* and I were forever.

"I'm ready..."

CHAPTER THIRTY-SEVEN

STORM

I hadn't rid my territory of all the Hunters, but they weren't showing their faces either. We had disposed of a couple more in the last month and the rest seemed to vanish. At this moment, I didn't give one fuckin' iota about them.

I brushed my tongue along Angel's spine, up to the covering of her tattoo. She tasted a little salty from the warm August day and smelled like heaven, and she was *mine*.

I had a stupid smile on my face, knowing what was beneath the plastic wrap. It made me ridiculously happy.

She'd gone through with it. My name and club's initials were inked on her perfect, delicate skin. I was so proud of her, given her fears. She dug the shit out of my skin with her nails at times, but she got through it.

"So proud of you, Angel. Fuckin' proud. You're officially a badass. *My* badass."

She giggled, face lying on the side of the mattress, and totally spent. The second we'd gotten into our room, I'd stripped the clothes off her gorgeous body and fucked her hard. We were both horny as fuck by the time Art had wrapped up her tattoo. Then he talked our ear off for half an hour. We were desperate for each other when we got home.

But I didn't just fuck her. I did, but after we both came, I spent the last hour worshiping her body with sweet caresses and tender words. I made sure she felt adored, respected, and *loved*. Only with Madeline had I ever done soft and tender. I only worshiped my Angel.

She was it for me. I loved her more than I could ever put in words. She owned my heart and was my everything.

My hands skated over her shoulders and arms, earning a purr from her lips. I tilted her chin up, gazing into her serene baby blues. They were like clear skies on a calm sunny day. One look from her and she could wash away the darkness inside me and fill me with peace. I hadn't known such a feeling in over a decade. But now, I would experience it for the rest of my life.

"Need anything, baby?" I ran my nose down the bridge of hers, cupping the side of her face.

Her eyes rolled back into her head, a sure sign she enjoyed my touch. "As long as I have you, I don't need a thing."

My heart slammed into my ribs. Her powerful declaration meant everything to me.

"Same for me, Angel. You are my heart. Without you, I couldn't live."

Her pretty eyes teared up, while she smiled. I'd only let her shed tears of joy from here on out. No pain. No sadness. No fear. I intended to make sure she was always exceedingly happy.

She bit her bottom lip, a nervous glint in her baby blues. "I have something to tell you. I hope you won't be angry."

"Nothing you do would make me angry, so long as it doesn't have to do with another man." I watched her worry fade.

She shook her head, smiling. "It doesn't."

"Then tell me."

"I stopped taking my birth control when I finished the last one… A week ago. I know the Dirty Hunters are still a threat, but I just thought—"

"Are you serious?" I said louder than I meant to. My heart raced with excitement and maybe a little fear. Would I be a good dad? Shit was about to get real. I wanted a baby with Madeline, more than anything, I just hoped I deserved her and our baby. Well, I'd do everything possible to be a worthy man.

Worry flashed in her pretty eyes. "Are you mad?"

I flipped her on her back and climbed on her so I could see her beautiful face clearly.

"Not even close."

"I can feel you hard again between my legs. Should I take it as a sign?"

"Damn straight, you should. My mission starting now is to pump as much of my cum into you until it makes you good and pregnant. Am I mad?" I chuckled. "Silly woman, you've made me happier than I've ever been in my entire life."

She pressed her small hand to my cheek, her eyes filled with love and adoration for *me*.

"Make love to me, Kaleb. Slow, passionate love. I want you deep inside me. I want our bodies as one. Just like our souls."

Damn this woman, she almost made me cry. Almost.

"Anything my Angel wants, she gets." I dropped my mouth to hers, kissing her like it might be our last. I wouldn't rush anything for the rest of the night. I'd love Madeline slowly, deeply, passionately. Just as she asked.

I wasn't a praying man. But at this moment, I prayed we'd create a baby, a little human who was pure just like its mother—*my Angel.*

CHAPTER THIRTY-EIGHT

MADELINE

On the evening of the party, I ran late by half an hour because I couldn't decide what to wear for the party. After an hour of trying on what was left in my closet, Tara forced me to pick something.

Last night, I spent the night at Tara to pack the last of my belongings. Storm and I argued over it, but eventually, I gave in and agreed to him staying with me. I wasn't stupid. The Hunters were still in the area. This morning he'd returned to the clubhouse to set up the party, leaving AJ and Hollywood to watch after me.

My man had texted multiple times throughout the day. I felt terrible, knowing Storm didn't get any sleep last night. I'd stayed in the living room with Tara gabbing all night.

Now I was running late.

At least my makeup and hair were finished. I went with loose beachy waves. I had on a little eyeliner to make my eyes pop, but on the whole natural. It was just who I was, a simple woman. Storm preferred me this way. He hated fake eyelashes, tarantula eyes as he called it, or caked-on makeup.

I had on my favorite tan boots with the cross on the front. They paired well with my white denim shorts frayed on the edges. These shorts made my legs look spectacular and tanner than they really were. An aqua blue off-the-shoulder crop top complimented them. The color made my eyes stand out even more, along with my tits.

"Let's go, let's go, let's go," I hollered, running out the front door with the last box of my clothes in my arms. AJ grabbed it from me and carried it to my car. It hadn't cooled off yet. The air felt thick, like scattered storms were on the horizon.

Tara snorted from behind me. "For the record, we're late because of you. I was ready an hour ago. Smells like rain."

"I was just thinking the same!" I laughed. Could she hear my thoughts? "Girl, Storm's texted me three times asking where the fuck I was." I hopped into the driver's seat and gave AJ and Hollywood a thumbs up. As AJ drove off, I followed him with Hollywood behind my Honda CR-V.

"What happens when you piss him off? I mean, he doesn't look like a nice, forgiving guy. He struts around with a permanent scowl on his face... Until he looks at you. He loves you, Mads. I can see it."

I gaped, turning toward her. "You can tell Storm loves me?"

"Uh, yeah. Hasn't he told you so yet?"

I worried my bottom lip between my teeth. Neither of us had said the L-word. "No, but then I haven't told him I loved him either."

"Why not?" Tara's shock made me squirm in my seat.

"I don't know. It's like we say it all the time but without words. It's in our actions, the way we treat each other. I feel his love every second of every day. It's why I got his mark on me. I know he loves me."

"But don't you want to hear him say it?"

I did want to hear Storm tell me he loved me, but it wasn't the be-all and end-all. Actions spoke louder than words, and Storm's unspoken words boomed like thunder every time he made love to me. "Sure. I wouldn't object to hearing him say, I love you, Angel."

"You know, now that I'm thinking about it, he never calls you Maddy. It's either Angel, baby, or Madeline."

"I don't see a problem. When we first met, he knew me as Madeline. I guess it stuck." I shrugged.

"Huh, just seems strange to me, I guess."

"Whatever. I love the sound of my name on his lips." Wild flutters sparked in my stomach, remembering his sexy baritone voice as he said my name.

We picked Steph up along the way, making me later than I'd promised Storm. I was getting a little nervous, knowing how he worried about me. But I had two prospects to protect me. Still, Storm wouldn't relax until I was in his arms.

After I confessed three days ago that I stopped taking the pill, we'd been going at it like rabbits. Having a baby wasn't something I took lightly. I was a planner, like most teachers. School started the day after Labor Day, and I wanted to finish the school year with my students. It would be my last year teaching for a season so I could be home to cuddle and love our baby.

Returning to work and putting the baby in daycare didn't appeal to me at all. Storm had told me I didn't have to work, if I didn't want to. If I did, Sugar and Tina could watch the baby at the clubhouse, where he would be around to care for it too. I thought his suggestion was sweet, but I also knew it had to do with keeping the baby protected.

"Wow." Tara's loud voice jerked me out of my thoughts. "I've never been out this way." Tara gawked out the window.

"Yeah, it's kind off the beaten path."

"Me either," Steph chimed. "Oh shit! There's an armed guard?"

"Mhm. He's a prospect." I gripped the steering wheel. "Storm told me there is no one better to keep at the gate, than Dodge. I guess he grew up with guns. He should get his patch before the end of the year."

Dodge had a large rifle in his hands. He didn't usually have it out in the open, but Storm had warned me about it. Again, because of the Hunters, security was amped up for the party. The celebration was a thank you and farewell for the Fallen Soldiers MC. Several members came up from Iowa to help with the Hunters. I hadn't seen much of them over the last couple of weeks. I think Storm preferred it that way.

I rolled down my window when Dodge approached my car.

"Hey, Madeline. Who do you have with you?" He ducked his head down, eyeing Tara and Steph.

"These are my closest friends, Tara, and in the back is Steph." I looked sidelong at Tara. Dodge wasn't much of a talker. The scowl on his face made me more than a little nervous most days. He took his job very seriously. I respected him for it. "Storm knows I'm bringing them."

He nodded to the girls. "Have a good time, Angel."

"Thanks, Dodge. Hope you can join in the fun later." I smiled as I drove the car past the gate. I knew he wouldn't be at the party.

The lot was packed with more bikes than I'd ever seen before. Finding a place to park might have been difficult, if Storm hadn't given me a designated spot near the front entrance. I pulled my car in between two sparkling motorcycles, careful not to hit them, then turned the engine off.

Steph gasped. "Shit, my heart is racing."

"Mine too," Tara said.

My heart rate skyrocketed, but it wasn't because I was scared about being on the compound. I was reacting to their reactions.

I checked my appearance in the mirror on my visor. "Ready?"

The girls nodded.

We exited the car, and AJ was waiting for us. "You ladies can follow me." He had a boyish smile on his face. He didn't have rough

edges like the patched members, but he'd probably get them…
eventually. The thought made me a little sad.

"Thanks, AJ."

Loud music and a warm glow came from behind the clubhouse.

Something occurred to me. I didn't know what had made Storm's
edges rough. Something in his life had to have made him a serious,
sometimes scary man. After two months of being together, I still didn't
know a lot about him. But we were official and trying to have a baby. I
should know everything about him, just as he should know everything
about me.

My phone vibrated in my back pocket. When I saw the name on
the message, I smiled.

Toby: Hey sis. I'm in your area. How about lunch tomorrow?

Madeline: OMG! Yes, yes, yes! How long will you be here? I
can't wait to see you!

Toby: Not sure. A few days, maybe. Looking forward to seeing
you too.

"Toby is coming tomorrow?" Tara peered over my shoulder as we
followed AJ.

"I guess so. Remember, Mom mentioned he'd be in the area, but I
never got a specific date." I put my phone in my back pocket.

Tara nodded, rolling her eyes. "That's right. What a stinker for not
giving you a heads up."

I laughed, feeling giddy with excitement to see my older brother.
"Typical Toby and his unexpected visits."

"I hope I get to see him too. He's so hot." Tara shimmied her
shoulders.

"He's handsome. But hot? Yuck, Tara. He's my brother." I feigned
gagging and elbowed her. She'd crushed on Toby since our second
year of college when they first met.

I missed Toby like crazy. He also avoided going home to
Garrison, our hometown, like I did. It was too damn sad there, too

many memories. We'd both broken our parents' hearts when we didn't return to South Dakota after college.

AJ stopped at the gate where another guard stood. As we passed through it, my eyes went wide. Lights were strung through the trees, multiple bonfires were lit, and a gazebo was also decorated in twinkling lights. When did the guys put it up? It wasn't there last week for the small cookout we had.

"Wow, this is fantastic." Steph nudged my elbow.

It was fantastic. I waved to Sugar, Tina and Emilee as I scanned the area. A row of tables was behind the building with what looked like enough food to feed an army—an MC army. Other picnic tables were scattered on the grass.

"Smells great too. I'm starving," Tara added.

"Not me. I'm too nervous to eat." My nerves were short-circuiting. I wasn't sure why. I felt like something terrible was going to happen.

"I don't see any kids," Steph whispered.

Tina's words rushed back to me, when she said she hoped the guys would start producing the next generation. I hadn't missed the look of panic on Storm's face. So much had changed in two short months.

As I focused my attention on the new wooden structure, I spotted a drum set, a few microphones on stands, and some guitars. Had they hired a band? Gosh, I hoped they had!

It looked like a party any family would have on a summer's evening. Shoot, grander than most I'd been to when I was little.

"There's my girl." Storm's voice boomed behind me. I whirled around. His eyes raked over me, leisurely. "Damn baby. You look good enough to eat." He grabbed my hips and tugged me to him, planting his lips on mine. He stole the air from my lungs with his delicious kiss. It was just what I needed to relax.

Tara cleared her throat. "Seriously, you two? Let's not do this here. I need food."

Storm smirked, not letting go of me. "I'd say sorry, but I'm not. Prepare to see lots of kissing. Even more from my brothers." He put his mouth on my ear and whispered. "I missed the fuck out of you last night, Angel. We might need to go upstairs after we eat. Or I could eat you instead."

Steph gaped. "What do you mean even more?" I was glad she interrupted Storm's dirty talk. He already had me breathing heavy and my thong drenched.

"These parties get wild. There will be sex and lots of it," he replied in a matter-of-fact tone.

"Outside in front of everyone?" Tara's eyes widened with intrigue. I figured she'd like the sound of raunchy, unapologetic displays of sex. She was the wild one in our friend group.

Storm snorted. "Yes. Outside."

Steph arched her brow.

"Oh! We won't be having sex outside! I swear." I prayed Storm didn't have other ideas. Ones I might be persuaded into after sleeping apart last night. I was just as horny as him.

"She's right. I'll be taking her upstairs to our room. Nobody will see my woman having sex."

"Of course not," I muttered.

His eyes flashed as he tugged me closer. "Missed you, baby," he whispered at the shell of my ear. "You really do look good enough to eat." His tone made goose bumps cover my arms. "I will later…"

CHAPTER THIRTY-NINE

STORM

Tonight was the first big club party we'd had all summer. A party had been the last thing on my mind while handling the Dirty Hunters. But this was good. I was damn grateful Turner, the president of Fallen Soldiers, sent his VP, Jack, out with his SAA, Deacon and a few patched members to help us. The Soldiers were a small MC of only thirteen. Aside from my dad's club, the original KLMC, our closest allies were my dad's cousin, Ben's club in North Dakota. The Knights were taking over the Upper Midwest.

My brothers were relaxed, drinking with their chosen lady. I could already tell it was going to be a wild night. Looked like we might get some rain, too.

Madeline was perched on my lap. I felt like a true king with my queen. For five years, I had ruled Knight's Legion. It hadn't been easy. I missed my Uncle Matt, struggling to do this job without him. Sure, Raul had been a great mentor, but he wasn't my uncle.

Uncle Matt had been the only person I trusted. Aunt Eve tried to fill the void in my life, but I couldn't let her in as I had Uncle Matt. I stopped trusting women after my mom took off, leaving my dad and me. After all the screwing around my old man did with the sweet butts, I couldn't blame her. She'd found a new man and had a new life and family. I was glad she was happy, but what about me? Her son?

The only person I had let close to me since Uncle Matt died was my best friend, Track. I trusted him with my life. He never judged me after confessing my greatest sin.

I hated dredging up the past. No matter how hard I tried to fake being over it, it all barreled back every June like a goddamn tornado, knocking me off my feet and tossing me around like the helpless pussy I'd been the day Tommy died.

The day I had killed him.

I was thinking a lot about Tommy tonight. It was because I was about to see Toby for the first time in twelve years. Finally, after all these years of hating myself and feeling like a worthless piece of shit, an angel brought the light back into my life. My avenging angel chased away the darkness.

"You didn't tell me there'd be a band." Madeline's baby blues glittered. I stroked her inner thigh with my thumb.

Her hand pressed against the side of my face as we stared into each other's eyes, heat smoldering between us. I knew all my woman's signs of arousal. Dilated eyes, rapid breathing, and a flushed face, were her tells. Indescribable energy seeped out of her pores and wrapped around me like a vice.

"You gonna sing for me, Angel?" I licked her bottom lip.

"What?"

Tara squealed. "Oh my God, yes!"

Steph clapped. "You betcha, she'll sing."

Madeline glared at them, then faced me. "Absolutely not."

"You chicken, Madeline?" Lynx taunted. "I've heard you, girl. You rock the stage."

"She sure does." Tara grabbed Madeline's hand and shook it. "Come on, girlfriend. Get your ass on the stage and show these bikers what you can do."

"They don't need to see what I can do."

"You sing?" Emilee asked, eyes full of intrigue. She and Madeline had grown closer over the last couple of months. I often found them talking about college and kids.

"I do, but not here." Madeline shook her head.

"Angel, just one song. Any song you want." I wrapped my arms around her waist.

"Storm—" she breathed my road name, eyes pleading.

Everyone at the table stared at my girl. I looked for Sugar. If she were here, she'd help me convince Madeline to sing. Sugar had a gift with people and could get most to do anything.

"Oh my gosh, sing 'Bleeding Love!'" Steph bounced on the bench with her blonde ponytail swaying from side to side. "I love it when you sing it. Tara can sing back up."

A weird pang in my chest appeared. For some reason, the song sounded familiar. I brushed it off, figuring I was just excited to hear my girl sing again.

"I'm in." Tara clucked her tongue, standing from her seat. I had no idea she could sing. Hero's eyes smoldered as he raked them over Tara's body. My brother wanted the redhead, badly.

"I don't think I know that song. Who sings it?" Emilee asked.

Madeline waved her off. "It's an old song. I'm sure no one wants to hear it."

"I want to hear it, and what the prez says goes." I winked, squeezing her thigh.

"He's right, babe. If the prez says sing, you sing," Lynx cut in as I knew he would. But calling her babe was pushing it. "I'll tell the band to prepare. Who sings the song?"

Madeline's head dropped onto my shoulder in defeat.

"Leona Lewis," Steph shouted.

"Thanks, babe." Lynx was off in a snap.

"Oh God," Madeline groaned. "Storm, I can't sing. People keep eyeing me." She put her mouth to my ear. "Carla's been shooting daggers my way all damn evening. I'm about ready to give her a reason for that tart expression on her face."

I chuckled at my little fireball. "All the more reason to get your fine ass up there and show her who's boss. Own the stage, baby."

Madeline frowned. "You're the boss. The president. The king. I'm just—"

I captured her mouth and kissed her hard, stealing her breath away. Possessing her like I had many times with just a kiss. I didn't stop until I felt her melt into me.

"You're *my* woman. My mark is on you." I lowered my voice for only her to hear. " Maybe my baby is growing inside you." I palmed her stomach. God, I hoped we'd created a baby already. "Every person here knows you're my old lady, my *queen*. Now get on the stage and fuckin' own it." I issued her a broad smile, then kissed the tip of her nose. "You're doing this."

Sugar appeared with a curious expression. "What's going on?"

"Please, Storm," Madeline pleaded. "Don't make me do this."

"Do you what, Angel?" Sugar narrowed her eyes at me. "What are you making my girl do?" It made me warm and fuzzy to hear Sugar call Madeline her girl. Since the day she met Angel, Sugar had treated her like a daughter.

Madeline frowned. "He's making me—"

"Have I got a special treat for all you fuckers tonight," Lynx shouted into a microphone from the gazebo.

"Oh Jesus," Madeline gasped.

"For the few of you who haven't met Madeline, she's the lovely lady on the prez's lap in the back. Ain't she a beauty?" Fuckin' Lynx. He knew I didn't like him or any other guy talking about my woman's looks. "Tonight, she's going to sing for us, and let me tell you, the girl is fucking awesome!"

Whoops and clapping ensued. There was even some loud whistling.

Sugar raised an eyebrow. "Sing?"

I nodded with a cocky smirk.

Madeline squared her shoulders when everyone turned toward her. I knew she wouldn't let me down. She took the bottle of whiskey on the table, filled her glass with more than a shot's worth, but before she tossed it back, I put my hand over it.

"Angel, what if you're pregnant," I whispered into her ear.

Her shoulders sagged. "I need some liquid courage. People know me here. It's not like singing in front of strangers." She made a pouty face. "Maybe I'm not…."

"And if you are?" A fierce protectiveness came over me for my unborn child. I didn't know much about pregnancy but I doubted drinking booze was okay.

Madeline sighed. "One drink won't hurt. After this one, I won't have another."

I exhaled, giving her a chaste kiss. "I guess one won't hurt."

Thank you, she mouthed, then threw it back. "Shit. That is disgusting." She coughed. "You like that?" She inhaled a deep breath.

"Yeah, baby, I do. You okay?" I rubbed her back as she coughed and cleared her throat.

"I'm fine." She patted her chest.

"Madeline, darling, get up here," Lynx called to her. "You too, Red."

Tara stood with a shit-eating grin. "Let's go, Mads."

"Can't wait to see you shake your ass, Roja." Hero winked, lifting his beer.

Tara scowled at him. "Dream on. If I shake my ass it won't be for you."

"Oh my God, I can't wait to hear you sing, Angel." Sugar dropped into Tara's spot.

Madeline gripped my hand. "Storm, please…"

"You got this." I kissed her again as clapping filled the air. All eyes were on us. I didn't disappoint, making the kiss extra passionate. I held her face between my hands, tilting it to my liking, owning her with my tongue. Fuck, and turning myself on in the process. I ended the show. "Go sing for your man."

She stood reluctantly. As she stepped away, I swatted her ass.

Madeline didn't flinch. She crossed the grass with Tara, who appeared to be talking a mile a minute. My eyes were locked on Madeline's behind. She never wore shorts. I gotta say, I liked how they clung to her ass like a second skin.

A table filled with gawking assholes watched my woman. It pissed me off. I yelled, "Hey!" One of them noticed, then tapped the guy next to him. Like dominos falling, every last bastard ripped their gaze off my woman.

"Storm, when's your security guy arriving?" Justin asked, taking a seat beside his daughter, Emilee.

"Anytime. I'll keep an eye out for him." I hoped he hadn't changed too much in twelve years. I sure as hell changed a lot and looked nothing like the fresh-faced teenager he once knew.

Toby agreed to work with Grizzly, giving him a crash course in advanced security systems for the clubhouse and our businesses. Toby was an in-demand man. When I called him back in June, he made no promises about coming out. Only saying he'd try. I'd forgotten all about him. Then the other day he called and said he was passing through the area.

We hadn't seen each other since the day of Tommy's funeral. The next day, my dad had shipped me off to Uncle Matt for causing trouble for him and the MC.

I feared the sight of Toby would fuck me up. The guilt I carried for what happened ran deep. But for Madeline, I needed to keep her safe. No matter the cost. I wanted the best security system for her, our future children, and for my club.

I needed to do this, even if it meant revisiting the past.

"Storm, do you know the song she's gonna sing?" Emilee steered my attention back to my girl. I'd bought the gazebo just for her, hoping she'd sing at every club party.

"No, darlin', sure don't." Although it sounded familiar, I couldn't place it by the title alone. Maybe hearing it would jog my memory. I rubbed my chest, feeling another weird twinge.

"Well, your girl is just about perfect." Sugar winked. "Is she hiding any other secrets?"

I chuckled, watching Madeline talking to the guys in the band. "Hell no. She tells me everything."

"Mhmm, I'm sure she hasn't told you *everything*."

I ignored Sugar's teasing. She didn't know Madeline as well as I did. My girl was an open book. We hadn't talked about our childhoods or stuff before we met. I preferred it that way, so I didn't have to tell her about the boy I killed. I didn't want her to think of me as a savage monster, even if it were true.

The crowd got rowdier, clapping for Madeline. Carla kept glancing at me. The woman pissed me off. She really needed to go. But Madeline had said she'd handle her. Sugar and Tina had been teaching her how to deal with the kittens. I didn't want to interfere with my old lady's business. Lynx hadn't done a damn thing.

But I was getting impatient and ready to take matters into my own hands. The bitch had no place in my clubhouse anymore.

"Here you go, Prez." Lynx handed me a beer, then gave one to Justin and Hero.

"I thought I told you to take care of Carla. The bitch is pissing me off." I lifted the bottle to my lips and took a long pull.

Lynx threw up a hand, shaking his head. "I did, but she's stubborn as hell when it comes to you."

"I don't give a fuck. Either you handle her, or I will. I won't have my woman feeling uncomfortable around here. You get me?" This was insanity. If Carla wasn't keeping my brothers happy with her mouth and Madeline wanting to manage the kittens, I would've had Carla gone the day after she called my woman a cunt.

"I'll take care of it." Lynx took a pull of his beer.

"She's been sucking your dick, hasn't she?" Hero narrowed his eyes at Lynx. "That's why you haven't gotten the job done."

Lynx flipped him off. It was no secret Hero didn't like Carla.

"Hey, y'all. It's a great night for a party, doncha think?" Madeline smiled at the crowd. My God, she was beautiful. "You probably won't know this song. It goes way back to my childhood when I was a silly, prepubescent girl obsessing over it… and a boy."

The crowd *oohed* like crazy, heads turning my way.

She wagged her finger, shaking her head. "No, no, no…. I know what you're thinking, but that was a *long* time ago. Storm is hotter than the fresh-faced, pretty boy I used to dream about. Storm is *my* man. Don't you forget it. You hear me?"

The crowd shouted *Yes* from every direction.

"Good." Madeline blew me a kiss, then nodded to the band.

Sugar nudged me. "I adore your girl."

My heart squeezed tight in my chest. It pleased me how everyone took to Madeline, especially my aunt.

But hearing how Madeline obsessed over this song because of *him*, the boy she once loved, didn't sit right with me. I wished her friends hadn't pushed her into singing it. Or Madeline could have flat out told them no. She tried. Why didn't I help her? Obviously because I wanted to hear her again. Angel sang like no one in this world. But I didn't want this. Shit, my gut was tight. Did she still think about him?

Her voice silenced everyone.

Sugar set her hand on my shoulder as if knowing I needed to be anchored to my seat. Emilee was in a trance. Steph swayed to the beat, and Lynx bobbed his head. Hero sat stoically but I knew my brother was more smitten with "Roja" than he let on.

As I watched Madeline, a memory from the past roared toward me like a freight train. I was transported back to Lake Waleska, where I'd spent the best week of my life with the Hamilton family. Why I remembered the song crashed into me. Toby's firecracker of a little sister had listened to it at least a million times at the lake. Toby had given her shit about it and made her cry. He was such an asshole, back then. We both were cocky and arrogant. When school started, we were going to be badass seniors.

That little firecracker had a massive crush on me. I adored that little girl...

Wait, what was her name again? *That little girl. Abby? Caddy? No. Shit. Um....*

Fuck.

Madeline's voice cut through my thoughts as she belted out "Bleeding Love." *Maddy.* That was her name. Madeline. Maddy. Basically the same name. It couldn't be, could it? Their names. This was all just a coincidence, right? It had to be.

But as she sang that stupid song, all I could think about was her intro and how she said it was about her childhood crush. A shiver worked through me. It couldn't be. She was Angel. Not little Maddy *"firecracker"* Hamilton. But fuck, what if she was? Why hadn't I ever asked Madeline what her last name was? Or what the silver H meant on the charm bracelet she kept in her underwear draw.

Shit... Fuck! The pang in my chest turned into a stabbing pain and my heart jackhammered against my ribs.

I studied my woman, trying to find similarities, but there weren't any. Sure, they both had brown hair and blue eyes. So did a lot of women.

My beauty sang her heart out, gazing at me with love in her eyes and swaying her body all sexy-like... Shit, it couldn't be the same girl.

They weren't the same.

They fuckin' weren't the same person!

"Woohoo, Maddy!" Steph yelled.

Maddy.

My gut twisted, nearly bent me over as bile crept into my throat. The sound of the crowd roared in my ears, but it wasn't enough to stop the memories of that fateful day from rushing back...

"Jump already, ya pussy!"

I stumbled over my goddamn feet, laughing at my stupid, drunken self. Toby hissed with laughter, holding his gut beside me. His fourteen-year-old brother Tommy looked scared shitless.

The little wuss. We were toughening him up. All year he'd been begging to tag along on our shenanigans.

Tonight, we'd teach him to think twice before whining like a baby to hang with us.

"Your dick is shriveling up, little brother." Toby howled with laughter. "Just jump in the fucking lake so Kaleb and I can get laid. It's our fucking graduation night!"

"It's too dark! I can't see if there are any fish." Tommy shook, peering over the edge of the dock.

"Fish? It's a lake, dipshit! Of course, there's fish!" Storm clouds were forming overhead. I chugged my sixth, or maybe it was my seventh beer. I'd lost count. We were saving Jack Daniels for Wendy and Suzie, knowing it loosened them up. "Are you seriously scared of some little fish?" Lightning lit up the sky miles away.

Tommy held his dick like it was made of gold, face tight with dread. He'd never make it in my dad's MC. He'd been showing interest the more I took Toby to the compound. It would never happen.

I grew up on the Knight's Legion compound, unlike the kids I went to school with living in neighborhoods. I'd been homeschooled

*through middle school. Then my dad felt I was tough enough to take
care of myself in high school. Even then, a prospect followed me all
damn day when I wasn't in the classroom. It sucked, but having a
big-ass dude on a bike was great with the girls. Once I had my own, I
didn't need a prospect to tail me.*

My sex life imploded then, too.

*"You think your dick will be mistaken for a worm? Probably
will, but then you can catch a big fish and take it home to Mama for
tomorrow's supper." I bumped shoulders with Toby, snorting.*

"Yeah, hurry it up, pencil dick!" Toby razzed him.

*Thunder rumbled as my cell phone chimed with a text. I finished
off my beer while opening it and instantly became irritated with this
bullshit. A raindrop hitting my eye didn't help.*

Wendy: *Where r u, K? You're an hour late!! Suzie and I are
heading to the bonfire.*

Kaleb: *Don't leave without us.*

Wendy: *I'm tired of waiting for you.*

Kaleb: *U stay put!*

*I waited for a reply. When it didn't come, I lost it. If I didn't get to
Wendy's house fast, she'd hook up with someone else. No fuckin' way
I'd let that shit happen. Wendy was an easy lay, a no-strings-attached
kind of girl. Just my type.*

*"Enough of this shit! Wendy and Suzie are going to ditch us!" I
stormed to the end of the dock, where Tommy stood naked, cupping
his junk. Clouds were moving faster, so was the rain. "Jump, asshole!
You're cockblocking me!"*

"And me!" Toby yelled a few steps behind me.

*"I changed my mind!" Tommy backed away from the edge. "It's
going to be storming any second. There's lightning." He wiped his face
and pointed up.*

*"Too late!" I blocked him. "Jump, or I'll toss your ass in
myself!"*

"I'll never beg to hang with you jerks again!" Tommy scrunched his face like a pouty baby.

Toby groaned. "Tommy, don't be such a sissy. Think of this as an initiation like into Kaleb's dad's MC."

"There aren't initiations into the club, dumbass. You prospect and get patched in after doing your time and all the menial jobs the members order you to do." I put my hands on my hips, irritation building inside me like a savage storm coming.

Toby shrugged. "Whatever. This is our initiation. Jump Tommy, or we'll help you in."

"Please guys. I'm sorry. I won't ask again. Let's just go. It's dangerous to be out during a thunderstorm."

"Too late," I yelled, tired of this pussy ruining my night. I threw my beer can over the edge and reached for Tommy.

He batted my hands away, screaming. "No, no, no!"

Toby laughed, trying to help me.

But I didn't need his help. I threw my weight into Tommy and launched him into the lake as electric bolts of light lit up the sky. I turned around, a victorious smile on my face, and high fived Toby.

Toby and I stared at each other for a tense second. Did he hear what I heard?

"About fucking time." Toby drained his beer and tossed it over the side.

I watched for Tommy to pop up out of the water, wailing like a baby. But all I saw was the rain pelting the surface. I waited and waited until a sick feeling crashed down on me.

"Why hasn't he come up yet?"

Toby peered over the edge. "Don't know."

I kicked off my shoes and jumped into the lake, frantically searching for Tommy...

"Thank you. Thank you so much. You're a spectacular crowd."

Madeline's voice pulled me back to the present. "I have one more for you. I want to see all of you on your feet and dancing. Do you like Gretchen Wilson?" Madeline smiled while clapping ensued. "Yeah? Excellent because I'm 'Here for the Party!'"

Emilee and Steph dashed toward the stage, and Lynx followed.

"I'm out. I'll catch you later." Hero left toward the clubhouse.

I couldn't move. Couldn't breathe. Madeline shook her hips with attitude, belting out the lyrics.

My throat constricted, and my hands trembled. I grabbed the whiskey and guzzled it straight from the bottle. *Shit. Fuck, no.*

"Storm? What's wrong?"

I heard Sugar's voice, but I was too far gone as I stared numbly at the angel on stage.

Madeline can't be the same person. Fuck, she can't be the same person.

"You okay there, Storm?" Justin asked next. "You look a little shell-shocked, son."

Sugar patted my shoulder. "Talk to me. What's happening?" The worry in her voice did me in.

"I… Ah…" I drank more whiskey, unable to speak as I heard the faint sound of thunder rumbling.

The song ended, and clapping broke out once again. I looked around at all the smiling faces but stopped on one perplexed man in the crowd.

Toby.

I glanced at Madeline. She was smiling and bowing. The moment she noticed Toby, the ground disappeared, and I was free-falling.

Life, as I knew it with my Angel, crumbled right before my eyes. I couldn't do a goddamn thing to stop it.

Excruciating pain rolled through my body, flooding my veins. It felt like my heart stopped beating as my world imploded.

And I couldn't fuckin' stop it.

"Storm, honey." Sugar shook my arm. "Justin, do something."

Madeline didn't blink, clearly in shock, staring at her brother. Her. Brother.

Her eyes swooped my way, then back to Toby, then back to me as if piecing the puzzle together. The mike in her hand hit the ground. A loud clanging bled through the speakers and the crowd froze.

She looked at me as she stepped down the stairs and ran into her brother's arms.

Every part of my body shut down. I felt numb and couldn't speak even though I heard Sugar and Justin calling my name.

I swayed as I stood from the bench, my legs weak, almost boneless.

Sugar grabbed my arm, but I ripped it away as my stomach spasmed. I took off, bursting through the gate and emptied my guts into a bush as little Maddy Hamilton's face flashed behind my eyes. Stomach acid burned my esophagus as a second wave hit, bending me over to spew into the shrub.

"Storm, please talk to me. What's going on?"

Sugar's words fell on deaf ears. I was in so much fuckin' pain as my world crashed and shattered, much like the day my life changed forever. When I'd savagely thrown a naked boy into the lake because of my own selfish desires.

Once I stopped puking out my guts, I bolted for my bike, needing to get far away. The shame and disgust I felt was too much. I might be Storm to everyone who knew me but to me, I was *Savage Storm*. A selfish, motherless, fatherless, worthless piece of no good shit… A savage bastard who had destroyed a loving family and the little firecracker who had made my life brighter.

Jesus Christ. My Angel was Maddy Hamilton, the little sister of the boy I killed…

To Be Continued…
In **AVENGING ANGEL**, where the mayhem continues!

Are you reeling after that cliffhanger? Do you want to talk about Storm and his brothers? Or maybe you want the inside scoop on KLMC? Join *Naomi's Knight's Legion MC,* a private reader group on Facebook!

ALSO BY NAOMI PORTER

St. James Billionaires

Breach of Honor (Part one of duet)
Bound by Love (Part two of duet)
Blinded by Loyalty
Battle of Wills (Releasing early fall 2021)

Bad Boys We Love

Neighbor Nik
Lifeguard Leo
Effing Eli
Fireman Fox

ACKNOWLEDGEMENT

First and foremost, to my super supportive husband and kids. I wouldn't be where I am without your patience. Thank you, thank you, thank you!

To my freaking fantastic editor, Marissa Gramoll, I love working with you! Reading your comments was the highlight of my day. Thank you for loving my characters and making their story shine.

To my proofreader, Beth at Magnolia Author Services, thank you for polishing my books. I appreciated your efficiency and professionalism.

To my author friend and fellow MC author, Stevie Lee. Thank you for commenting on that Facebook post. Your friendship and support have meant a lot to me. You are a treasure! XO

To my dear author friend, Sarah Bailey. I feel like we've been on our writing journey together every step of the way. I couldn't have asked for a better person to share this incredible experience with. You've gotten me through some rough moments and made me cry-laughing many other times. Thank you for always being there for me. I love you, friend!

All the love,

Naomi

ABOUT THE AUTHOR

Naomi Porter always had a knack for storytelling, and she's finally putting pen to paper to share with you, the reader. Whether she's trying to stay warm during freezing winter weather or cool in the sweltering heat, she's pounding away at the keys of her laptop to bring you the latest gritty motorcycle club romance, decadent billionaire saga, or heart-stopping sexy drama.

No matter what story she's telling, you can bet it has sexy as sin men, sassy and confident women, and plenty of sizzling passion.

Printed in Great Britain
by Amazon

54736829R00189